THE DOLL

JOCELYN DEXTER

BLOODHOUND BOOKS

The tiny fingers curled around my index finger, the thumb latching on with a gentle grip meaning I could lift my hand and the rest of his body would follow.

Stroking the rounded curve of his soft tummy, I swirled the palm of my hand in gentle circles, delighting in the physical touch of Harry's flawless perfection. His face was that of a cherub: two rosy cheeks and dimples either side of his cupid-bow lips. There really was nothing more beautiful than one's own child.

Cooing at him, I changed his nappy and fastened up the poppers of his blue dungarees. Yellow letters spelled out HAPPY on his bib. Shiny eyes gazed up at me, unblinking – his long lashes turned skyward like a brush, as if in a grand sweeping gesture.

I had to admit to a certain amount of anticipatory pride. Harry and I were going for a walk, me pushing and he in his buggy.

We both smiled at the other children being steered upon wheels along the park's pathways, but I was annoyed with myself because I was hot and sweaty from such a busy morning

– I hadn't stopped – and my hair was a mess. All the parading mothers in their Sunday best were so perfectly dressed, not a hair out of place, cool in their stylish clothes and with their manicured nails – and not one of them covered in baby vomit.

But I told myself it didn't matter. Not really.

Back home, exhausted, a bad temper threatening, I picked up my special little boy. 'Come on, Happy Harry. There, there, shh. There's a good boy.'

Cheek to cheek we stood, me gazing out of the window and Harry relaxed, quietened – but still holding on tight, his arms around my neck, peering over my shoulder into the room behind. I relaxed, tired after hours of cleaning and dusting and cooking, running about and playing with Harry. It was sometimes hard being a single parent, but hugging my child to me, I knew it was all worth it.

Tiring of the view, I wanted Harry to play.

I was bored.

And vaguely irritated.

It was never good when I became bored. In my mind, boredom meant bad, and I dodged and avoided tedium of any sort. It often spelt danger.

Keeping it together was what I had learned I must do. For everyone's sake.

And so far, I'd done just that.

Shifting Harry around on my hip, I held his chin gently and pointed his face towards the window, letting him see the big wide world through those bluest of blue eyes. 'See, Harry? See all those babies and children in the park – see how they play and laugh and run about? That was us, just an hour ago. Look. Watch. Can you see? They're all tumbling and toddling around quite quite happily. And what are you doing?'

Harry's expression didn't change, but his eyelashes fluttered, and his blue eyes stared at me.

I placed him in the playpen and settled him so he was comfortable and safe, resting back against the bars, and I took a few calming breaths. Regaining my composure, I carried on my Sunday morning routine. Eventually, I turned my attention to him again. 'Here, Harry. How about Carrot?' I waved the stuffed fluffy ginger cat back and forth in front of his face. Not a lot of reaction. Smiling tightly, getting more pissed off, I waved Doggie at him. 'Look, Harry, Doggie's here. Want to play?'

But he just sat there. Not playing. Not playing at all. Sitting stiffly with his stuffed toys, Carrot and Doggie, both ignored in his lap. For all the interest Harry showed, I suddenly questioned why I bothered.

It was difficult maintaining a Loving and Caring and Nurturing environment under these circumstances.

I leant over the bars, feeling disproportionately infuriated, took him by the shoulders and shook him hard. 'What is fucking wrong with you? You're two years old and you do nothing. Absolutely *nothing*. I can't do it for you. *What is wrong with you?*' Grabbing him by his hair, I lifted him out of the playpen and threw him against the wall.

It wasn't the dull thud of flesh hitting stone, but more a resounding shattering, a clattering of china as Harry exploded into a million tiny fragments.

An eyeball rolled across the carpet and came to rest at my feet.

Panting with rage, I kicked the eye into the furthest corner. *The carpet would need bloody vacuuming again.*

I stomped across the room, threw open the drawer containing my miniature dolls, ran my fingers over them – and discarded them all. I wasn't in the mood for one of my personal four-inch china-dolls-to-go.

From one of the shelves in the cupboard, I selected a new proper-sized doll – an even better one than Harry. A more grown up one. Perhaps three years old. Four, if I were being generous. A girl, this time.

'Hello, Sally. It's me. You remember me, don't you, Sad Sal? Why so Sad? We're going to play. Not now, because I'm tired. But next weekend. Won't that be nice? We'll wipe that Sadness clean off your face, yes, we will.' Crooning and clucking softly, I whispered into Sal's soft pink ear, tucking her red hair behind it. 'I know you'll be better than Happy Harry. Much better. You'll be perfect, and I'll be perfect. Together we'll be normal and talk through your sadness and as one, we'll understand it. We *will* get to the bottom of it, trust me, Sal. I just know we'll get along splendidly.'

2

ADELE

Adele Snapp fretted and quietly panicked. There was still such a lot to do to organise her husband's sixtieth birthday party. There were little things that needed finessing with the catering team, but Adele had been meticulous in her planning and was confident the party would go smoothly tonight.

It had to be just right, because Adele liked things to be just right.

Even though she'd failed to make her son right. He wasn't right *at all*, and she'd known early on, even when he'd been a toddler, that there was something most definitely very wrong with her child. She'd tried, really tried, and it had been hard to change him. At first, it had been impossible.

And frightening.

Generally speaking, now that he was a grown man, she thought she'd achieved all that she could. She had reined him in, and he managed himself – with little reminders from her if and when necessary.

This morning, Adele had stood outside the door to his self-contained flat upstairs and heard him shouting at one of his dolls. Had heard him throw the doll against the wall. And had listened as it shattered.

She'd felt an all too familiar chill as she'd contemplated her son's rage, and what he might one day do with it.

Up until recently, Barney had been able to keep his fantasy doll world alive in an appropriate way and had kept his brooding always-there fury under wraps.

As far as she knew.

The dolls had always been an absorbing and *good* outlet for him. A safe outlet. Seemingly, not anymore. Now that suppressed anger was leaking out. And she worried he was drifting out of her control – a ticking time bomb, waiting to go boom.

And that terrified her.

Adele jumped as Barney appeared at her shoulder in the kitchen, catching her off-guard. Looking up at her son, she gave him a smile that didn't seem to fit on her lips. Ignoring the uncomfortable sensation of the false expression, she said, 'I popped up to your flat earlier – was wondering if you wanted lunch down here with me?' She waited a beat. 'But you were busy with one of your dolls.'

'You should have texted me. The answer would have been a resounding yes.' He smiled at her, full of charm and gentleness. As she'd taught him.

Nodding, she kept the tight smile in place. 'It's your father's sixtieth. You haven't forgotten, have you?'

He laughed softly. 'Course I haven't forgotten. Need any help?'

'Just promise you'll be here this evening. Your father would be heartbroken if you didn't come.'

'I'm coming, Mum, relax. Eight o'clock do you?'

'It does me.'

She watched as he busied himself making a sandwich.

Gnawing the inside of her cheek, and running her hand through her short hair, Adele felt duty bound to voice her concerns. 'I heard you, you know. Earlier. Upstairs, in your flat. You broke one of your dolls.' Her brow creased with concern. 'I'm sorry.'

He loved his dolls, and she loved that he loved them. It made everything safe for him. She didn't love him breaking them. It was uncharacteristic and worrying.

Barney straightened up from crouching in front of the open fridge, cheese in one hand, a cucumber in the other. Placing them gently on the worktop, his eyes wavered and he threatened to shut them, using that glazed look she hated so much. It was something she'd endeavoured to eradicate very early on in his life: that unfocusing of his eyes that so frightened her.

And made him unreachable.

They continued to stare at each other: she waiting; he, she assumed, thinking. Finally, he nodded and managed to look contrite. She could only hope it was a genuine expression and not merely a much-practised one – he was highly skilled in mimicry, primarily due to her one-to-one teachings throughout his life. 'Yeah sorry, Mum. I don't know why I lost my temper. I've got so used to controlling it, but it didn't work today.' He rubbed his chin. 'And ironically, I broke Happy.'

'Did you do your breathing exercises? Go through as many emotions with your dolls as you could to counteract how you felt? Did you try Calm Karen?'

'No, I was way past using Calm. But of course I went through my intellectualising routine. Those glib statements that aren't glib or trite at all. Not when you've really studied the true meaning of the words, as we have. About right and wrong and good and bad.' He ran his fingers through his hair. 'On an academic level, I understand all truths and emotions. After a *lot* of practice with you.'

He beamed at her, and as they stood in the kitchen, she

recalled the hours and hours she'd spent with him as a child, endeavouring to rewire and totally reprogramme her emotionless son. Playing with the dollies. Practising with the dollies. Until he was doll-perfect. Controlled and harmless.

With military precision, she'd taught her strange little soldier to change his skewed moral compass and to study feelings: as many as she could think of. An impossible ask, but they'd both worked hard at it, using the dolls as various versions of people in different moods. Countless scenarios with countless permutations of potentially right and wrong responses to everyday life, until he'd understood what was acceptable.

Academically speaking.

He swept his hair from his eyes. 'I don't know why I couldn't connect with what I *know* are facts, but Happy Harry really pissed me off this morning. I was weak. I recognised my anger and couldn't control it. Sorry.' Barney raised his eyebrows. 'I'm a bit surprised my rationalising it didn't ground me. It all just seemed like words today, not real, not something I could actually relate to, not like normal.' He shrugged. 'But don't worry, Mum, it's nothing to worry about, promise.'

In the silence, Adele told herself it was far better her son's anger was directed and taken out on a doll than unleashed on a real woman. His propensity for violence at such an early age had meant she'd taken action swiftly. As a two-year-old, it was Barney's utter lack of a bond with her and his father, Timothy, with *anyone*, that had been the first red flag.

Later, that disconnect had solidified into a shocking inability to communicate on any real emotional level, and that was what had frightened her the most. As a young boy, his eyes blank, his face expressionless, Barney would simply sit and stare at her, as if he really didn't understand what it was he was meant to be feeling, showing, demonstrating or doing.

'I love you, Mummy,' he'd said as she'd cried in frustration when he'd refused to play or laugh with her. She'd told him that saying 'I love you' was important. So, he'd said it.

But Adele knew he'd never really meant it. Pre-doll, it had merely been a phrase that he'd churned out robotically. With no understanding of the words. He'd performed the sentence, instead of experiencing the meaning.

After complaints from his nursery, and later his primary school, that her son was disruptive, bullying, violent, and often excluded himself, Adele had got down to serious work with him.

It wasn't difficult to spot that he seemed to have no comprehension of kindness, gentleness, softness, and had an alarming lack of empathy. Once she'd seen the flaws in his personality, the gaping holes in his psyche, she'd made it her mission to fix him. To help him. To make him love her and the world, as much as she loved him.

Adele had decided to take him out of official formal education, and homeschool him herself. For his sake. And for everyone else's. *Her* curriculum. Her judgement.

Please God, let my assessment and treatment of Barney be right, she'd prayed. She'd remained confident of her own maternal skills. Never had call to really question them, for everything given to Barney came from love. And how could that be wrong?

A solitary boy, Barney had found solace in drawing. Spending hour upon hour creating beautiful pictures of, ironically, people. He was very talented. She'd had his IQ tested and it turned out it was extremely high. He was gifted. When not sketching, he was always reading, and Barney's vocabulary was extensive, making his brain easy to engage with: all intellect. But an empty heart. The plus side: it meant they could talk on a higher level. Really *talk*.

Now he was thirty and she had intuitively felt him slipping away from her for some time. Adele couldn't stop him becoming his own man who was inevitably less reliant on her, and incrementally, year on year, she'd been aware of him drifting, quietly but surely, further and further away. Inch by inch.

She adored him and didn't want to let go.

The dolls had been his idea, and it had proved something of a breakthrough for both of them. Inventing his doll fantasy had, Adele thought, saved him from God only knew what.

He'd been twelve when he'd walked in from one of his daily walks, thrown his rucksack on the floor and kicked off his shoes. He'd simply stood there, holding on to the arm of a plastic doll.

'What have you got there, Barney?'

'A girl in the park had a bunch of them. So, I took one. And yes, I know I can't just take stuff I want, because it's wrong, but I didn't think you'd mind this time. This is important. For my remoulding.'

She hadn't questioned his phrase: remoulding. But was surprised he'd used it. He was so young, but so mature in his language choice – mostly what he'd learnt from books.

'What's so important about a doll?' she'd asked.

'I realised something when I was watching the girls playing with them.'

'Realised what?'

'I wanted the doll because I thought it was like me.'

'What do you mean?'

'Dead inside. Perfect on the outside but dead and empty on the inside – where it matters.' He'd shrugged. 'That sounds so simple, but it's actually a very profound happening. I want to understand dolls, and why I'm so like them. I feel like this...' He'd waved the doll by its wrist in front of him. '...is like my little soulmate. A little version of me. And together, me and this doll can learn to be real. You can teach us *all* the emotions, using the doll as a tool. What do you think?'

She'd wanted to weep with the tragedy of it all.

And so it began. His fascination with the inanimate object, his role-playing with it, his real connection with it, seemed to cement his knowledge that he was indeed emotionally lacking so much. Together, Adele, Barney, and a series of beautiful china dolls, which he'd chosen and she'd bought for him, had set off on a weird but as healthy a fantasy as was possible: role-playing and learning how to be human.

Adele had always known her son was capable of killing. She knew this because she was his mum, and a mother knows these things. Deep down, however hard she'd tried to bury the knowledge, she'd always known.

She wasn't a trained psychiatrist, but equally she wasn't a fool. She was a parent with a deeply disturbed son. Ever since Barney had been able to talk, she'd known her son had the potential to be bad. Very bad.

If Adele had anything to do with it, nurture *would* overcome nature.

Sometimes she thought she'd succeeded.

Sometimes, especially recently, perhaps not.

So far, she'd made sure, as much as she could, his life had been blessed with happiness and calm, and as luck would have it, free from trauma.

But it was only a matter of time before something out of her control set him off.

Because that was the nature of life.

My handsome, beautiful, gifted son.

My son, the psychopath.

3
—
ME

I wasn't a great fan of parties. Too many people, too much to take in, too many personalities screaming to be dissected and then subsequently, mostly ignored. Some, however, held a modicum of interest for me and so I indulged them, as courtesy dictated I must. As I'd been taught. Although, if I were being honest, the interest was all too often fleeting and transient, and I quickly tired of others' company.

I truly had difficulties in seeing the point of people and found it hard mixing with them. They were simultaneously uncomplicated and complicated. They confused me. I pursued no social life at all – why would I? My interaction with the human race was minimal and I only engaged when absolutely necessary.

But I did love learning, sucking up everything there was on offer. Desperate, absolutely bloody desperate to find some reason, some point to it all. *Surely, this isn't all that life is? This mediocre going through the motions, engaging in shallow relationships, mimicking being alive – there must be more. Surely. There* has *to be.*

Very brief one-to-one interactions were much easier for me to deal with. It gave me enough time to see the person for who they really were. Overall, it was often disappointing: so many of them were superficial and transparent.

And I certainly wasn't keen on the number of people here tonight. So many of them – brushing past, rubbing shoulders, clasping hands and proffering cheeks to be kissed. I discreetly patted my inside breast pocket, where my doll-to-go Polite Petra was. She was my reminder to always be courteous in a coming-together of people like this. Not that I didn't know that – I wasn't *completely* socially crippled. But still, her hidden presence made me feel better.

A drunk man bumped into me, the alcohol almost masking the fact he was Sad. His female partner could not disguise Anger at him, and with amusement, I watched them awkwardly pretend, Fun.

Years and years of tutelage from Mum had made it surprisingly easy to fool others with fakery.

I often wondered if I was really fooling myself.

A touch on my arm made me turn. Knowing there'd be lots of people at the party, I'd mentally prepared to be physically touched by strangers. Trying not to grimace, I turned my painted bland doll-face to the speaker, and waited to adjust my expression accordingly.

'Barney? Is that really you? I haven't seen you in years. How are you?'

One of my father's oldest friends, a woman, all crinkled and wrinkled, held my elbow in a vice-like grip. Smiling and feigning Delight at seeing her again, I put on Bashful, with a smidge of Coy, and dipped my eyes to her, throwing in a little Shyness. 'I'm well, thank you, Cynthia. Lovely to see you. You look very well.'

'I most certainly do *not*, young man, but thank you for lying. I'll take it.'

Oh, how we laughed. Me, one big polite sham; she, seemingly, enjoying our exchange – as trivial as it was. It wasn't particularly difficult to keep up this mockery of a conversation: it was what I'd been doing all my life. I pretended to be normal, along with the rest of them: we were all different levels of normal, after all. Bluffing had become habitual, and I did it without conscious effort.

Although recently, for some reason, I'd really rather lost track of who was fooling who.

'Barney-Boy, there you are.' Dad slung an arm sloppily around my shoulders. 'Got yourself a drink?'

I waved my glass of untouched champagne at him and nodded. 'Happy birthday, Dad. Having a good time?'

'It's bloody brilliant. Your mother's outdone herself, as usual. It's perfect. Everything's perfect.' He looked at me, his eyes filling with alcoholic weepiness. 'And thanks for coming. I know you hate this sort of thing.'

'No, not at all, Dad. It's great. Loads of people, though. Sensory overload and all that.'

'Don't know who half of them are myself if I'm being totally honest.' He laughed and swayed a little on his feet. 'Shit, I'm pissed. Need to sober up before my famous birthday speech.'

I watched as Dad stifled a belch, and he looked at me – for a moment, very sober. 'You know I love you, don't you, Barney? You're the best son I could wish for.'

I felt sorry for him if that was really the case, but I knew Mum adored him, so I politely accepted his very big compliment to me. I recognised it as such, because I wasn't a *complete* knob. He was a good bloke – kind – and he loved me. And I appreciated his sentiment, I really did.

'And I love my silver tankard. Bloody great present.' He

waved his hand wildly in the air, indicating that my birthday gift was somewhere in the house.

'Good, I'm glad you like it. I could picture you in front of the fire, drinking out of it, when I bought it.'

'Exactly. It's bloody perfect. Thanks loads, Barney-Boy.'

He clasped me to him unexpectedly and I felt wooden in his embrace. I tried to feel Love, but all I came up with was genuine gratitude, and that wasn't a bad thing. I liked Dad, but really, he was just a nice man who lived in the same house as me. I saw him as a very good friend, who happened to be my father.

Mum appeared behind Dad and she wrapped her arm around his waist. 'What are my two favourite men planning?'

'I've made a decision and sod it, Adele, I'm going to do my speech now. Fuck the buffet. People can eat afterwards instead of waiting for the old fart to do his boring "Welcome all, thank you for coming" spiel. It will only spoil their appetites. Speech, then eat – that's what's happening.'

Mum rolled her eyes at me. 'Is your father drunk?'

'Certainly not,' I said, playing the annual game. 'Dad's not drunk, Mum. As if.'

Laughing and swaying, Dad made his face look sober. 'Well, colour me bloody shit-faced.' He giggled. 'I'm as un-drunk as un-drunk could be.'

Mum whispered into his ear and Dad shook his head. Standing away from her, grinning, he walked towards the long flight of stairs. 'You can't stop me, Adele. I'm drunk and I'm doing my speech now – like it or not, and as pissed as a fart.'

Laughing uproariously, he slowly went up the stairs, holding the banister, and trying to give a good impression of someone who wasn't drunk.

'Your father's a fool, Barney. Please don't let him make a complete idiot of himself. Again.' But her voice was full of laughter.

'Who cares? It's his birthday. Sod the lot of them if they disapprove of his celebrations.'

Mum shrugged and laughed more, not really caring. 'You're quite right. Let him have his moment.'

I grinned and pecked her on the cheek, relaxed with her by my side, not having to mimic my posture. 'I do love you, Mum.' And this time, out of all the emotions crammed into the room, housed within so many people, *this* was a real feeling, instead of an intellectual acknowledgement of what I'd been taught I should feel. It was the one true effortless pulse that came from my heart, and it wasn't merely an habitual feigning of a feeling created in my brain. The love for my mother – *that* was real.

It didn't need initialising inside my head.

Both Mum and I raised our eyes and watched as Dad reached the top of the very long and curved staircase. Beaming with delight at the conquering of such a tricky obstacle, he finally stood and turned around carefully to face his audience. Coughing loudly and theatrically, he waved his hands in the air to get attention.

'Hello, dear friends. It's that time again. The time you all dread – my birthday speech, which has become something of a tradition. Whether you like it or not.' He paused for the riotous drunken laughter to die down, although I heard it more as a polite, discreet but audible murmur of affection at an old joke.

'My huge thanks to my beautiful and marvellous wife, Adele, who has, once again, put on the most delightful party.' He held his arm up. 'Later, later, Joan, stop heckling me, you can eat *after* I've finished yabbering.' Raising his glass to Mum, she reciprocated the gesture.

'I also wanted to say thank you to my wonderful son, Barney. Cannot *wait* to use your present.' He lowered his voice to a loud whisper. 'Tonight, just you and me and...' He pantomimed knocking back a drink from the tankard, and a few more real laughs sounded. Dad winked at me and I held my thumb up at him, smiling.

'Now, here's the part where I get soppy and nostalgic and go over the events of the past year, and my hopes for the next.' Groans and giggles and what I thought was a real Sad smile from my father, although, as it was loaded with subtlety and nuance, I wasn't one hundred per cent sure.

And I call myself an expert.

Before he went into his practised speech, he looked down at my mother and I, and blew us a kiss. 'I'm so proud of my beautiful wife and my fantastic boy, Barney. Proud as bloody punch.'

Back to his party piece, Dad lifted his chin in a melodramatic way and looked at the ceiling as if remembering. Putting his hands on his hips, he stood there. Everyone had quietened down, not sure if he was being silly, or if in fact this was a heartfelt memory that he was endeavouring to vocalise. His mistake was deciding to go for comic, and he tried to cross his ankles quickly and deftly, right over left. Deftness had deserted him, though, and the movement unbalanced him.

His body, when it fell, had some momentum behind it. He'd tripped over his own foot and he propelled himself down the stairs with his own weight, head first. The unexpected horror of it, the pure unadulterated shock of it, made people utterly motionless, and we all watched his long, crashing descent. You couldn't help but hear it as his head bounced from banister to wall, his breath whooshing out of him, his limbs, like a doll, flapping around him loosely – acting as a hindrance instead of being helpful in any way. Staccato grunts punctuated his downward tumble.

Dad gathered speed and landed at the bottom of the staircase, coming to a very final full stop. Everyone heard the crack of his neck as it snapped.

The sharp retort of his broken bone had been as loud as a gunshot.

And then there was a complete lack of sound, and I swore, if someone had had a pin, I would have heard it drop.

Eventually, there was a delayed collective gasp, a woman I didn't know fainted, and then there was a mad rush to Dad's crumpled side.

Mum didn't move.

I didn't move.

And I realised, with a nasty shock, that me and Mum had never covered Grief. Not in any real meaningful way. We'd done Sad, but not Grief. If I'd never experienced it, how could I replicate it and understand it with any degree of accuracy?

Mum and I had never emulated the death of a loved one with the dolls, so I wasn't well-acquainted with the emotion of Loss.

I was shocked but I gratefully allowed my intellect to take over. I turned to Mum and held her. I definitely experienced empathy for her, thank God, and genuinely wanted to comfort my mother. I just hoped she didn't notice my lack of real sorrow.

But my mind kept on repeating, over and over again, my father's last words, 'I'm so proud of my beautiful wife and my fantastic boy, Barney,' and couldn't stop an inappropriate thought as it piped up in my mental background. The bad, hidden side of me wanted to laugh, because it turned out that pride really *did* come before a fall, after all.

Mum and I stayed in an embrace, me quietly, greedily, *desperately* taking my cue from her behaviour and I started copying her, waiting for Grief to show itself. At the moment, Shock was stopping it, so I wasn't required to do much on the demonstrative front, other than hold my stunned expression in place.

I was an imposter, posing as human, but with very little normal inside.

I am still *like a doll – nothing's really changed – except the façade I wear in public is more practised, polished and credible now.*

I think.

4

————

ME

1 MONTH LATER

'We are gathered here today to remember the life of Timothy Snapp.'

Dressed appropriately in a black suit, grey shirt and a thin black tie, I clasped Mum's hand in mine. And got no response back. As if her fingers were as dead as Dad.

My other hand rubbed Grieving Gregory, who nestled in my pocket. Tempted to lift his head from the depths of my jacket, so he'd be able to actually *see* the proceedings, I restrained myself, knowing it would be inappropriate.

I zoned out the words of the vicar – trite, banal and meaningless as far as I could ascertain – and gently but sporadically squeezing Mum's lifeless fingers, I held a conversation with Gregory in my head. As I'd done since a child with all my dolls, irrespective of their size, I'd go back and forth in conversation with whatever doll was being used, and use applicable voices for each different character. Sometimes, I'd speak out loud, but clearly this wasn't the place to try out my new funereal voice.

Surprised, I was genuinely disappointed that the voice I'd conjured up was so unimaginative: Gregory's voice was a deep baritone – it reverberated with the melancholy of a glorified cinematic death – although its imagined dramatic effect only made me want to giggle like a schoolboy.

Having only encountered death on the silver screen and, of course, in books, my head had automatically gone for the overused, melodramatic, dirge-like deep pitch adopted by film stars finding themselves within scripted tragic events. It didn't really matter – actors were only faking it anyway – they were merely suitably dressed dolls in makeshift wardrobes in manufactured scenarios. Little Grieving Gregory was simply and frantically treading the proverbial boards within my pocket. Same difference.

'Do you feel me, Barney?' I boomed on Gregory's behalf inside my head. Answering so only I could hear, in my own well-modulated tone, after some thought, I simply said, 'Explain. How should I feel?'

'Lost. Empty. As if your whole world has come to an end. Do you feel any of that?'

Digging deep, concentrating, eventually I admitted defeat. 'No. I feel nothing. In fact, I'd declare myself as to be verging on the wholly disinterested. I'm having difficulty emotionally connecting to the whole thing.' Internally, I shrugged. 'Except for Mum. Of course I feel for her.'

'And how do you suppose your mother feels?'

'All of those things you mentioned. I know because my mind tells me so, but *I* don't feel any of it.'

'What else does she feel?'

Tuning back to the service, I glanced at Mum. Her face was white but I could see a smudge of rouge where she'd attempted to colour herself undeathly. There were no tears, just a faraway look in her eyes and a tight line to her lips, her jaw set as if it were a mould cast in plaster.

'Mum has buttoned herself up, Gregory. For appearances

sake. Or else because she fears if she cries, she might never stop. She's cut herself off and is all alone. Even though I am sitting right next to her, holding her hand.'

'Good, Barney. At least you recognise how she is dealing with Grief. But there are many *many* ways to cope with bereavement and each person manifests their sadness in different ways. Which I can guarantee, you will witness for yourself in the coming weeks and months as you watch your mother.'

As I sat there, feeling decidedly nothing-in-particular, I was tempted to tell Grieving Gregory to fuck right off with his stupid booming voice – all dark and mysterious in my head – but I didn't. I wanted to learn, I really did. If only to help Mum. Usually, I could offer her whatever was necessary – up to a point and perhaps not as fully as others, certainly not like Dad – but this whole Grief thing left me cold. It was something so far off what I'd ever encountered, we were complete strangers and I had no inclination to want to familiarise myself with whatever Gregory had to offer.

But I had to. I was all Mum had left, so for her, I'd make a concerted effort to investigate it further.

Fully focused now, I absorbed the entirety of the funeral: the stained-glass windows; the coffin, pre-flames; the congregation; the mourning mourners, dabbing delicately at their noses with small but clean hankies; and I couldn't help but notice there was an awful lot of head bowing. Although again, I'd seen this on the screen and read about it in books, it was worth remembering. A minor detail, but the posture definitely *looked* good and knowing I could use it in the future, I gratefully adopted the pose now. Tried it on for size. I thought it a good and easy fit.

'How would you feel if Mum died?' Gregory whispered in my head.

'Frightened. Very frightened,' I answered automatically without any conscious thought, and only when I heard the words, did I realise how wrong they were. *That, would be my reaction, not how I'd feel* emotionally *about Mum's departure.* It was a selfish answer: clinical. Embarrassed I'd got it so wrong, I closed my eyes and channelled my thoughts. 'I'd feel lost, abandoned, scared. Helpless, cheated, angry. Fucking angry.'

'My, what a self-centred boy you are. Wouldn't you miss your mother on a personal level?'

'Fuck off, Gregory. What do you even know about it? I invented you, you're in my head. Go away.'

Softly, I placed my forefinger and thumb around the neck of my four-inch pocket doll. And pressed until there was a sort of cracking, snapping noise. I'd broken Gregory's neck and for my efforts, I felt a small shard of china cut my finger. I smeared the blood on the inside of my pocket, feeling it sticky and knowing it red. But I'd made Grief go away. Thankfully. For now.

Mum glanced at me, her eyebrows furrowed. 'What's wrong?' her voice hissed.

'Nothing, Mum. Don't you worry.'

Again, I squeezed her hand, wanting to give her solace, but turning her face from mine, she blanked me out and I realised she was in a world of her own once more – and it didn't include me.

I might as well have been holding the hand of a ghost.

All on my own, I worried I'd lost Mum forever.

That couldn't happen.

Without her, I really didn't trust myself, so I squeezed her hand even tighter, not wanting to let her go. Grimacing, she pulled her hand from mine and continued to look out into space – without me.

It might as well have been me that had died, and not just stupid old Dad.

I bowed my head and held on to my fury, gripping my hands in my lap until they hurt, and my finger bled invisibly onto my dark trousers.

5

———

JODIE

3 YEARS AGO

Jodie Box's daughters, Katie and Emily, were in bed.

Jodie prayed they were asleep as her fingers trembled and fumbled at the straps of the new black dress Tom had told her to put on. Looking at herself in the en suite bathroom mirror, she sucked in her breath at her reflection. *What a pathetic mess I am.* She could see her ribs and her hip joints jutting through the clingy material and her face was thin – and terrified.

Tom hadn't bought her anything for so many years she'd lost count, and instinctively Jodie didn't trust the gift, even though it *was* their anniversary. Twenty years together. Instead, she thought it the prelude to yet another sick game of his. But how could she refuse his demand that she wear it? He was bigger and stronger than her, and she had no choice.

For a moment, she allowed herself to entertain the notion that perhaps this time he meant it. A nice present to please her, a real anniversary present – nothing bad – going back to how their relationship used to be when they'd first met, so desperately in love with each other. She couldn't really believe they'd been together for over twenty years. She'd been childishly excited when she'd awoken this morning, knowing it was their anniversary, and she'd asked Tom, 'What have we got planned tonight?' She'd offered a worn-out smile, already defeated and really only expecting a non-answer from him. 'Or is it a secret?'

He'd nodded, not really listening, and she'd been horribly disappointed that he hadn't even acknowledged what should have been a celebration. She'd gone to the trouble of buying him a horrendously expensive gift – for his stupid car, which was his mid-life-crisis baby. She'd bought him a pair of handmade, outrageously expensive Italian leather driving gloves. He'd loved them. She knew he wouldn't be able to resist putting them on later that evening. Tom was a child like that. But he hadn't really thanked her for the gloves.

Because he was a bastard.

Things had changed between them so quickly in the years that had followed the birth of the children: she hadn't been prepared for it. *Whatever I touch, I always fuck it up. Always. It's my fault. It must be. It always is.*

She watched her reflection in the mirror as a smile landed on her lips at the memory of their once-shared love, but the curve of her upturned mouth only tentatively settled in place, as if like an aeroplane, it might at any time take off to some distant place.

Knowing Tom was waiting on the other side of the door, probably lying on the bed, impatiently waiting for her to carry out his instructions, she tried desperately to flatten down her hair that seemed to fly away at the slightest touch.

She'd had a drink earlier, a shot – or three or four – of vodka, and for a reason she couldn't explain, every time she'd had a sneaky drink recently, she was tempted to hum. The tune didn't matter: it was more a way to make her believe she wasn't actually disappearing from this world. It was also proof that she was functioning. As if only sober people were capable of knocking out a melody. *Stupid*, she thought. *Ridiculous.*

I'm a hummy mummy. Normally, that made her smile. Now, it made her want to weep.

Her mouth dry, she ran her tongue over her teeth, trying to get enough moisture to unstick her lips from her gums. Bracing herself, pulling her shoulders back as if in preparation, she came out of the bathroom. Despite her knowledge of Tom, Jodie so desperately wanted to believe this time it would be different.

The dress really is a gift. It is an anniversary present. He does love me. He's bought me something special. Because he loves me. He wants to see me looking beautiful and desirable again.

And here I am, thinking he's forgotten.

Maybe this is a new beginning for us and he is being kind and this won't be a trick.

Jodie stopped self-consciously in front of Tom, and his expression didn't change. Not one bit. Only his eyes moved as they roved over her body. 'Turn around. You know, do a twirl.'

She forced out a laugh. 'No, I don't want to. Don't be silly.'

'Go on, darling. For me. Do a twirl. You look great.'

Reluctantly, tugging nervously at her hair, feeling awkward, she turned in a circle, her feet tripping clumsily in stuttering little steps. She knew she should have pirouetted elegantly and sexily in a fluid movement, but embarrassment made her stiff and ungainly.

'Take it off. The dress, take it off.'

'No, I–'

'For me, darling, take it off. I want to see you.'

Gritting her teeth together so hard her jaw ached, she tried to unfasten the dress but her fingers couldn't find the zip. Couldn't get a proper hold of it. She started sweating. Started blushing at her own inadequacy. And then she felt hands on her shoulders and she tensed.

'Let me.' Tom pulled the zip down. Slowly. Very, very slowly. Jodie thought she might throw up with the not knowing what was coming next. Anticipation swamped her, making it easy for him to manipulate her physically with his touch. Her limbs were floppy with an anxious limpness.

'There, and don't you look lovely in your bra and knickers.'

She whispered out a laugh, hoping he wouldn't smell the vodka. 'Do I?'

'Most certainly you do, my darling. Really lovely.'

She stood there, not knowing what to do next, not knowing what not to do.

'Take them off.'

'What?'

'Take off the bra and knickers.'

Shaking her head, she stared at the floor. 'I don't want to.' Even to her own ears her voice sounded child-like in its terror.

'For me. Take them off. Please. Go on. Pretty please. I want to see you properly. I want to see you naked.'

Closing her eyes, Jodie unclasped her bra and let it drop to the floor. Squeezing her eyes tighter, she slid her panties down over her bottom and past her thighs. And all the time she waited for it to change. Into something nastier. Something that over the past year had become horribly familiar.

'Now do a twirl for me. Again. Do a naked twirl.'

There was no point in protesting – she had to obey because they were the rules and they both knew it. Stiffly, she rotated on the spot.

When she heard Tom laugh, she flinched.

He wouldn't stop. Louder and louder he laughed and she closed her eyes again. Something hit her in the face. Automatically she opened her eyes and gazed down at the ball of socks he'd thrown at her. Two tears trickled from her eyes, one from each side as if symmetry in shame was somehow important.

'And there you stand before me, Jodie. The woman who promised so much but delivered so very little. Just take a look at how very old you look. Your skin is saggy and baggy and you've acquired crow's feet. I'd say you were a little on the young side for wrinkles, but that's what you get for being a lazy bitch. You do nothing to help yourself.' He laughed. 'And even less for me. You're totally worthless. To me and to everyone. Even the children wouldn't miss you if you suddenly disappeared, and don't you think that's just too awful to even comprehend? Can you get your stupid head around *that* little fact? You're a useless mother.'

She stood, head down, and let it wash over her. She knew it was wrong, but she felt she deserved his hatred and felt like crying when his voice carried on. She wept silently.

'How dare you, Jodie? How fucking dare you even dream that I'd ever want to touch you again.' He laughed. 'Just shows how off your mental capacity is. You have no idea at all how I feel about you. I loathe you and I will *never* forgive you. Never.'

Stepping nearer, Tom stood right in front of her, his nose touching hers. 'You are one sad and tragic woman, do you know that? Do I keep on having to remind you?' He jabbed her in the chest with his finger. 'Do you really think I don't notice how I've taken a back seat since the bloody girls came along. Playing second fiddle to two stinking brats. You belong to me. I am the provider, but all I do is give and give and give with no fucking thanks at all. I don't forgive you for making me second-best in my own house.'

He punched her. On the shoulder. Hard enough to make her stagger and fall.

Never on the face where it would show.

'You will make my meals and wash my clothes and do exactly what I say. Because that is your job. The kids can look after themselves – I don't like the space they take up. It's *my* space.'

She could only gaze in horror at the veins pulsing in his neck, his face flushed and twisted, full of hatred. 'And don't think I haven't noticed that Katie – our elder child – is a better mother to Emily than you are. I'd have thought even you would be able to see that.' He wiped his hand across his mouth. 'At least Katie makes sure the two of them are presentable for public scrutiny. They look the part: nice and polite and from a good and decent family. *Because they are* – no thanks to you. You should take a lesson from your oldest daughter.'

Jodie knew in part Tom was right. She'd failed abysmally. Lifting her eyes, she watched his mouth move again.

'Seems you need to remember *I* am the one who needs catering for. Because I own you.' He smiled and his tone softened. 'Jodie, Jodie, Jodie. You are one serious fuck-up. But you're my fuck-up, Jodie. All mine.'

Jodie tuned him out, her mind instantly turning to her daughters. Especially little Emily.

I won't make a noise when he really starts beating me.

I'll make sure I scream quietly. Promise.

I can't let Katie and Emily hear me.

Especially Emily. She's only eight but young for her age.

So, that's why I will not scream, because I don't want my children to hear.

I know ten-year-old Katie calls me Shadow Mummy, because she hasn't learnt to whisper properly yet, and I've heard her say it. But she's right. There's nothing of me left. I have been reduced to a grey silhouette.

As the second punch landed on her ribs, Jodie had time to think, *I hate you, Tom. I hate what you have become.*

I love you, Katie.
I love you, Emily.
I do not *love myself.*

31

6

———

ME

NOW

It had taken me months to find the appropriate group to attend. These days there were groups for everything – it was just a matter of finding the right one that would cater to one's needs.

I'd found it online and had eventually been asked to join after telling my story, incrementally, over several weeks and months, tapping earnestly away on my laptop. It was as if I'd been softly caressing these people with my lies – bad me – and I realised I'd essentially groomed them all. My laptop was my buffer and I hid behind it, no one ever guessing they were conversing with a personalised living, breathing doll.

It had felt a very natural process enticing in the women, and a relatively easy ruse to pull off. I wasn't actually doing anything Wrong or Bad, *not really*, but I was taking advantage of them, and for that, I should have been Ashamed.

After a couple of months of saying the right thing, being furiously Kind and Gentle and Vulnerable, I'd been accepted and they'd invited me to this little gathering of three women. A splinter group of their own making, they had split off from a larger corporate counselling organisation and now met at a face-to-face weekly meeting.

I hadn't known whether to be pathologically early, or psychopathically late, but had plumped for the former. I loitered outside the doors of a sad-looking community hall, which I'd had to take the bus to. Adopting the correct expression for the occasion, Nervous and Apprehensive, I sat on a wall and hung my head and clasped my hands together in between my knees.

As I waited quietly, I decided this really was a good idea. It had come to me quite unexpectedly after Dad's death, and it had felt right. I'd be killing so many birds with one stone, it was brilliant. The only drawback was, I wasn't well-acquainted nor entirely comfortable with socialising – Mum hadn't included that in her homeschooling. I'd always prowled around on the outskirts of the human race, but rarely got *involved*. Deep down and dirty involved: because I didn't really know how.

Nor did I see any need. I was fine on my own.

Affable and Amenable Annie sat in my pocket and I touched her for good luck. When I looked up, I realised several cars had parked and people, some in couples, some on their own, were making their way to the entrance. A disparate but steady dribble of men and women, walked in an untidy crocodile of human chaos. None of them was who I was looking for, but I watched anyway. I liked watching people. From a distance.

Most of them were smiling and I hid my desire to smile with them, so excited was I. But I didn't want to appear Rude or Unsympathetic should my trio of mourners arrive unnoticed by me in all the hustle and bustle, although I had seen them already on Zoom.

But in the flesh might be quite different.

Not being a cruel man, I was genuinely interested in the outcome of my little experiment, and standing, I effortlessly merged into the pushing and excited clump of the moving mob as they entered the building. I assumed they were here for something Fun, like an art group, karate, or singing.

Watching them disperse into various rooms, I leant against a wall and waited.

My three ladies arrived together and one of them made a point of looking around, presumably seeking me out, although I was the only person in the empty reception area. I held my hand up and approached. 'Hello, Jodie?'

'Yes, of course. I recognise you.' She held out her hand and I shook it. She was tall and slim with wispy blonde hair, well-dressed and well-spoken. In her early fifties, I estimated. If that. 'How nice to meet you properly, Barney, face to face.'

I nodded and smiled and looked a little Needy and potentially tearfully Grateful at her introduction. She patted my hand in hers and then let it drop. 'This is Grace, and Odette, who you've already met online.'

Odette nodded curtly and managed an underwhelmingly tight smile, not bothering to hide the fact the effort nearly killed her. She clearly wasn't impressed by my inclusion in the group.

No problem. I'd win her over. At least she was unnecessarily rude, which made her instantly more interesting than the other two.

The third woman, a redhead, was Grace, probably in her mid-forties, who was a vocal gusher. Gushed all over me, speaking without taking a breath. 'Hello, Barney. How lovely to meet you at last. You're our honorary male member, so we're honoured to have you. Really, we are. Yes, most definitely.'

'Thank you so much for allowing me to join you. *I'm* the privileged one. Really I am.'

Am I overdoing it? No, they were lapping it up – except Odette. She simply stared and her expression was unreadable. Odette kept her face neutral and I really quite admired that. It made me smile inside. She would be my immediate challenge, but challenge was really the wrong way to look at this.

I was here to study. I was the student, and they, my teachers in Grief and Misery.

There was also the small matter of what else I wanted, but first I had to ingratiate myself.

Jodie steered me by my elbow into a small room with a tatty sofa and three armchairs. 'It's hardly the lap of luxury,' she explained, as if embarrassed, 'but they let us hire it weekly, and it's cheap and cosy, which is perfect for us. I hope you'll feel comfortable here too.'

'It's lovely. Don't worry about me, Jodie.' I knew the repetition of someone's name made them feel instantly special and it was a tool I used when I had no option but to mix with the masses. Something I tended to avoid, wherever possible.

I allowed myself to be pushed into one of the armchairs, and Gushy Grace asked how I liked my coffee. 'As it comes, Grace. Black, no sugar, please.'

Odette threw herself down on another armchair, crossed her legs, and unashamedly studied me. Her hair was black and swept back in a severe bun, which was so taut it risked pulling her face from her skull. She, I guessed, was in her thirties. I had three women spanning three decades – all the more interesting as a control group for me to study in their natural habitat.

'What do you do, Barney? I mean for a job. You never said in your messages in our chat room.' Her glare didn't waver. 'Or when you were allowed to join us in our personal Zoom calls.'

Jodie tutted. 'Leave him alone, Odette. This isn't an interview for Christ's sake.'

'No, I don't mind at all,' I soothed. 'I'm an illustrator. I spend my life drawing pictures.' I shrugged. 'For my sins. Pictures of this and that. Nothing in particular. Just stuff.' I smiled Modestly and rolled my shoulders Cutely. I was actually uncomfortable having to talk about my real self. To strangers. It was unnecessarily exposing.

'Do you have many of those?' Objectionable Odette asked, her face still a mask. 'Sins, I mean, not pictures.'

Grace gushed out from the remaining armchair. 'Stop being horrid, Odette. Leave the poor man alone. Let him drink his coffee in peace. He doesn't have to take any of your shit.' She gasped and put her hand to her mouth. 'Excuse the swearing.'

'Yes, I've never heard the word "shit" before. I'm shocked.' I smiled, deadpan.

It took a while, but finally Grace, like a child, squeaked with laughter. 'Sorry. I'm not used to someone else being in our group, that's all. I'm a bit nervous.'

'Stop behaving like a fucking child, Grace. *He's* the one who should be nervous,' Odette said, standing up. 'This is *our* group, just us three, and I for one, never okayed you joining, Barney. In fact, intuitively, I'm against it. This is private, and you don't belong here. We don't even know you.' She drew back her lips, her skin so tight the movement produced was a rictus grin at best. 'But I'm happy to vet you in the flesh, if that's okay by you?'

Ignoring her sarcasm, I nodded. 'Go ahead. Your reluctance to accept me on face value is wholly Admirable.' I lifted my shoulders, as if visibly Upset. 'You know my story, Odette, and I'm Sorry, but that's all I can offer at the moment. But I understand you feel as if I've just barged in on something special and private. And I am truly Apologetic for that.'

'Shut up, Odette.' Jodie sat on the sofa. 'And sit down. Stop with the threatening. I invited him, Grace approved, majority rule and all that. What is your problem?'

Sitting, Odette was very clearly still Angry. 'Why did we have to take anyone else at all? We were fine, just the three of us.'

This time, *I* stood up. 'Perhaps I should go and wait outside – give you time to consider my inclusion here. I understand completely. Let me know when you've decided.'

Before any of them could stop me, I exited the room and stood outside, my back leaning against the wall again. Fair enough, I thought. I was the interloper, and if I'd been Odette, I'd have been put out. Change is never good.

Never. I had discovered I hated change.

Dad's death had changed everything. It had definitely changed Mum, and it had changed me. Irreparably. Because I didn't know how to behave or how to fix my mother.

For the first time in years, I wasn't there to understand and offer my support to Mum in general, and now, specifically, I couldn't help her Grief. I had no comprehension of what she was feeling. I missed Dad about the place, but I'd got over it. I'd been a bit sad, but he was gone. The end.

On my own, without Mum's administrations and assurances and advice, I was floundering.

Fucking *change*.

But I'd work with what I had, despite my anger.

My fury had to be kept in check. I didn't need Mum to tell me *that*.

My plan was simple. Once I'd been officially accepted, and there was no doubt I would be, however loud Objectionable Odette's objections, I'd let the three women lead the conversation, but would refuse to join in. I'd show Softness whilst listening to their stories and would Respect their collective Sadnesses. Not joining in was the privilege of being a first-timer in the group. They knew the gist of my story anyway, so there was no pressure for me to elaborate on it straight away. No one could or would force me to speak of Dad's death in any greater detail, and it was my own business after all. I also highly doubted my business was the same as anyone else's in the room.

The women had no idea what I wanted and for the moment, that suited me just fine.

They were feeling the emotion, and I was assessing and evaluating it. The Grief was theirs, not mine. And I was interested to see how they all handled it. And I'd learn how to do it. In an effort to help Mum and not be left on my own.

I couldn't be left on my own – *some*one had to look after me now that Mum had run off with Grief, and that person was me. I had no choice in the matter.

Meanwhile, these women's feelings were mine to play with.

Although, granted, that wasn't strictly how Mum had taught me to use and explore new emotions. But things had changed and I was now effectively working solo.

Mum had fallen into a big dark hole of Grief, and as she drowned, I stood by and watched, sad and helpless – totally unable to save her from her feelings of bereavement. I told myself I was doing this for her, but part of me, a big part, was genuinely excited at what I might find out from my three little guinea pigs: Jodie, Grace and Odette.

For the first time, I was going to allow myself to have some honest-to-goodness Fun.

Something I'd never really experienced for thirty years. The prospect, in itself, was Fun.

This was my maiden voyage – chatting, socialising and making chums. All on my own. Without my puppet-master Mum pulling my strings. I was personally orchestrating a *good* change because I thought I deserved that. And I had a most very definite plan. A good one. One no one would see coming. It would be a great big wonderful surprise – for one of them.

And I could hopefully achieve that which I'd always wanted.

A normal life.

With all the trimmings.

7

ODETTE

1 YEAR AGO

Odette walked home and dumped her shopping in its allocated spaces, and sat down. She could bloody murder a drink, but couldn't be arsed to get one.

Here I sit. Alone. Single. And an orphan. How bloody pathetic is that.

She couldn't really articulate how the death of her mother two years ago had affected her – only that she now felt as though she'd lost her identity. Without her mother, she was no longer a daughter. So, what did that make her?

It made her insignificant: a nobody. Lost in her own space that only consisted of herself.

She'd been left behind.

Odette had lost her sense of belonging in the world and sometimes wished it would all end. Not actually, truly, really – not in any concrete sense – it was just a thought she played with in her head now and again, when all she wanted was for this emptiness to finish. When all she craved was oblivion.

She had friends but they said all the wrong things and pussy-footed around the subject of her mother's death, or didn't bring it up at all. It was as if they were embarrassed by her loss, so avoided the topic entirely.

And, of course, there had always been those unspoken words that no one dared utter out loud, but Odette knew they were all thinking it. *Why hasn't she got over it yet? Her mother's been dead for two years.* Two whole years. *Odette really does need to move on and get a grip.*

Odette didn't care. She felt alone, so actually being alone didn't make much difference. So what if it was taking her so long to get used to Mum dying? There wasn't a law that put a time limit on the amount of days permitted for mourning. It was just her way. She couldn't help it.

It was true when they said cancer was a silent killer. Her mother had taken her diagnosis screaming, wailing, hollering. Bloody outraged. Until she hadn't, and she'd been silenced by the disease and had accepted. She'd wanted to die at home and Odette had nursed her. It was that silent suffering that Odette couldn't forget. Days that seemed to never end, sitting next to her mother, holding her hand, not being able to take away and ease her pain – it had been like witnessing her die in slow motion. Eventually, quietly, Mum had welcomed death, and Odette had watched as it stole her mother. They'd held hands until her mother's fingers went cold in Odette's grasp. And still Odette had held on.

Feeling relief that at least she'd followed her mother's last wish.

So, now, Odette carried on in cruise control – remembering to eat occasionally, remembering to go to bed and sleep, remembering to get up and do it all again. But mostly she just remembered her mother. Not in any real specific way, but in a fluid swirl of emotion that left Odette blank and unreceptive to the rest of the world.

She couldn't quite believe that when she did go out, people

didn't stare at her. It was as if she were wearing a hat with a flashing beacon on the top, screaming out, *Look at me, my mother's dead,* but no one seemed to notice her – the change in her. The world carried on rotating on its axis and people carried on with their lives. It was as if her mother had never been.

In the grand scheme of things, no one had really noticed her departure.

Only Odette's world had ground to a halt.

Which made a mockery of life. And death. There seemed little point in living, but Odette carried on with the best of them, hoping that she'd eventually be able to crawl out from this yawning empty chasm which had swallowed her whole.

The only place where she felt alive was when she visited her mother's grave.

At least Mum was still there, in one piece, under the ground, and not scattered in some random place in a waft of ashes. Burial was the most respectful way to treat the dead, in her opinion.

Odette didn't believe in cremation.

It was *too* final.

She closed her eyes as she sat at the kitchen table and, ashamed, admitted she couldn't wait to go back to the graveyard. It belonged to her and was the only place that felt even remotely like home. Which was just stupid. Odette knew it, but couldn't shake the feeling that when she was at home her mother was all alone, under the soil, with no one there to hold her hand.

It never changed – a monotony of grief-filled days. Odette would awake to a day which felt like all the others that had come before it since she'd watched earth being thrown onto her mother's coffin. Ashes to ashes, dust to dust, alive to dead. She could still hear the sound of the soil as it landed on wood, the sobs of the other mourners a dreadful background noise that she'd tuned out. Nothing had changed from that moment on.

Everything was the same. She was the same. And Mum was still dead.

Odette would make an effort, make coffee and sit, sipping and staring into space, thinking of nothing – her mind a blank. A blissful blank.

Internally, she would go through the day that yawned before her – like a bloody great big hole, which she could fill how she chose. But she had no choices. So no thinking involved. Problem solved. Off to the graveyard. Off to her new home. Off to talk to her mother. Again. She was surprised she still had such a lot to say to Mum.

Shit.

Odette didn't know how to get out of this routine. It was killing her and she knew it, but she didn't know how to change it. Putting her head on her crossed arms on the table, she would close her eyes and try to think positively. The radio always blared in the background and she'd try to listen, wanting a distraction, but she could never engage.

Nope. Nothing good to be found on the radio. Or in her mind. Absolutely nothing. Sighing, she'd get up and shower and dress. Tick. Those exciting jobs accomplished, she would move to the sofa in the sitting room and again, sit with her eyes closed, pretending to herself if she couldn't see anything real, then she'd be able to picture nothing – just blackness, which would be an improvement.

Although, in her imagination, her fixation on picturing her mother's rotting corpse six feet under the ground, was wedged firmly in her mind. In fact, closing her eyes, only made the image more vivid. Not knowing what to do with herself, she'd sit, eyes stretched wide open in order to ward off the dark film reel that played in her head on an endless loop, giving her up-close visions of her once-mother. She gazed at nothing in the sitting room. In total and frightening silence.

Waiting until she couldn't put it off any longer, she'd gratefully give in to her need to visit the graveyard. It really was the only place she wanted to be. And she'd often last a whole two hours after waking, before giving in to what felt like a compulsion.

Hurrying, once the decision had been made and Odette had given herself permission to go to the cemetery – she didn't know why she always played the stupid putting-it-off game, the outcome never changed – she left the house and went to the graveyard.

Immediately outside the cemetery, there was a florist. Odette handed in yesterday's vase and collected another, a fresh one – a stupid thing she insisted on, to show her mother she was making an extra effort – and bought some flowers. She and the shop had an arrangement and it worked well for both.

Quickly, she powered through the headstones, until she reached her goal.

'Morning, Mum. It's me.' Odette smiled and settled down to pretty up the headstone.

Squatting there, arranging the flowers into something beautiful, she finally made a decision.

I need help. I really do.

I need someone to talk to. Someone who'll understand.

I'll start looking tomorrow. There must be a group out there where at least one person will understand me.

Although she wouldn't be completely honest with whoever it may turn out to be. How could she? Odette had committed an illegal act, but no one needed to know that whilst they were holding her hand, comforting her.

Decision made, she smiled to herself.

Onwards.

Tick.

8

———————

GRACE

NOW

Before going to the group, excited as ever by the prospect of it – even more so, knowing they'd be welcoming a new recruit, Barney, into the fold today – Grace had sat in her armchair at home, looking out into the garden through the window, and let her mind drift back to the *accident*. It was an indulgence she practised often.

Being the youngest of two siblings, Grace had never been without her older sister, Polly.

Until Polly had died.

And then there'd only been one child. That had been years ago. Six years to be exact.

I've changed a lot *since then*, Grace thought. *I'm much stronger and more assertive now.*

But six years ago, in the most brutal way, Polly, almost inexplicably, had gone forever, and Grace had been left all on her own. All she had for comfort was the strangely not-awful memory of that day. She'd never told anyone what had *really* happened. Until she'd met Jodie. Up to that point, she'd kept quiet about her not actively doing *any*thing – apart from

44

watching. From shock. That was the story she stuck to. Still. She'd done nothing to stop it and nothing to help.

Without Grace even realising it, mourning her sister's death had ironically become a way of life. Like a personal crusade. A profession. She'd become a full-time freelancer in mourning, until finally, nearly two years ago, Grace had been recruited by Jodie into the special group of two – as it was then – and after meeting Odette sometime later, the three of them were as close as close could be. Grace had also had to tell Odette her secret.

Because that was how it worked.

Quickly, after Polly's accident, Grace had been grateful to shed the burden of her parents' grief. They were devastated and destroyed. She'd been unable to help them, and they, her. The death of one of their children had cut like a cleaver through the blood that bound them, creating a deep ravine between her parents and herself: the sole remaining child. The family break-up had been inevitable.

Grace was pretty sure she'd never really loved Polly truly, and she'd known Polly most definitely had never even pretended to love Grace. Grace had been an irritant in her older sister's life and Grace had simply always accepted that. Because she was weak.

To add insult to injury, Polly's death had been such a stupid accident. It should have been tragic or melodramatic. But it hadn't been. Life shouldn't end *accidentally*. It was all so unlucky and unfair.

Grace had been forty and together, she and Polly had been celebrating Polly's forty-sixth birthday. It should have been the perfect day. The weather was perfect, the river and its leafy bank was perfect, their picnic in its perfect hamper with perfectly folded napkins, all had been perfect.

Including their sharing of the day, mostly because Polly hadn't been able to rustle up anyone else – that was the truth of it. There was nothing other than family commitment that put them on the riverbank together to celebrate. But Grace had hoped, as she always did, stupidly and in such a needy way it made her blush, that one day, Polly would acknowledge her and say she loved Grace. It was childish of Grace, but she hadn't stopped wishing for some show of affection from Polly ever since she'd been a child.

Grace always wondered why she carried on this charade. She'd known early on it was a futile wish and nothing would ever change between the two of them. They didn't like each other – never had – why lie about it? Sometimes it was hard to believe they even came from the same household, let alone the same parents.

'Pour me another glass of champers, Grace. It's my birthday and I'm celebrating. With knobs on.'

Laughing, Grace had rolled her eyes. 'Don't get pissed. I'm not carrying you back to the train station.'

'Don't be such a bloody prude. God almighty, it's my birthday. Forty-fucking-six. How depressing is that?' She'd laughed with her head thrown back, but it wasn't a laughter full of joy. It had sounded jagged, jaded and joyless. Grace had poured her another glass anyway because it was easier to go along with whatever her sister wanted – *demanded*. Poured her a small one. Polly had picked the glass up and inspected it. 'No. I might be old, Grace, but I'm not blind. That's half a glass. Fill it up. To the top.'

Laughing, wanting Polly to approve of her and not think her boring, Grace had relented and poured herself another one as well – pretending to be carefree. *I am* never *carefree. I worry about everything.*

Sitting together, their backs touching and facing away from each, they'd chatted about everything and nothing. Grace had enjoyed the proximity, forcing herself to see it as closeness, but knowing it wasn't. Deep down, she knew Polly was simply using Grace's body as a physical upright support – nothing more.

Popping the cork of the second and last bottle of champagne, Polly had become quieter and quieter. Grace had watched as her older sister had tipped the drips of bubbly from her glass into her opened mouth.

'Don't you think it's a bit bloody sad that neither of us is married, Grace? Two spinsters. What are the chances? Neither of us is ugly or stupid or horrible. And yet, here we both are, two single women in their forties, alone on a riverbank, cheering on another year. How sad is that?'

'You're drunk and maudlin. Stop it. This is beautiful. Look around you. It's heavenly – all this grass and water and stillness, away from London. What better way to spend your birthday? We don't need men. We're fine on our own.'

Polly had sneered. 'I wouldn't say no to some male company. Any old man would do, I'm not fussy. A fling definitely wouldn't go amiss; sex however it comes and with anyone. I'm like a dried-up old prune.'

Grace had looked around her and quietly acknowledged to herself, not for the first time, that she wasn't in fact perfectly happy being single. Desperate, bloody *desperate*, to find a man, she'd hidden that needy side of herself. All she presented to the world was forty, free and single. As if that had been her plan all along.

Grace rolled onto her back and had pulled a mock-sad face, feeling slightly pissed. 'Yeah, well, what's a girl to do? We just haven't found "the one". We will, though. Don't worry about it. Really. What's the point? Once you stop looking, a man will come along. Guaranteed.'

'God, you're so sickeningly positive. So bright in your outlook, you make me want to puke. You're all sugar and spice and rainbows and prancing ponies and heavenly sparkling fairy tales. Don't you ever feel like complete shite? Like the rest of us? Don't you want some excitement in your life? Don't you want to do something bad and fuck the consequences? For once in your life, don't you just want to do whatever you want?'

Polly's face had twisted and contorted and looked ugly. 'You're such a conformist, Grace. Too frightened to ever rock the boat, you pretend you're a fucking angel.' Polly glared at her. 'And don't you think it sad that I'm here, with my bloody sister, no offence intended, instead of having a raucous party with a thousand friends hanging on my every word?'

Grace had sipped at her drink, hurt. She knew she had a tendency to being boring and predictable. In fact, she was the complete opposite to Polly, who followed nobody's rules but her own, and revelled in spontaneity and frivolity and saying what she thought – there was never any sugar-coating with her. Polly had never minded if she hurt or offended others. Unlike Grace, who admitted to herself she was always afraid of being disliked. It wasn't something she was proud of, but it was too late to change her nature now. She was a doormat, waiting to be trodden upon.

What an unexciting woman I have become. Have always been, Grace thought. *Truly, painfully dull.* She'd tried and pretended to be fun, but couldn't really pull it off and didn't fool anyone. Certainly, hadn't ever fooled herself – hadn't even come close. She'd come to terms with being run-of-the-mill, ten-a-penny, not worthy of inspiring passion in someone else. She couldn't change her banal accepting personality – it was who she was and she was quite happy with it.

Am I?

Who am I fucking kidding?

Even my relationship with Polly is a going-through-the-motions habitual lie, because there is no one else. For either of us.

Her older sister stood up. 'I'm going for a swim.'

'Don't be stupid, you can't. You've had too much to drink.'

'Oh, get a life. It'll be a laugh. You stay here and watch, then. Don't do anything out of the ordinary, Grace, someone might see.'

Her sister was a selfish bitch. And a cruel woman. Why did Grace so desire a loving relationship when there clearly was none? How bloody cringingly needy was she? Shrugging internally, she sighed and said, 'Do what you want, Polly. I'm staying here.'

'What a surprise.'

Polly walked, unsteadily, towards the river. Even from her seated position, Grace could see the water was high and fast-flowing. A slight unease settled in her, but she didn't move – only watched as Polly peeled off her top, kicked off her sandals and pulled down her jeans, leaving her clothes strewn behind her on the grass. She was so arrogant and self-assured, and for a minute, Grace was seething, absolutely furious. It was at times like this, Grace allowed herself to embrace her hatred of her sister's self-importance and boastfulness, thinking herself above everyone else.

The bank sloped steeply down to the water and Polly had slipped. Grace had heard her laugh and then swear, but undeterred, Polly had entered the river until it came up to her stomach. Turning, wobbling slightly with the force of the current, Polly held her hand in the air, and waved. 'It's bloody freezing. Freezing but great,' she shouted, and Grace automatically waved back.

The first time Polly's head dipped below the surface, Grace had assumed her sister was just being silly. She'd been submerged for perhaps seconds, that was all, and Grace told herself not to be so uptight, such a kill-joy. As she came up for air, there were more whoops of delight from Polly, and then her head had disappeared again. For longer this time.

Much longer.

Grace had hugged her knees to her chest. Waited. Held her breath. Until Polly popped up again, much further down the river now. Still arrogant and overconfident, Polly fist-pumped the air. 'Come on in, you boring old fart.'

But Grace remained on the grass, watching and waiting.

And a little bit of her, hoping.

When Polly's head vanished for the third time, it had taken a while before Grace had stood up. And suddenly her heart had pounded painfully in her chest, her breath had come in gasps, and only then did she start walking, trotting, *running* to the river.

Polly had never resurfaced.

Her body was found hours later, after Grace had rung the police and an ambulance and anyone else she could think of in a total panic. She'd said she'd fallen asleep on the grass and when she'd awoken, Polly hadn't been there.

Gone forever and Grace could never quite get to grips with how she felt about it all.

She'd never permitted herself to probe too deeply under the surface of her emotions.

It was too frightening to imagine what she might find if she really looked properly.

Of course, Jodie and Odette knew the truth of that day. But not *all* of the truth – not the juicy part of it. Jodie – the leader of the three women, the one who'd recruited Grace into the special, most elite group – had been wonderful and supportive and caring. Precisely what Grace had needed. Still needed.

Although, when Grace was feeling mean, she'd admit to herself that Jodie had that same bossiness her sister had. And it irritated the fuck out of her.

Grace wondered if the new man, Barney, would be able to see through her little white lie.

She hoped to God, not. Not yet.

For what would that make her, if he knew she could have saved Polly? She'd need to get him onside before she told him the truth.

Grace could have saved Polly, or at least attempted to, but she simply hadn't wanted to.

And that was her big secret – the *not wanting to*.

Finally, Grace had beaten her sister at something – had come out the winner. The fact it had been life over death only made it more satisfying. More final and definite.

A real victory.

9
———

ME

I had been collected from the hall, like a new treasure, by Grace, who told me not to mind Odette. 'She comes over as a little harsh, but really, she's very nice. I'm sure you'll grow to like her.'

'I'm sure I will. Thank you for being so Kind.'

Grace gently took me by the hand and led me back into the Grieving room. I was alarmed to feel her hot clammy fingers softly give mine a little squeeze. As if she owned me.

Or wanted something.

This was precisely why I had little to no contact with women. Apart from the prostitutes who catered to my sexual needs, I avoided females. At least whores didn't lie. Money for sex: it was a simple transaction – no conversation, no arguments, no lies – just a physical coupling. No more complicated than buying a bag of potatoes.

Other than that, women were unnecessary and an unknown quantity as far as I was concerned: way too complex for me to deal with. Plus, I had no inclination at all to mix with them, as I wanted nothing from them.

Having not anticipated the sudden physical intimacy from Grace clutching my hand, I hadn't enjoyed the forced proximity of her, and felt unnerved by it. *Why hadn't Mum taught me how to be with people? Unchaperoned. Instead of only allowing me to skirt around the edges of society.* I was suddenly horribly hyper-aware that I might be at a disadvantage. And it made me angry.

Back in the room, the women, with their unfamiliar rules by which I had to abide, made me more unsettled. I wasn't used to the feeling, and it was most certainly a very real emotion I could have done without. I hadn't expected it, and so was careful to manage my expression. In truth, I was as near fucking completely freaked out as I'd ever been. This was new territory for me, and I didn't like it. A fine balance, teetering on a knife edge, I put on a camouflage of Receptive to all of them, and kept my mouth firmly shut, covertly caressing Affable and Amenable Annie deep in my pocket. I would allow Jodie to run things.

Whilst I got my breath.

'Glad you hung around long enough that we could get you back.' Jodie beamed at me, and ran her hands through her hair. 'Shall we start again? Odette has promised not to be rude, and for the moment, she has promised to give you the benefit of the doubt. She has also promised not to hit you. So, that's a relief. What more can I say?'

Odette scowled and Jodie laughed too loudly, which was my only indication this was meant to be light-hearted. Once realised, I Gaily laughed along.

Weirdly, despite Odette's aggression, I feel more at ease with her than with Jodie. And Grace makes me nervous. She seems... overfocused on me. Predatory, and I am not used to that. I think things are getting out of hand. I am not in control. It is the squeeze of Grace's hand on mine that has thrown me. The physical touching.

Slapping her hands on her knees, Jodie bent forward, elbows on her thighs. 'Really, Barney, sorry we got off to such a tetchy start. We'll move on.' She nodded at me, so I nodded back and endeavoured to look Enquiring and Interested, although felt off my game.

'This group is an opportunity for us three, and now you.' Jodie smiled again, and although my repertoire of facial mouth-stretching was being pushed to its limits, I managed an upturned tilt of the lips. 'It's a safe place for all of us to talk. It doesn't have to be about who we've lost, although obviously, if that's what you choose to speak of, please feel free.'

Jodie crossed her arms. 'We're a group of *four*...' She stressed the number as if I should be terribly Grateful for being included. 'We meet weekly and we use the time to be open, friendly and warm with each other.' She shrugged her shoulders. 'It's not really very complicated. We support each other, and are always there if any of us needs anything. Grief brought us together, but without wanting to sound too sickly, it's friendship that binds us.'

Another fucking smile. 'And that's it. It's simple, Barney, but it works for us. Knowing there is always someone to talk to. It doesn't sound like much, but believe me, and I think we'd all agree that as a group, we've made our own individual survival possible.'

Bobbing her head quaintly, she simply split her mouth open again: clearly it was her stock-in-trade go-to expression. I was running out of appropriate matching facial contortions. I felt very uncomfortable and embarrassed by the sheer... the sheer and very real *crappiness* of the entire thing. What a crock. I was disappointed. I wanted more.

This wasn't reality, not this show of hand-holding fake Love. This was a Mockery. They didn't know what they were talking about. My mother, who was *really* Grieving, didn't look like any of these women. She looked utterly *Ruined*. I could see it and that's why I was here: to help her get over it. Which was obviously going to be harder than I'd anticipated, but as I was here to study, I gritted my teeth and slipped back into intellectualising – my safe place.

Perhaps my special trio needed a gentle shove in the right direction, just to get things moving, although I knew I had to take things slowly so as not to unnecessarily alarm them.

It was when Grace stood, in order to pull her armchair next to mine, that I was again startled, not used to what I assumed was "normal" interaction between *friends*. Sitting back down – much too close to me now – Grace snaked her hand over the two arms of both chairs, and rested it on my knee. Patted it. 'Of course, Barney, if you want to specifically talk about your sadness, I'm here. We're all here, aren't we?' Grace added this last part as she remembered Jodie and Odette.

Gratefully and thankfully, Odette scoffed. 'Take your bloody hand off his leg, Grace. Leave him alone. This isn't a dating service.'

I wanted to laugh with huge and very genuine relief that Odette was already onside. Catching me completely off-guard, she winked at me, and I almost blushed – no one had ever done that before, except Mum. Clearly this was a very different wink, and I was unsure as to the meaning, but thought it definitely a positive one.

Playing it Cool, I glanced at Grace. With her red hair, she reminded me of my doll, Sad Sal. Except Grace didn't look Sad at all. Not like Sal, whose face, as a child, I had beautifully and very carefully painted, adding a down-turn to her mouth and a blue teardrop beneath her eye – truly Sad. When Mum couldn't keep up with making relevantly emotion-named tops for every new doll, painting their faces had sufficed. More than sufficed. It had brought them to life.

But I wasn't looking at Sadness now. All I could see on Grace's face was... Greed.

She wanted me and I couldn't understand why.

Ignoring Odette, Grace tightened her fingers on my leg. 'Come on, Barney. Tell me how you're feeling now. I'm sure it all must be very overwhelming for you. Three virtual strangers waiting to hear you speak. But trust me. I'm here for you.'

She bobbed her head inanely and I wanted to scream.

Gently but firmly, I put my hand over hers and removed it from my leg, repositioning it on the arm of the chair. Really, I wanted to hit her, to make her stop crowding me, but I followed the rules of the world, and stretched my lips yet again – an empty nothing-smile. She took my physical repel well, but couldn't hide the flash of Hurt as it skittered across her face. Out of the corner of my eye, I saw Odette nod. Unsmiling, but understanding me. Progress.

Keeping my face blank, I swept the hair from my eyes. 'I wouldn't know where to start. I don't know any of you. Not properly. Not yet.' I shrugged in a boyish fashion. 'Only from our chats online. Perhaps someone else could help me and say something. Just to get me going.' My face did Sheepish.

Seemingly recovered by my rebuff, Grace clasped her fingers in her lap. 'Suppose I could kick things off by seconding what Jodie said, and reiterate how nice it is to have you in the group. And you know my story, but I'll remind you. To get the ball rolling. My sister died, she drowned in a river and...' She dipped her eyes. '...I never really got over it.'

Immediately, I knew Grace's words were deceitful. It wasn't real Sadness, and most certainly not Grief, she was portraying, but a cheap mock-up. And *I* should know. Nothing of Grace's expression was right. Politely, trying out *Mixing Easily* with women, freewheeling on my own without any hand-holding from Mum on how to deal with a crowd of strangers for more than five minutes, I nodded at Grace, ignoring Odette's not-so-discreet rolling of her eyes.

Mum had told me people always love to speak about how

they *feel. Ask them how they are, and you won't be able to stop them talking. That way, you give little away about yourself.*

Clenching my jaw, I made my eyebrows curl in Sympathy. 'I'm so sorry, Grace. Death is awful and such a permanent thing. Of course, it's permanent.' I crinkled up my face Endearingly, and sort of tittered at the stupidity of my statement. 'Obviously, permanent. But it's so very final, isn't it? Those that haven't experienced it first-hand have no idea of the ever-lasting effect. It really is a Dreadful thing. How do *you* Cope?' Remembering what I'd learnt, I quickly dipped my head, as if in mourning for my new friend's Grief.

Back to gushing, Grace inhaled, ready to explode with her lies. Falsehoods were easy to spot. *I* am a falsehood. If she was trying to trick me, she stood no chance. The cards were stacked against her.

'Exactly, Barney.' She puffed the words out, her lips all-a-quiver, and her eyes rounded. 'I knew you'd understand.' She lifted her shoulders. 'I cope.' She was playing Indulgent, Feel-Sorry-For-Me. It was so blatant I wondered how the other two women didn't notice it.

Odette shifted, her face rigid, but I realised with relief her expression included me, in a partnership type of way – like we both *knew*. Should *I* wink at *her*? No, not necessary. We appeared to have a very real and immediate understanding – after our initial brief clash. Keeping it safe, I didn't respond overtly, but turned my full attention back to Grace. 'You said your sister drowned, Grace. Were you there?'

Instantly, her body closed down and a strange furtiveness covered her, like a very literal web of deceit. Grace was a useless liar.

'I was there, yes. I told you that. But I was sleeping, you know, after the food and everything. I didn't even know she'd gone. I woke up and there she was – not there.'

Jodie stood up. 'Tea, anyone?'

It was a strange and clumsy request, and I wondered if Jodie, as well as Odette, also had trouble believing Grace. I held my hand in the air, warding off the offered beverage, not wanting to allow Grace off the hook. 'But what did you do, Grace? How simply awful for you. Did she wander off into the river on her own? Was she drunk? Why didn't you stop her?'

Careful. Don't be overly Inquisitorial. Don't be Aggressive. But I want to hit her. I don't like Grace. Lying, Greedy, Gushing Grace.

Nodding her head vigorously, Grace's face flushed. 'Yes, drunk, she was very drunk. Silly woman. It was awful. Really. Imagine what a shock it was to find her gone. Forever.'

'Were *you* drunk?' I nodded and shrugged at the same time, keeping it open and vague. Giving her permission to admit to being drunk. *I cast no blame because I am good.*

Blushing a little, Grace nodded. 'Course. Well, a bit. Not *drunk*, drunk. Obviously. But it *was* her birthday, so we'd both had a bit to drink. And I couldn't *stop* her. *Because I was asleep.*'

'Didn't she make a noise as she left? I mean, stumbling drunk and all, you must have heard her. Even if you were a little tipsy.'

'No. No, I didn't hear her. I was in a deep sleep. Because of the sun, and everything. And I never said she was stumbling drunk. Just merry. She was merry. Much merrier than I was. I wasn't drunk, I told you. But I was definitely asleep. Fast asleep. Dead to the world.'

Putting my fingers to my chin, I stroked it in a thoughtful way. Keeping my silence would tempt Grace into overexplaining. Sure enough, she piped up after a second, talking without breathing. 'I *wasn't* that drunk, but I was definitely very tired. And it was so hot. So, I really didn't hear her leave. Of course I didn't. How could I have? I never saw her again, because I was asleep. Fast asleep.'

And there it was – protesting far too much. Always an indicator. She *had* heard her sister leave. Had probably *seen* her. Drunk or not, Grace's sister hadn't simply and mysteriously disappeared. In Grace's quest to cover up how much she *hadn't* drunk, she'd instead incriminated herself in terms of what she hadn't *done* – because she hadn't been asleep at all. That was her lie.

This is child's play. She thinks being drunk is the crime here and so, vehemently denying it, she inadvertently admits to the bigger crime of negligence. Or something else. I don't really care what she had or hadn't done – I only wanted to prove her a liar. Job done.

Letting the silence build, her words hung in the air, and the more time passed, the heavier they became with Deceit. Everyone heard it. Even Grace did. Eventually. I made a hmmm-ing noise, which conveyed volumes of Complete and Utter Disbelief.

'What are you saying, Barney?' She stood and stamped her foot. 'Stop being so mean.'

And all she looked was Guilty.

'I don't know what you're talking about, Grace. Don't be silly. I was Sympathising with you, that's all. I can't imagine the horror it. Well, I can, because you paint such a vivid picture. It really must have been a shock. I'm so Sorry.'

There was a silence, which I assumed the women found awkward, and I had to make myself appear Mortified. 'I hope I haven't upset you, Grace. It certainly wasn't my intent.' Forcing myself to do the unthinkable, I stood up and, breathing in and bracing myself, I hugged the stupid, lying redhead and let her sob on my shoulder.

'There, there, shh, it's going to be all right. We'll talk

through your Sadness and as one, we'll understand it. We *will* get to the bottom of it, trust me, Grace. I just know we'll get along splendidly.'

Grace was just another lying dolly.

She'd lied.

And she wasn't even any good at it.

I was bloody furious.

10

JODIE

Jodie had initially liked Barney. Had immediately warmed to his boyish and vulnerable exterior. There was something wholesome about him, as if he ate a lot of fresh vegetables. Although Jodie wasn't normally one to grade a man on his diet alone.

Her past record of relationships with men wasn't good: she didn't trust her own judgement of *any* man. Ever. She was hardly an expert. She was a fool, for who else would have put up with an abusive husband for as long as she had? *No one strong*, she thought. Equally, she wasn't stupid. There was something about Barney... *dishonest* wasn't quite the right word, but Jodie couldn't pinpoint it any better than that. But dishonest was what she was looking for.

She conceded she could be very wrong about him though. Because there was something about Barney that was more than a little different. Something charming, something endearing, but also something unrecognisable. *Something*.

Watching him with Grace, Jodie wasn't sure of anything anymore, doubting both herself and Barney. Grace had certainly sounded as if she'd been lying, which Barney had highlighted quickly and succinctly, which both she and then in turn, Odette, had also done previously. So, theoretically, Jodie was heartened by Barney's ability to pick up on Grace's deceit. Quickly. Intuitively. Precisely what she was looking for.

Grace, like Odette and Jodie herself, merely needed help coming to terms with all of it. But it was slightly worrying that Grace had so obviously buckled, visibly unnerved at Barney's questioning. She was a potential weak link. Always had been.

Barney had been slick and efficient in his instant understanding of Grace's patchwork full-of-holes tale of Polly's drowning. And he'd been harsh, pushing for the truth. They all had their own burdens, secrets, little lies that made themselves feel better. Who was he to come in and destroy them in such a cavalier way? She'd tried to intervene with an awkward offer of tea, but he'd been relentless in his questioning of Grace. Jodie would not tolerate cruelty.

But the truth was what it was all about, after all, so Jodie wasn't *too* angry with him. She was pleased and surprised. Only slightly concerned at this stage.

This group was all about the ugly truth of things. Of life and death. Jodie felt happy, relaxed and content with Grace and Odette, purely because they all knew everything there was to know about each other. Jodie needed that reality. It was like fresh air and enabled her and them all to move on. There was no point in lying. None at all.

But the group had been cruising for some time, not really getting any further. What they needed, and what Jodie was looking for, was new blood. And here was a man who looked like a very possible new recruit. Barney had arrived and dissected and disembowelled Grace in a matter of seconds.

And that was a good thing. Although his lack of softness could be a problem.

But there still remained a certain something about Barney,

again *something* that might be cause for alarm, but she couldn't identify it. Yet. Perhaps Odette would be better at diagnosing the possible unnameable problem that might be Barney.

Jodie revelled in her honesty about her own story of loss, and looked forward to sharing it with Barney, and to hear *his* story. She was ninety-nine per cent sure he had one. The women needed something new to talk about and all looked forward to helping another lost person, struggling with what they had or hadn't done.

It was impossible to know if she was being premature in choosing Barney, but Jodie was uncharacteristically impatient, wanting desperately to hear someone else's story and, of course, retell her own story. It was always a cathartic experience.

At this precise moment in time, however, he was definitely a risk.

But Jodie liked a risk.

Risk was familiar – her marriage had been one long interminable and terrifying risk. But she'd understood her role in it, and how to respond to danger. And of course, Barney wasn't like Tom, wasn't going to hit her, nor, she thought, did he pose any obvious danger. He was simply different. So, overall, her decision *was* a good one. Barney *was* right.

Turning to Odette, who had remained seated throughout Grace's performance, Jodie waved her fingers in her lap, getting Odette's attention. Jodie raised her eyebrows in query, asking the silent question, *What do you think?* Odette shrugged and then made the faintest of nods. *Okay then,* thought Jodie, *We'll keep him. For now.*

Coughing loudly, wanting to break the embrace of Barney and Grace, needing Grace to break free of him instead of holding on – far too tightly – Jodie said, 'Why don't we take this to the pub? Have a drink together and just chat. Like people do. Happy people.'

Instantly dropping Grace as if he'd been pronounced a free man, Barney swivelled quickly on the spot, leaving Grace in a state of sudden emptiness, the arms around her gone. 'That sounds like a great idea, Jodie. I'll buy. As a thank-you to you all.' Jodie watched as he remembered Grace, and turning to her, he patted her on the shoulder. 'A drink will sort you out, Grace. And a nice chat. Sounds just the ticket.'

Jodie slipped on her jacket. 'Great, let's go. I'll lead the way. The pub's not far, Barney. It's a nice amble. Five minutes, tops.'

'No worries. I love walking. A good brisk walk always clears the mind. And it'll work up a thirst.' He smiled at her. 'I could murder a pint.'

The ten-minute walk was quiet but not awkward, each of them seemingly lost in their own thoughts. They reached the pub and found a table, told Barney what they wanted to drink, and watched him as he went to the bar.

'I don't think I like him,' Grace said, wriggling her hips deeper into the red velvet banquette.

Odette snorted. Jodie thought she was a much-practised and expert snorter – she did it so effortlessly. Odette, her voice withering, said, 'That's because he called you out on your story, Grace. And of course you like him. You like all men.'

'What do you mean by that? Why are you always so aggressive, Odette?'

'I'm not. Just truthful. And you lied to him. And he knew. And that's something to think about. How did he know so instinctively that you were lying? You're not the best liar, but he knew straight away. Interesting, don't you think?' She patted her bun, making sure it was all in place. 'But, granted, we don't know him properly.'

Before Grace could protest, Odette held her hand up. 'Don't know him *yet*, thus the decision to include him is pending. And that's fine, don't get your knickers in a twist. I reckon Barney might be just what we're looking for. You know, in terms of shaking us all up a bit. Instead of going over the same old crap we always do, and never questioning each other anymore. Not really. We've become too comfortable and cosy as a threesome. Too safe.'

'So what? What's wrong with safe? Safe is good.' Grace's voice had become shrill.

Ignoring her, Jodie put her mobile on the table and quickly texted her babysitter, she spoke without looking up. 'I agree with Odette. He's refreshing. Different. But if we all agree we don't like him after tonight, we'll tell him to leave. It's not a problem, Grace. Don't fuss.'

'*I* never talk crap. What do you mean, Odette? You're so mean.'

Odette leaned forward. 'Don't be so bloody precious, Grace. You did lie, and rightly so – until we know we can trust him. But we need to hear his story. All of it. I'm withholding judgement until I spend more time with him. There's no need to be hasty. At least he has a backbone: I was unnecessarily rude and aggressive with him, and he didn't back down. That's a good sign. We could do with a bit of that. Something new. And solid. *Dependable.* Anyway, relax, here he comes.'

Jodie watched Barney with interest as he returned to the table. Weirdly, he seemed nervous in their company. Perhaps it was the three of them specifically – but she didn't think so. He was not dissimilar to a child at his first birthday party, wearing new clothes, unable to keep his swathe of nicely combed hair from falling into his eyes, but he was completely unsure as to how to behave, as if no one had told him the rules. Again, she convinced herself it was endearing and an attractive quality. A social virgin. Who ate vegetables. *What's wrong with that? At least he's different from the norm, and clearly not bonkers. Always a plus.*

Sipping at her drink, Jodie leant forward so she could be heard over the raised voices around her. 'Do you live near here, Barney?'

'Not far.'

Odette picked up her glass and looked him in the eye. 'Is there a Mrs Barney?'

'No, no. It's just me.' He paused and Jodie studied him. For a moment he stilled and it was as if he were thinking furiously. Then he smiled. 'But recently I've moved back in with Mum. After... you know, after Dad died. My mother needs me and I'm happy to be of help to her. As much as I can, anyway.'

Grace couldn't help herself around men and she exhaled loudly. Jodie hoped it wasn't an orgasmic letting-go of breath, so throaty was the sound.

'Good for you, Barney. How kind,' Grace whispered. Barney leant back, out of reach of her. He seemed embarrassed and busied himself with his pint, closing his eyes as if distancing himself from all of them. Jodie didn't blame him. She wasn't surprised that an obviously gentle but troubled man like Barney might very well find the three women slightly overwhelming.

Jodie was now adamant she *was* happy Barney was in the group. Anyway, she could always change her mind if she wanted. Laughing internally, she berated herself. *I am right about Barney – he is a good choice, stop questioning yourself. I'm not a teenager meeting my first real man. I was right the first time. Barney will be a welcome addition to our club. I am right.*

Jodie truly wanted to openly speak of her secret again, and she thought Barney might enable her confession as he seemed in great need himself. Because if she was right, he was carrying a dark secret of his own. He was slightly odd, but would bring a whole new dynamic to the group. He was also most definitely lying – a prerequisite for admission to this particular gang. They all had their own specific tells. Grace, when she lied, rounded her eyes slightly, as if in surprise. Odette lowered her own lids, before making her face completely neutral. Jodie wasn't sure what her own tell was, but was pretty sure she had one.

And Barney? Well, he was just bursting with tells – there were so *many*, Jodie couldn't keep up, so full was he with odd but slightly off mannerisms. Overall, she thought him strong, but strangely naïve. An interesting if strange mix. She didn't know why she'd ever doubted his rightness for the group – he was perfect.

After she and Odette had a quiet word with him – without Grace – they'd know for sure.

Jodie quickly reminded herself why she was doing all this. She made herself recall when Tom had died, after the initial shock, and the immediate comforting of the children – and once the funeral was over – how she had allowed herself to examine how she'd really felt.

And it hadn't been hard to label. She'd discovered herself to be overwhelmingly happy.

How bad did that make her? To be actively joyous that her abusive husband was no longer breathing? However, Odette, in whom she'd confided, having already told Grace, accepted it for what it was. An undeniable truth, and wholly understandable under the circumstances. And with both Grace's and Odette's acceptance had come such relief – like jumping from a great height and realising your new wings *did* work.

Of course, that wasn't really the *only* thing that she had to break to Barney. That was simply a taster, before revealing her real truth. But it wouldn't be for much longer, she was sure.

Her very careful selection of the members of this small but elite club was ultimately hers, and she took it very *very* seriously. It was the most important choice she had to make, and making a mistake wasn't an option. Lives depended on it.

It still really rather depended on the secrets of Barney,

however. She was confident he *had* a story. But would it measure up to hers and the other two women in terms of *badness*? Jodie was content to wait and see. For the moment. The longer she spent with him, the more confident she became that he was hiding something. Something about the death of his father. The accident. The falling-down-the-stairs story. She recognised the signs.

Of course, she hadn't got it right every time and had had to steer more than a few potential candidates on to other more suitable bereavement groups: Clare, Mary and Freddy had been rejected. And many many more. It was *that* hard picking correctly. All of the non-starters had only been sad, in denial or simply lost – but none of them a liar when it came to their mourning and their involvement in their individual losses.

Jodie needed to trust this group. Really trust them. With her life.

So, talking openly of her glee at Tom's demise would only be a teeny admission for Barney, when he'd proved himself – but it would be enough for him to absorb, as a taster. If he was appalled that Jodie admitted to her happiness, no harm done. It wasn't criminal to be happy, and he could move on.

The rest of her story, she'd keep to herself until Barney had been officially accepted into the club and was ready to hear the full horror of it.

For what she'd done was unspeakable.

11

ADELE

Normally, Adele would be keeping an eye on the clock, subconsciously noting what time her son left and how long it was before he re-entered the house. Although, she'd never really had to question Barney as to where he'd been, what he'd done, as he rarely went anywhere for long and would always pop down for a quick chat and tell her what he'd been up to. As if he were checking in. Proving he'd been a good boy. Usually, he'd been off on one of his walks, popped into a pub, done some shopping. Nothing wildly exciting.

And thus far, his travels had never given her cause for concern. He was a natural loner and avoided people as much as he could. Because it was easier for him.

Adele knew he also intellectually acknowledged it was safer. For everyone.

He had his own front door at the side of the house, and it was rare that Adele heard him as he came and went about his business, except when he slammed his door, or raced up or down the back stairs, uncaring of the noise he made. Essentially, he spent most of his time, happily, she hoped, pottering around his own spacious flat, drawing and working on his dolls.

Today, yesterday, for days, for weeks, for months and months and forever, since her husband's death, she'd stopped worrying altogether about the whereabouts of her son, because she was too full of missing Timothy. Her grief consumed her and left no room for anything or anyone else. Timothy had truly been the love of her life, and without him, she felt she was drowning.

His absence was a very real presence. Adele missed him so much she sometimes thought she couldn't bear it. It had been Timothy who had always been her light – a calm, loving backdrop to the chaos that was their son – who had shone quietly in her life, a source of joy, masking the darkness that was Barney. In bed together at the end of the day, he'd hold her and his kindness, his wit, his very loud sense of fun – softened as he embraced her – was like an antidote to the child they'd created together. Without her husband, she was lost in a very black blackness.

When Barney walked into her sitting room, she jumped. Glancing up, Adele couldn't fail to miss the physical change in him. The very way he moved, his shoulders back, his chin up and his walk, which had become an out-of-character sort of swagger – full of boast and self-confidence – seemed massively exaggerated. Her heart dropped. She couldn't deal with him. Not now. Not on her own. Tiredness and sadness made it almost impossible to play the never-ending game that was Barney.

Now, without Timothy, she wasn't sure she had it in her to keep the world safe from her son. Because it was a fact that only she really understood: Barney wasn't normal. If she'd ever thought any different, she'd only been fooling herself.

He was never *normal, and will never* be *normal. The only thing I achieved was to delay the inevitable. I did my best. But now I give up. I can't and I won't carry on. There is no stopping him. I know that, have always known that and I have lied to myself, pretending – all these years.*

'Evening, Mum. How are you?' He beamed and bobbed about on the balls of his feet.

I'm suffering. I'm heartbroken. I'm alone. Leave me alone.

Taking in his body language, she shuddered. 'What have you done, Barney?'

Laughing, his eyes gleaming, his entire being seeming to twinkle with a strange delight, he put his hands on his hips, showing off. 'Why do you suppose I've *done* anything? And don't lie to me.' He threw himself down into an armchair. 'You're assuming it's something bad, aren't you? Oh, ye of little faith.'

It's as if he's forgotten his father is dead. Truly, out of sight, out of mind. As if Timothy had never been.

'Surprise me.' Her words sounded flat and emotionless – ironic, considering who she was talking to.

'I've only gone and done it, Mum. I've made some friends. Three of them. Women. And I'd go so far as to say, they liked me. They accepted me. All that life tuition you gave me, finally it paid off. It worked.' He punched the air in celebration. 'I passed myself off as normal.' He waited a beat. 'And it was easy.'

Adele let the words sit there and she slowly digested them. She found she couldn't swallow the true meaning of what he'd said, as the implication of his announcement stuck in her throat. *I do not want to know. I want to scream out to these innocent women, to run and keep on running and not look behind them. My son cannot be trusted.*

'That's nice, dear.'

His face flashed anger at her dismissal, at her not wanting to know more.

'*That's nice, dear?* Are you joking? I thought you'd be pleased for me. *I'm* pleased for me.' Glaring at her, she noticed his hands as they balled into fists. 'You couldn't give a rat's arse, that's pretty bloody clear. I've finally cracked it and that's your response, *very nice, dear?* What the bloody fuck?'

She shifted in her seat. 'I'm sorry.' And she was. 'If you can grasp this, then that will please me more. I am struggling without your father. I loved him. At the moment, nothing else matters. Not even you.'

Strangely, his face crumpled in on itself – shock and yes, hurt. Real hurt. At least he responded to *her* in a normal way. *But it is only with me because I am the one person he genuinely loves. Because I have given my entire life to him.* Adele was acutely aware his emotions were superficial and transitory. So fleeting – if you blinked, they'd be gone, and something else would have replaced it.

Sighing, automatically switching back into her mother role, she loosely held her hands in her lap. 'Did you connect with them, or was it all a pretence, with you internally initialising what you were meant to be experiencing? All your practised emotions and mannerisms?' She shrugged. 'I'm pleased that you can at least show real understanding with me. But can you do it with real people, in the real world? That is the real test.'

He stood up, so unexpectedly that he frightened her. Involuntarily, she shrank back into her chair and held a cushion up against her chest. As if that would stop him.

'Yes, I bloody can. We all got on and my reactions and responses were all real. I know they were.'

She knew him too well and recognised his lies. And he'd ignored and already forgotten her saying how she missed Timothy. It was all about him. Barney Snapp. The boy trapped in a plastic bubble of nothing. For a moment, she hated him. For his total lack of... his lack. Full stop.

'Who are these women, Barney? Where did you meet them?' She tried to add lightness to her tone, wanting to calm and soothe him. Wanting him to stop being angry. Slowly, she watched as he relaxed and gently sat down again. Trying hard to behave in the right way. *I have* taught him well, *she thought. But it's not enough. He's dangerous and he's made friends with three women – what can I do?*

'They're great, Mum. And I did it for you. I know I'm not able to help you... you know, Grieve for Timothy. Dad. So, I joined a bereavement group to learn about being left alone, without the person you love. I admit I can't feel Grief, because we never covered it, *but that's not my fault.* It's yours. Why didn't we do Grief?'

She could only look at her son, suddenly so scared of him she couldn't move. Timothy had taken her heart when he'd died, and she'd been left incompetent. Unable and not wanting to help her son anymore. It was all too much.

But she played the game, needing to keep Barney placated. 'That was a kind thing to do. And thank you. Really. And of course I'm proud of you. It must have all been so overwhelming for you, but you did it.' She faked a smile. 'Who did you take with you?'

He grinned, back on safe ground again with his mummy guiding him through life. 'Affable and Amenable Annie.' He shrugged it off, as if it wasn't important – although it was. *She* knew it was important, too. 'I enjoyed it, Mum. I really did. We're meeting again next week. I don't know why I didn't do it before – I was a natural at it. And the funny thing is, it appears *I* can actually help *them. That's* a twist neither of us ever thought we'd see coming. Me, helping other people.' He stopped and thought about what he'd just said. 'It's bloody amazing.' And he laughed.

It wasn't a nice laugh, but a triumphant one, and Adele closed her eyes.

She opened them again when she heard Barney's mobile go

off. That was odd in itself. Nobody ever texted him. His preferred communication was by email.

'Who's it from, Barney-Boo?'

For some reason, Adele's heart was thumping and her mouth was dry, and she'd resorted to using his childhood nickname. Barney glanced up at her briefly and then down again, reading his message. His face had shown delight when his mobile had gone off, and then a downturn of disappointment, as if the wrong person had messaged him.

'Is that one of your new friends?'

'Yeah. One of them. I'd have preferred a text from one of the other two, but it's good enough. It's a start.'

Eventually, as if he were loath to put away his mobile, he gently slipped it back into his pocket.

'What did she say?' Adele waited. 'Was it an invitation to meet again? So soon?'

'No. It was nothing really, Mum. Don't worry about it.' He tapped his temple. 'I've got it all planned out up here.'

Their eyes met, except they didn't really – his glance had that glazed, disconnected look that remained utterly unfocused on her. She questioned whether he'd actually ceased to see her at all, as she sat, suddenly mouse-like in her chair. She was invisible to him, so lost was he, playing games in his mind. Preparing, scheming, plotting.

A ripple of fear crept through Adele's body and she sat there, chilled and so very alone.

12

ME

Trying to ignore my mother's weird behaviour, *as if she were frightened of me*, I'd gone for a walk. After returning to my own quarters, I worked late into the evening, furious, but endeavouring to calm myself down by painting and repairing the face of a china doll. It soothed me and enabled normal breathing again. With my tongue sticking out from the corner of my mouth in concentration, I went about bringing real life and depth back to the damaged, cracked and ruined dolls with which I was surrounded. This one in particular needed a full paint-job – her vapid expression had worn and peeled with age.

On opening one of my drawers in The Rehab, as I liked to think of it, I examined row upon row of eyeballs: different colours and shades gazed up at me in glassy adoration, wrapped carefully in their own individual boxes. I picked up a pair of perfect blue orbs and let them roll around softly in my palm, then opened the next drawer with my other hand, and let my fingers trail over the perfect rows of eyelashes.

These were one of my favourite accessories for expression – a girlish flutter of over-large lashes; smaller, dipped ones intimating a more demure look. Shorter, less curled ones managed to convey an innocent spray of childish wonderment. Or surprise. Add in eyebrows, my speciality, and it was possible to birth a whole new dolly with a brand-new face and outlook.

Restoration was power.

I particularly enjoyed the solitude of my job – just me and my little darlings together, in utter silence – not having to listen to the babble of stupid and dishonest people. I loved my dolls. It was that simple.

If and when I was offered the task to not only paint a new face on a once-perfect doll, I very occasionally offered to touch up a chipped nose, a missing lip, a faded eyeball, a missing eyelash or two. Gratis. On the house. I have even been known to suggest a completely new hairstyle.

Don't even *talk* to me about the hair. I loved weaving and threading in new locks and tresses – it was often the ultimate transformation of a doll – a finishing touch which completed the image I was creating. It was a real mood-changer.

Like being God.

My life-teachings from Mum had worked well, in tandem with my dolls, and often I'd use pen and ink on paper as my dry run, before putting my specialised paints to china. Over the years, as new emotions came to light, I'd had to modify my own dolls' faces to replicate newly discovered expressions, emotions and moods. I'd created a whole range of reactions, forever captured on their features, and I had brought each and every one of them alive. It was like recreating mini versions of myself, again and again and again. It was as important to me as breathing.

Essentially, the bulk of my income came from selling my pen-and-ink drawings, depicting children's faces wearing a myriad of emotions. I recognised, for the millionth time, what an extraordinary gift I had. People loved them and having built up an extensive body of work and followers online, it had been inevitable that success would follow.

Holding the doll at arm's length and studying my handiwork, slowly, quietly, I started to forget my mother protecting herself with a bloody cushion, cowering in her chair, as if she really thought I'd *do* something to her. She'd been genuinely scared. What the hell was wrong with the woman?

She'd deserted *me*, so it was me who should be bloody emoting all over the place, and I was *furious*. Rage sat in my belly, and would remain there, until I allowed myself to become wholly immersed in my doll and forget the outside real world where dolls didn't live.

Miniature Professional Pete was propped up against my drawing board, overseeing my work. It was the biggest joke on earth that I should be so blessed with the talent of portraying a full range of exquisite expressions onto little faces. The irony of it all never ceased to amuse.

Everything, from initial contact to finished product, was carried out on online. I'd courier back reborn and revamped dolls, to grateful owners – presented perfectly packaged in velvet cushioned boxes – a little like coffins. And my reputation spread.

With success, I had created, quite naturally, a pseudonym. I had no wish to be known for anything using my own name. Attention was not something I craved: I wasn't so shallow.

Social media had proved a lucrative platform for my art. And once my business was up and running, and sales were booming, I now signed all my work as Rhapsody Snapp. *Rhapsody: an ecstatic expression of feeling.* That was the dictionary definition. My false name was a fingers-up to the world that judged me as odd. My own little private joke.

Mum had always supported and encouraged me in my

pursuit, and had been unable to hide her pride. The house was filled with framed pictures by yours truly.

Although I made a lot of money selling my pictures, it was my work on the dolls that captivated me, and what I considered my main profession. Every time I was working on a doll, I'd become so engrossed, I was lost to anything else. Including people. *Especially* people. Mum obviously loved this aspect as she battled to keep me from actually going out there into the big bad world, amongst real live breathing men and women.

I was Rhapsody Snapp, a doll-man fixing and beautifying dolls for other people.

But mostly for myself.

It was my calling.

I'd lied to Odette when she'd asked what I did for a job, as even to my own ears, fixer-of-dolls sounded a strange career for an adult man to do, so saying I was an illustrator was as near the truth as I was prepared to go. I wasn't used to mingling with normal people and I'd panicked, not comfortable giving anything away about myself.

My affinity and love for my dolls was between me and my china lovelies. It wasn't something I would ever share with anyone else.

Calmer now, putting the doll down on the worktop, I allowed myself to think about my mother. I'd made three new friends – for the sole intention of *helping* Mum – the fact that she'd been so clearly frightened, at *what I might do to them,* enraged me. What was going through her mind? Even I hadn't quite decided *exactly* what I was going to do, but I wasn't leaping to unwholly evil conclusions, like Mum. I wasn't thinking or planning anything *bad.* Suffice to say, I had a new trio of women, and it was all going to plan thus far. I did not need any negative input from my mother.

Admittedly, I'd gone a little off-piste with my recently

created agenda for Jodie, Odette and Grace, but that wasn't the point. My *intentions* towards my mother had been good – originally, I'd been doing it all for her. I was still doing it for her.

And she didn't even care. *Very nice, dear.* For the first time as an adult, I had to force myself not to go downstairs and berate her. Shout at her. Scream at her. *This is all your fault. You left me on my own, this is all your fault, you stupid bad mother. Because of you, I don't even know how to really speak to people. You never let me try.*

I again found myself bunched up with anger at her betrayal. Here she was, no longer really with me anymore, and she'd left me with nothing.

I still loved her, naturally, but my anger at her caused me real distress. It was unfamiliar and yes, *Frightening*, because it was new. And something I'd have to come to terms with, because I recognised, whatever Mum was feeling wasn't a temporary thing that I could happily paint over and make better – it might very well be a permanent state of affairs.

I considered going downstairs and confronting her about her casual abandonment of me, but knew, by this time, Mum would have slunk off to her empty room and taken sleeping pills to knock her out. Because, guess what? After all her talk, throughout my entire life, it turned out she couldn't even handle her *own* emotions. Granted, I didn't fully understand what she was going through, but still – if it wasn't so sad, it would be comical. Mum at a loss as to how to deal with Grief. And she, the great omniscient teacher of all that was touchy-feely.

She should practice what she'd been preaching to me all these years. Otherwise, it made a mockery of the entire thing. Mum couldn't even deal with something that happened to everyone – death.

Mum was still the focus of my anger, as I pondered the sheer unfairness of it all. I couldn't shift the rage.

Only as a child had I shown her anger. Over time, as we'd worked together on my remoulding, I'd grown to truly love her.

And I still did.

But now I was angry with her because I realised she'd cheated me.

Mum had left me.

For a dead man.

I was on my own.

So, fuck her.

13

———

ME

That was the text I'd received last night. I was definitely disappointed that it was from Gushy Grace, *Guilty* Grace – Guilty at being caught out in a lie. She was already seriously irritating me with her pushiness. She was even too wordy on her grasping, greedy text. *A quick one* – disgustingly flirtatious. Stupid woman. I'd much rather have received a text from either of the other two – preferably, Odette. I admitted to being just a little fascinated with her and wondered if she was more like me than I dared hope.

But I was happy enough. We'd all swapped mobile numbers last night, at Jodie's encouragement, and I really couldn't believe my luck. It had all gone so smoothly – a little awkward for me at times, not surprisingly, and I'd had to stop myself and control my temper now and again, mostly ignited by Grace, but overall, I'd fooled them all.

I was in.

Not bothering to say "Goodbye" to Mum, still irritated with her, I left the house. It was time for Grace. Trying to be positive, I knew this was a great opportunity, handed to me without me even having to ask.

Grace was a good one to practice on, for she was the most stupid and the most transparent of the three – good for rehearsal purposes – passing myself off as a man casually chewing the fat with a new friend as if it were a daily occurrence. Nothing out of the ordinary. No problem here at all. I could get away with saying or doing the wrong thing and put it down to nerves at meeting her on my own. She obviously wasn't the one, but a good starting point. Just the two of us. Little old Sensitive me. The woman would believe anything I said. Already, I'd dissected her sham of a story, and she'd known it. It had hardly been taxing.

Misbehaving was certainly not my intent today. I confidently self-diagnosed myself as Cheerful as I set off – on my first official lunch date with a woman. I was uncaring that my companion wasn't one of my choosing – I accepted it. Sometimes, it was necessary to do unpalatable things with awful people, in order to get what one truly wanted.

Looking through the windows of the pub, I saw Grace had arrived early and was sitting on a chair, rummaging through her handbag. She applied a little lipstick to her lips, and taking out a small mirror, she plumped up her red hair with the heel of her palm. Settling my expression into an open, Happy-to-see-you face, I entered, listening to the clatter of the bell above the door as it announced my arrival. Already annoyed, I gave my mini doll-du-jour, Charming Charles, a pat on the head with my thumb as it sat in my back pocket, and approached Grace.

Turning and seeing me, Grace's face exploded into Delight. I did my best to emulate it. 'Barney, I'm so pleased you agreed to come. And at such short notice. Lovely to see you again.'

I saw you last night. It's not like this is a long-awaited reunion. It is a task. For me, a tedious but necessary task.

'Lovely to see you, too.'

She leant forward, giving me her cheek to kiss. I ignored it, sat and picked up a menu, glancing disinterested over the pedestrian food on offer. Focused as I was on the dreary descriptions of unexciting nourishment, I saw Grace's fingers, with their red-painted nails, land on my forearm. I looked pointedly at her hand, and then raised my eyes to her – my face a blank. Blushing, she pulled back her arm and dithered, unsure. She tittered Nervously. *This is too too easy. I should have socialised much earlier in my life. Had I done so, I'd be unstoppable.* Take note, Mum. *As it is, I know I have Grace exactly where I want her. She is mine and I am almost disappointed at the ease of my acquisition.*

Putting the menu down, I looked Grace straight in the eye, my face as innocent as a baby. 'I'll have the tomato soup. How about you?'

'The same. Good choice. Drink?'

'Just water for me.'

She couldn't hide her disappointment, as if she really thought that a drunk me would be more amenable to her advances. And I wasn't that stupid not to understand her intentions. But let her try – it would be fun – fencing with an idiotically transparent woman with her desires directed in my direction, so nakedly on display.

Deliberately, I remained quiet until the soup came, and waiting Politely for her to pick up her spoon, I then joined her. I could see the silence between us made her Uncomfortable, but I refused to relent. Vaguely smiling at her, I remained silent. It wasn't long – two horribly loud and uncouth slurps of soup later from her sucking puckered lips – before she was unable to help herself. 'How did you enjoy meeting the girls last night? It was fun, wasn't it?'

Quickly angling my eyes down, I tried to ignore the red smudge of tomato soup that rimmed her lips, making them look sore. Equally, I knew I had to answer. 'Yes, it was Lovely. You were all so Welcoming – it was much easier than I'd Anticipated.'

That relaxed her, and her teeth shone whiter, still surrounded by her thin moustache of red soup. Her tongue flicked out. 'Why not tell me about the awful time you've been through? If you're ready, that is. I want you to know, I'm here to help you. What you told us on Zoom was so sad. I do so feel for you, I really do.'

Wanting to tell her to use her napkin, I spoke into my bowl. 'Yes, it was all such a shock. Seeing Dad like that, falling, right out of my embrace, and then... you know. It was awful.'

Despite her horrendous tomato lipstick, I chanced a look at her. I shook my head in Sadness. 'Really awful.'

Her hands clutched at her face. 'It's too ghastly to think of, your arms around his shoulders as he gave his birthday speech. I can't even imagine how dreadful that must have been. What a terrible, terrible shock.' She could barely conceal her Delight.

I didn't really know why I'd added that detail on Zoom. Perhaps I thought it gave the whole incident a more personal and Tragic touch – a sense of Melodrama, with my father plummeting to his death, falling from my Loving birthday hug. It had made it seem so much more real. It had become so vivid a picture in my head, I almost believed it myself, and imagined I could feel him topple forward, leaving me, with my arms outstretched, grasping only at empty air.

And, of course, I'd realised early on that lying was the thing to do in this group. All of Jodie's hints and innuendos about her husband's not-so-tragic death – I'd taken a chance and I'd been right.

Scrunching up my eyebrows, I wished tears into my eyes, but I couldn't do it. So, I closed them instead. 'All I heard, Grace, was my father's loud fall. It was a noise I'll never be able to forget. It was so very Final. I heard him hit every step, his body thudding down the stairs, one by one. Every. Single Step. I'll never forget it. Never.'

This time I allowed her hand to rest on my forearm as she grabbed at it Earnestly, wanting to Comfort me. Clenching my teeth, I pushed my soup away and found my breathing had become tight. As if my chest was caving in. It was her look of silky Sincerity and Compassion, the we're-all-in-this-together tilt of the head, that shrivelled my insides with distaste and horror. I had to stop myself from punching her expression clean off her face. Everything about her, this entire conversation, it was all so False – one big Bluff. I was disappointed at the dishonesty of her. She, who'd shown Guilt when caught out in her lie. Not because of what she had or hadn't done, but because I'd caught her out. Simple. Shameless.

A doll would show more integrity than she.

Exerting pressure through her fingers, she tightened her grip on my arm, and I swear to God, her eyes welled up. 'But it must have been absolutely *the* worst. How do you feel about it now? You must be devastated. And your poor mother – I can't even begin to think how she's feeling. She saw the whole thing, right? How truly sad. Words fail me.'

If only *words failed her. She just wouldn't stop.*

Wiping her mouth with the back of her hand, Grace leant forward and for an awful moment, I thought she was going to kiss me. Instead, she smiled a wet and watery smile. 'And you came back to live with your mother? Moved back in, to help her? What a selfless thing to do. That's the kindest thing I've ever heard. How does your mother feel about you moving back in? How do *you* feel?'

I wanted to scream at Grace to stop asking me questions. To stop bombarding me with ridiculous meaningless platitudes. I also regretted my second unnecessary lie that I'd run home to be by my mother's side. I'd thought it made for a better story. More heart-wrenching for all to imagine. It made me the Good boy. Grace just made me feel like a Stupid, Out-Of-My-Depth boy. I wanted to hurt her. Because I couldn't cope with this conversation. And it was all her fault.

I was failing miserably with this encounter, feeling everything I said or did was wrong or misplaced. Made exposed and vulnerable and out of control by an idiot: Grace had highlighted me as a social fraud, making me frail and useless.

Standing, I pushed back my chair. 'Will you excuse me for a minute, Grace. I'm so sorry.' I bowed my head. 'I just need a minute.'

'Of course, Barney, take your time. I'll be here waiting for you, don't you worry. Take as long as you need. And then we can carry on our little chat. Just you and me.'

I had to stop myself from running as I escaped to the toilets, and I sat on the closed lid of a lavatory in a cubicle, avoiding a puddle of urine on the floor. Keeping my feet off the ground in a sort of gymnastic hover, I took out my mobile.

I couldn't bear Grace any longer. Not on my own. I had discovered that prolonged one-to-one conversations with someone was harder to maintain than I'd expected. It was exhausting. Thinking and hoping there was safety in numbers, I scrolled through my non-existent contacts and, giving it a little thought, finally put my thumbs to work. Wanting to be honest, I really wanted to say, *I need rescuing from Grace – her and I alone together is too intense. I can't cope. Please come, come now.*

But of course I didn't. I made my texted request slightly

Comedic, as if I didn't really mean it. Wasn't really desperately panicking and thinking I couldn't do this whole people-thing at all. My own social ineptness was like a very loud and weird type of musical instrument in the room, playing all the wrong notes for the unfortunate listener. Maybe Mum had been right all along and I'd be better off on my own – away from the public. *Do not approach this animal. He may bite.*

I didn't think I'd been particularly Charming either. It had been my intent, but Charm had fallen by the wayside, drowned and gushed away by the saccharine that had oozed from Grace. Feeling dispirited, I typed out:

> Odette, Please join Grace & I in the pub. Same one as last night. We're having lunch. HELP!!! ☺ Barney.

Putting my mobile away, I covered my face with my hands and silently screamed in fury. Biting down on the inside of my middle finger to stifle the escaping keening noise that leaked out, I drew blood.

I tasted it, coppery and metallic in my mouth.

Furious, I savoured its saltiness – and found it strangely comforting. I sucked at the wound, like a baby on a teat. The very distinct flavour of blood in my mouth finally quietened and calmed me.

A bit.

14

ODETTE

It wasn't often Odette got messages on her mobile, and she didn't like being disturbed whilst flower-arranging at her mother's grave. She felt the phone vibrate in her pocket and took her own sweet time before she read the text. Today was a bad day. Sometimes she was still lost in darkness and despair, and other days, she thanked God she'd met Jodie and had the beginnings of a possible, very tentative new life. Like catching a smell on a breeze – there, but only if you concentrated.

Today wasn't one of those days.

The message made her raise her eyebrows. And then it made her scoff. Grace had captured Barney, and Odette pondered leaving him at her mercy, but knew she couldn't. It was too easy to imagine the scene at lunch: Grace, non-stop talking; he, polite at first and then squirming as Grace laid her hands on him. The woman couldn't help herself – so needy and wanting... wanting. Grace just wanted.

More to the point, what the bloody hell was Grace doing having what amounted to a clandestine rendezvous with Barney? That was against the unwritten rules of the club. Jodie hadn't okay-ed it. It wasn't how it went. Jodie vetted potentials, and Odette advised. Grace did not come into it at this stage. Jodie had admitted Grace had been a mistaken selection, but now she was impossible to get rid of – under the circumstances.

Odette gathered her mother's grave accessories and stood up. She stayed in the same spot, out of the way, standing at a respectful distance from a sad huddle of mourners, who walked past, hugging and stepping simultaneously – as if unable to mobilise independently.

Bereavement only gets worse, so get used to it now as you're in it for the long haul. Time doesn't heal – that's a lie.

Since her mother died, Odette had become consumed, and yes, *obsessed* wasn't too strong a word, with the whole concept of death. Death was inescapable, but was it random? Why did some people, some seriously unpleasant people, live happily until they were in their nineties, unplagued by disease and pain? Why did death feel the need to steal the young and the innocent, and why had it made her mother's final departure so rudely premature?

All deep and meaningful questions and asked a million times by philosophers and great thinkers. She didn't consider herself a great thinker, only a great daughter. And now, not even that. It enraged her.

Very occasionally, when Odette saw groups of young drunk men and women, rolling home from the pub, shouting, pushing and shoving, being rude and offensive and uncaring, she'd want to go up to them and say, *You don't get how lucky you really are. You have no fucking idea. You lucky bastards. You're alive and if I had anything to do with it, you wouldn't be. That's how lucky you are.*

And even more occasionally, Odette would wonder *how* she would take the life of someone whom she thought undeserving and ungrateful for their life: the privileged, the entitled, and had she had their names and addresses, the rapists and the paedophiles. Usually, she'd plump for concentrating on graphically violent ways to murder them, in the coldest of blood. She'd allow herself to become lost in her fantasy of killing and wondered if she ever really could. If push came to shove.

And more often than not, she found the answer was, yes, she probably *could* kill. If she was pissed off enough and she was having a bad day. Shit happened and some people wouldn't even be missed. They'd be better off dead, and Odette would be more than happy to oblige. At which point, she'd take a mental curtain call – *You're welcome.*

Odette looked at her watch, knowing Grace was always back in her shop by two o'clock, so even if Odette was willing to save Barney, she'd never get there in time. She only prayed that Grace hadn't done too much damage already with her runaway mouth.

Jodie had to be told. Worried, she forced herself to calm down and relax. Odette always enjoyed seeing Jodie: her happiness was as obvious as the sun shining in the sky and it always brightened Odette's world. She envied Jodie's ability to be happy about Tom's death, but was nowhere near able to replicate the emotion for herself and her dead mother. However hard she tried.

I wish I could be like that and move on from Mum's death. I wish it with all my heart.

Knowing Jodie would be at home, probably nursing a hangover after last night – she was such a lightweight when it came to alcohol – Odette texted her quickly.

> I'm coming over. Grace is having lunch with
> Barney. He just texted me. Wanted rescuing!!
> We need to talk.

She waited for a reply. Within two minutes, Jodie texted back.

Come now.

Just two little words and yet it screamed out the panic Odette knew Jodie would be feeling at the news of Grace and Barney's secret tryst.

Meeting confirmed – tick – head down, Odette walked briskly to the bus stop and then the short distance to Jodie's home.

When Jodie opened the door, her face was pinched with worry.

'Come in, come in. Bloody Grace. What is she *thinking*? How dare she jeopardise everything without consulting either one of us.' Her cheeks coloured in rage. '*And* I WhatsApped her after you texted me, and she hasn't replied. I know she's read it and she's ignoring it. She always answers immediately.'

Nodding, grimacing, kissing Jodie's cheek, Odette walked into the kitchen, sat on a stool at the island, and hooked her feet around the lower strut.

Jodie waved a bottle of wine at her. 'Drink?'

'Are you hungover?' Odette couldn't help a smile.

'I am. I have a headache, a dry mouth and feel a bit sick. Sicker knowing Grace saw Barney on her own.'

Odette nodded. 'Yeah, stupid not-amazing Grace. And yes to the drink. A small glass of red if you have it, please.'

'I have.'

Odette waited a beat, choosing her words carefully, not wanting to freak Jodie out more than was necessary. 'What do you think Grace is playing at? You don't think she's *testing* him, do you? On her own?'

Jodie's head whipped round as she crouched over the wine rack. 'She wouldn't dare. Even Grace isn't that stupid. She knows what it could mean. She wouldn't dare. *Would she?*'

'I've been thinking about it all the way over here, and I

reckon she's just taking the opportunity to be with him. On her own. To put it simply, I think she fancies him.'

'For God's sake, she fancies *all* men. But I'm surprised she has the cheek to sound him out without my express permission – whether she fancies him or not. She knows how dangerous it could be for all of us. Surely she's not *that* stupid?'

Glass now in hand, sipping at her wine, Odette considered the situation. 'Grace *isn't* that stupid. She really isn't. She likes to play at being a total idiot, but she's not. The police believed her story about her sister's death, and that's saying something. So she knows when and how to reel it in. To save her own skin.'

'But we don't even truly know Barney yet. We haven't talked to him properly, so it's risky her meeting him, talking to him. One misplaced word, that's all it would take. It's outrageously stupid. I can guarantee she'll be quizzing him, trying to get a head start on us. Wanting to know all the details of Barney's life. If he indeed has details that would interest us.'

'She wouldn't put *herself* at risk, Jodie. Really. She just wouldn't. I think she's game-playing. As you say, wanting to get one up on us. It's juvenile.'

They sat in silence, until Odette couldn't stand the lack of sound. 'What should we do?'

'We don't want to frighten Barney off. And we don't even know if he's bloody eligible for our club, anyway, which makes the whole thing even more ludicrous. He could be a fine upstanding member of the community, who's simply had the misfortune to lose his father. Imagine if Grace let something slip.' Jodie shook her head. 'No, she wouldn't. God, she's a fool. A selfish fool.'

Sliding down onto the floor, Jodie sat and rested the bottom of her glass on her drawn-up knees. 'She's a liability. And we need to stop her. We need to text Barney. *You* need to text Barney and suggest we meet him for drinks tomorrow night. At a different pub, The Pig & Whistle, just in case Grace feels the need to lurk, linger and loiter at our local.'

'Sounds like a plan.' Odette nodded, always feeling better and stronger when with Jodie.

'We can't get it wrong.'

Head bent to text Barney, Odette could feel, without even looking, Jodie's concern, which was echoed in her next words. 'I haven't got time to talk now – the children need picking up early and they've got friends staying the night for a sleepover.'

'No worries. I've texted him. Stop panicking, it's contagious.' Odette laughed but it sounded shrill, with a hint of hysteria, even to her own ears. 'Honestly, Jodie, please stop. You're worrying over nothing.' *She's not.* I'm *worried. We* should *be worried.*

Leaning her back into the wall, Jodie crossed both her ankles and arms, her knees together, and let her wine glass dangle from her fingers. 'I really did hate Tom, you know. He was a bastard. He beat the crap out of me. So, yes, I couldn't be happier the shit is dead. Consider me full of joy at his demise.' She raised her eyebrows at Odette. 'Yes, definitely very happy. Grace wouldn't have repeated *that*, would she? If we're wrong about Barney, that would be disastrous.'

'I'm happy you're happy, Jodie. Good for you, Miss Not-So-Goody-Goody-Two-Shoes. I'm...' She grappled for an appropriate adjective. It wasn't hard. 'I'm pleased for you. Genuinely.'

Jodie nodded, her face serious. 'I know you are and I love you, you know that, and you too will accept what you've done. That, I promise.' Jodie's body slumped. 'But I don't want to screw this up with Barney. Wouldn't it be easier just to let him go? We don't even know he's a liar, do we? Not for sure.'

Odette recognised this was a stupidly dangerous game they were playing. Unnecessarily. She went and squatted in front of her friend on the floor. 'Shouldn't we think about it more before we plunge in and do something stupid? I don't like rushing.'

'We have to rush. We don't know what Grace said to him. She's reckless, self-obsessed and she's always so silly around men. Supposing she said something about *us*? We need to find out exactly what Barney knows. As soon as bloody possible. I wouldn't normally pressure him, I don't want to force him into speaking to us, but what else can we do?'

'You're right, of course. We need to nip it in the bud. And pronto. But it seems mean to push him, don't you think?'

'I do, and I'd never normally do it, but we don't have a choice. We just don't.'

Odette put her mobile back in her bag and nodded. 'He's definitely lying about his father's death. His story sounded too... rehearsed. Unnatural. As if he was choosing his words too carefully. Like a practised routine: *And Dad just fell out from under my arm and I couldn't catch him. I tried but I couldn't.* I didn't believe it when he first said it on Zoom, and I don't believe him in general. He's a bit... different, would be a polite way of saying it. I can't really get a handle on him.'

'I agree. To his being different and, instinctively, I think he's lying too. Hence, his probable inclusion into our club. Because, let's face it, Barney *could* have pushed his father. He sort of hinted at it, but he never said he did, so we can't know for sure at this stage.' Jodie ran her hands through her hair. 'This isn't just any old bereavement group, Odette. It's by invite only and if and when he chooses to speak – tomorrow night, hopefully – then we'll know we made the right choice. We can deal with Grace when and if.'

'Let's not panic. He may not even be suitable for our gang, and Grace may simply have been throwing herself at him. No harm done. Barney could go on his merry way, and we'd return to normal.' Odette finished her wine. 'But I agree, we need to know.'

'All I want to do is help others who need the same sort of... support as us. That's why I'm pushing it and trying to save Barney from being put off, derailed, bloody terrified by Grace. That's all.' She breathed in sharply and, holding Odette's shoulder, pushed herself upright. 'And if she *has* said something, we'll need to act. To save ourselves. Damage limitation and all that. Although, God knows what.'

She kissed Odette on the cheek. 'I need to get a grip. Have more bloody confidence in what we do.' Jodie smiled weakly. 'Trust me, it'll all be fine. If Barney needs us, I won't allow Grace to ruin it. If he's just a nice, normal grieving man, we'll let him go, and it'll be over.'

Odette didn't bother smiling. In her world, nothing was ever as simple as that.

Ever.

Not since Mum.

15

____

GRACE

Grace was bursting with joy. She'd done it. Barney had actually liked her. He'd been unable to hide his feelings and it had been as plain as plain could be. How he'd squirmed as he revealed his real self, how he'd bent his head, not wanting to cry, how he'd shyly shown her his smile and, unable to cope with their very tangible coming-together of their souls, how he'd had to escape momentarily after the soup to gather himself.

He *liked* her. He really did – she could tell. As she hurried down the road, she couldn't stop herself from smiling. How easily they'd bonded, really connected: as if they'd known each other for years. Barney was so boyish and vulnerable it had made Grace want to swoop him up and hug him to death.

And he'd spoken in depth about his father's death. Only to her. Much more than he had on Zoom. She'd felt every bump as his father had fallen down the stairs to his death, as Barney had so eloquently but brutally described it. She was honoured that he'd opened up to her.

And not to Jodie or Odette.

Together, she and Barney had created something special and secret and only for them.

For once, none of it involved the other two, but it was Jodie's exclusion that really pleased Grace. In some ways, in *a lot of ways*, Jodie reminded Grace of her sister, Polly. That same supercilious air, that holier-than-thou attitude, that I'm-better-than-you air of confidence. And Jodie *wasn't* any better than Grace. Barney had proved it by choosing to share his innermost feelings with her instead of Jodie. It was clear it was his first deep and meaningful telling and he had chosen her for his reveal.

Quickening her step and worriedly glancing at her watch, knowing she'd be late opening up the bookshop at two o'clock, Grace carried on regardless and felt as if she were walking on air.

Exactly as she had been with Polly, Grace was finally triumphant over Jodie. Oh-so fair, oh-so kind, oh-so fucking perfect Jodie. She wasn't all that she claimed she was. Barney had confided in Grace, and he liked *her*. He most definitely did.

Grace was prepared do anything to make him hers, and to stop Jodie catching him in her clutching, grabbing talons.

That's why Grace was following him.

Hurrying, panicking, she saw him get on a bus. Thankfully, there were about half a dozen people who also boarded at the bus stop, and she fell into step with them, averting her face and holding her hand like a fan to hide behind as she saw him settle in his chosen seat. Bravely, but finding herself almost tiptoeing and holding her breath, she walked past him and sat two rows behind. It was thrilling and exhilarating.

Not dissimilar to watching Polly drown.

And getting one-up on the supremely marvellous bitch that was Jodie.

Her mobile beeped and she took it from her bag and read the message.

What are you doing, Grace? Why are you
meeting Barney on your own? Txt me back. J

Who *precisely* did Jodie think she was?

She was *precisely* like Grace's sister, Polly, that's who, and here Jodie was, proving it with her sheer arrogance, informing Grace in her high and mighty way, whom Grace was and wasn't allowed to text. Grace let that thought settle and niggle and eventually turn into real anger inside her head. She'd had to put up with Polly's arrogance and overconfidence all her life, she'd been shamed into following everything her sister wanted, and what had Grace done? She'd stupidly and naively replicated the relationship with Jodie. They'd known each other for five years, had met one year after Polly's death, and Grace had thought herself the luckiest person on earth. Finally, she had a best friend. A person in whom she could confide. And had. In depth. After Jodie had tricked her into telling her story. About the accident.

The accident she could have averted.

The sister she could have saved.

But once Odette had come onto the scene, just under a year ago, Grace had recognised, with an all too familiar resignation, her place in the pecking order. She was playing second fiddle again. Kowtowing to the great and the good and the better, Jodie. Both sister and once-best friend, used that same tone with her, as if she were stupid and unworthy and an embarrassment.

Who was stupid now? Jodie had clearly texted Grace in desperation, astonished at being left out for once. Not the one in charge now, but shouting out orders, expecting Grace to jump to it and drop everything.

Well, fuck her.

Odette hardly even registered nor acknowledged Grace, so fuck her as well.

Fuck them both.

Grace was more than ready to show Jodie who was boss now, and took great pleasure in not answering Jodie's text. *And she was following Barney right up to his front door.* Smiling happily, keeping an eye on her man, she glanced out of the window. It took a while before it hit her. *How did Jodie know I was with Barney?*

It slowly dawned on Grace that Barney must have texted Jodie when he'd gone to the loo. Probably saying what a great time he was having, and thanking Jodie for the introduction. The image of Jodie reading *that* text made Grace laugh. It made her conquering of her new man better and better. It made it perfect.

So caught up in her glee, she almost lost sight of her goal as he suddenly got off the bus. Again, Grace was lucky that three others also alighted, giving her enough cover to carry on where she'd left off, trotting behind Barney. Frightened that he'd turn and see her, she kept her distance. Although, if he *did* turn around, well, she wouldn't expect him to be *that* surprised. After all, when he'd made his departure from her in the pub, he'd bowed his head, paid the bill and taken her hand in his: quickly and delicately, as if he thought her so fragile he was mindful not to hurt her. And then a sweet smile in farewell. As if he were already imagining seeing her again.

She was going to go for a big splash ta-da moment when he was at his front door, and suddenly she'd pop up, smiling with arms outspread. *Here I am, Barney.*

Could she be that brazen?

Either way, she had to hurry. She was never late in opening her shop after lunch, or indeed at any time. It was her baby, so she hoped that Barney didn't have far to go before reaching home.

Leaving the high street, he turned onto a side road – more of an avenue, really, with beautiful houses lining each side. Slowing even further, she waited until finally he pivoted on his heel and disappeared through a gate.

Putting on a spurt, she managed to catch up, then peeping around a large bush she saw Barney go not to the front door, but instead around the side of the building to a red door. He opened it and stepped into the house.

Tapping her foot with anxiety and now dithering, Grace realised she'd missed her moment. She needed to rethink her plan. Looking at her watch again, she decided she couldn't be late opening up, it just wasn't her. It made her nervous simply imagining it. If she hurried and the buses were on her side, she'd only be about fifteen minutes late, but she would have to leave immediately.

Grace would come back early tomorrow evening, rat-a-tat-tat on his red door, and oh, how she'd surprise him.

That was a *much* better idea.

And Barney would be hers.

For keeps.

Whatever it took, she'd get him all for herself.

16

ME

Breathing in deeply, I looked at my trio of party guests. We were all sitting cross-legged on the floor around a small table, cups and saucers and a steaming pot of hot tea on coasters arranged neatly before us. A fruit cake sat in pride of place on a silver salver.

It was good to be home amongst familiar and friendly *safe* pleasures, happily together in the dolls' room, the morning light shining through the window.

I sat opposite Furious Phil, and he sat next to Guilty Grace – formerly Guilty Gertie –artistic licence and reality allowed me to invite who I bloody well chose and change the guest list as I saw fit. They were my rules, after all.

Calm Karen sat opposite Furious, or Fury for short, and I hoped her mood would win the day. My intellect wished for that, but my real self backed Fury. Always and forever. Because I knew him the best.

Although in my current frame of mind, I seriously fucking doubted Calm would rein in Fury. Clenching my fsts and reopening the wound on my middle finger, I banged them on the table, hearing the clatter of the cups as they rattled in their saucers. 'Why were you so mean, Grace? And so obscenely grasping at me? Hiding behind your transparent guilt, why so insincere and interrogatory?' I unclenched my teeth. 'And what are you fucking guilty of, anyway?'

My voice sounded out, soft and gentle, coming from Calm Karen: 'Language, Barney, language. There's no need to swear.'

'Oh, why don't you just fuck off, Calm?' Fury shouted. He always shouted loudly and made the veins in my neck stand out with the effort. I liked him. We were sympatico.

'Barney waited forty-five minutes before he admitted Odette wouldn't be coming to rescue him. Fucking pathetic or what? And Grace stuck to him like glue. It made me sick. No wonder I turned up – invited or not.'

He sort of leered and I laughed with him, baring my teeth and drumming my fingers on the table – harder than was necessary, and I watched as red drops of blood fell onto the white tablecloth. Ignoring the crimson splashes, I matched Fury's expression: the two of us inextricably linked since I'd been a young boy. We understood each other. Not like soppy Calm and horrid Guilty Grace.

It turned out Guilty Grace had a simpering girlish voice, and her round eyes and her red hair looked absurdly Comic as she lied. Not so gushing now, but still Guilty. Still, having tea with me, Grace lied. 'I wasn't mean, Barney. I like you. And I'm not guilty of anything. You have my word.'

I moved the fruit cake and plates, and poured tea for all of us, adding milk. I shook my head, trying to keep my voice level. 'You *are* a liar. Everything about you screams out one big untruth. And you don't even have the grace to be aware of your total lack of grace. You tried to dissect me, pick my emotions apart, you tried to *help* me – how dare you? I don't need your help.'

Sweating, I wiped my brow. 'And there you were, hiding

behind your own Guilt the whole time. Hiding your Guilt in plain sight, you fool. You *bitch*. And you know what, I don't even care *why* you're Guilty. I couldn't care less.'

Dipping my index finger into the milk jug, I flicked it at Grace, and watched as drops of white landed on her face and a spray settled on her hair in a fine mist, tinged pink with a flying drop of blood. Fury laughed. 'Go, Barney. You tell her.'

Calm's hands rested in a Placatory manner in her lap, and she tutted theatrically. She opened her rosebud lips to speak – Calmly. I rolled my eyes as I waited for her gentle reprimand. 'I will not tolerate this behaviour. You need to Calm down, Barney. Don't listen to Furious – Fury gets you nowhere and gives you nothing positive. I can stop him.' Her eyes gazed into mine. 'If you'll let me, I can Calm you and the whole situation down.'

Fury shouted, 'Don't listen. There's nothing wrong with Anger – it keeps people at bay, keeps you safe, it protects you, and it is justified. It is powerful because it makes you, you.'

Sweat beaded on my upper lip and in order to unclench my fists, I forced myself to pick up the small cup of tea and brought it to my mouth. Blowing on it, I played for time. It was always like this, Furious against Calm. Fury had the most wins under his belt, and I naturally warmed to him. Calm, I found a pain in the arse and really very boring. And soft. And useless. Most of all, especially recently, I found Calm to be a total waste of fucking time.

Calm's treacly voice whispered out oh-so quietly, I had to lean forward to hear her, her expression all sweetness and light. 'Why are you so Angry with Guilty Grace? What did she do, exactly?'

'She wouldn't let me be Charming, she didn't give me enough space, she wouldn't stop asking and asking and digging and delving for more information. Personal, private stuff. She fucking wanted me to kiss her, and I bought her lunch. She overwhelmed me by being... being *her*. She got a free lunch and a quick thrill with me. Grace was obscene and overtly disgusting in her grasping Wanting. And all I got was a bloody finger and a tension headache.'

'That's because I was there, mate.' Fury dipped his head as if expecting thanks for his intervention, and I couldn't help but smile and was rewarded with a smile back. 'At your service, Barney.'

'And lest I forget, I was abandoned by Odette,' I shouted, full of Fury. 'She didn't come and she didn't even text me. What a bitch. Why are people so difficult? I don't understand them and I don't like them.'

Guilty Grace raised her hand. 'Please, Barney, listen to me. I only wanted to make friends with you. I... well, you know, I'm not great with men and I admit, okay, I *admit*, I'm a little on the Needy side. But all I want is a partner. A man. To Love as my own.' She blushed. 'That doesn't mean I'm *too Needy*. I'm just naturally Giving.'

That made me laugh. 'Giving? I don't think so, you're too self-obsessed. But Needy? You're so fucking needy, you're *leaking* desperation from your pores. So, you want to be Loved. Join the fucking queue. Get in line. But you're not the one, okay? Get that into your Stupid, Greedy, Guilty head and understand it. It's not you I want. You're just a rehearsal woman. *Okay?* You just happened to be there.'

I leant back on my hands. 'But I do want one of the other two: not fussed whether it's Odette or Jodie. It doesn't matter.' I held a finger up and wagged it at them all. 'And never again, and I do mean *never*, will I do a one-on-one meeting with either of them. Until I'm good and ready. More established. More me.'

'Good,' crooned Calm. 'Really, very good, Barney. Well done for admitting you want to be Loved.'

I was more than surprised at this turn of events and Fury's blue glassy eyes blazed with a frightening and sudden rage. 'He never said that. You inferred it. He doesn't need to be Loved. Do you, Barney? Not when you've got us. We're your family, not those people outside. They're a con, a trick. *They're* the fraudsters. Don't listen to them.' He laughed. 'And definitely don't listen to stupid Calm – she's always sticking her fucking oar in and getting in my way. It's always been you and me, Barney. Remember that, I'm your best friend and always have been.'

Calm went quiet, Guilty went quiet and finally *I* went quiet.

I admitted to being slightly shocked at the outcome of the tea party. Who would have thought I wanted Love? I let the idea settle in my mind. Later I'd give it the consideration it deserved. It was a novel concept and most unexpected.

All four of us sat there in silence until I raised my head. 'Stop with the Sad faces,' I said. 'Come on, this *is* a tea party, after all. I've even made cake. I'll cut you each a slice – it's got extra glacé cherries and dried fruit. Delicious.'

'Get a bloody move on then, you moron,' Fury said, but more Petulant now, rather than downright Furious. 'Fucking tea's getting cold.'

Ignoring Fury, I gently put a piece of cake on a side plate for each of them and topped up their cups, Politely, I wiped away a few fallen blood drops. 'Now, isn't that better? All Calm again. As Adele isn't here, I'll be Mummy. One lump or two, everyone?'

I'd been so busy losing myself in dollying after my disastrous lunch date with Grace, that I'd missed reading the text from Odette until late afternoon. I couldn't have been more thrilled and it softened the whole sham that had been Grace and her lying, imbecilic, probing, pressing non-stop chattering questions.

Having not slept properly due to nervous excitement at the prospect of the next day's thrills and spills, I found myself clock-watching as soon as morning broke. Unsure as to what to wear, never having considered this a problem before, I realised I was actually enjoying myself.

I laid out a few different shirts from which to choose, and a couple of jeans and two different pairs of trousers – one casual, one smart. I'd mull it over. Maybe mix and match. Either way, I'd give my attire the serious consideration it required. I wasn't meeting Jodie and Odette until eight o'clock this evening. A different pub. A different me. More prepared, I thought.

And I was meeting *two* of them at the same time, so no chance of getting bogged down in the intensity of a one-to-one conversation, which I'd discovered could make me feel trapped. I'd always been a quick learner, so recognised that particular set-up should be avoided. Until such time as I was more accustomed to people and their weirdnesses.

This time, I had the advantage: I understood what I wanted, instead of simply *Hoping* for all the trimmings. I'd broken it down, with the help of my dolls, and now I *knew* I was seeking Love.

With Odette. She was the one. And Jodie would act as my buffer, if I found myself out of my depth. Everything was slipping nicely into place.

At this point, I appeared to be experiencing Hope – not a feeling I was familiar with – so I gratefully welcomed input from my brain. Was I being incredibly naïve, immature and premature in feeling excitement? Just because the dolls had spoken, didn't make it law. They were sometimes wrong. Could I really expect to get it right on my very first outing and meeting with people? Was I really that childish that I could even entertain the notion I might have the possibility of actually finding Love?

I smiled to myself. I *did* think Odette liked me. We'd had an instant connection from the off. *And she'd winked at me.* She was more sophisticated than I in these matters, but I suspected she was exercising discretion, and being subtle in her show of interest in me, nothing overt nor vulgar.

Intellectually, I recognised this was all a little far-fetched and highly unlikely, and yet, I remained quietly confident, if somewhat apprehensive. I was more than aware that I held no Romantic feelings for Odette, but hoped they could be manufactured – given time. It was unusual for my brain and the one emotion – that of potential Love – to be in conflict and at such odds with each other.

Needing a bit of grounding and normal, more familiar angst, I went looking for Mum.

I found her lying on the sofa, her face and body partially hidden by a heap of cushions and a large heavy blanket.

'What's wrong, Mum? Are you all right?'

She plucked feebly at the cover and managed to extricate her face from its cocoon of soft furnishings. And seeing her, I was shocked. Not a bad-looking woman normally, her face now was puffy, her cheeks pasty and her eyes swollen and bleary. 'Mum?' Shaking her gently, my hand on her shoulder, I whispered, 'You look dreadful. Is there anything I can get you?'

Running her tongue around in her mouth as if it were a strange object that shouldn't be there, she finally spoke. 'Hello, Barney. What's the time?'

Time you fucking pulled yourself together and got your life back. Stop being weak.

'It's lunchtime. What can I tempt you with?'

Already shaking her head before I'd even finished the sentence, I knew she'd want nothing from me. Thinking of Jodie and Odette, mostly Odette, as much as I knew of their bereavement stories, I was pretty sure they hadn't given up and lain on the sofa, pretend-dying. Granted, my mother's loss was recent, but still. I didn't think she was making a real effort.

Annoyed, I stood up and went to the kitchen, and threw together a cheese and cucumber sandwich. Remembering a napkin, I brought it all to her on a plate. 'Eat, Mum. You're not dying. You need to eat. Here, I'll help you sit up.'

Manoeuvring her, I finally got her into a sandwich-eating position, albeit a sloppy and messy one. Biting my lip, I wanted to shout at her for giving up, for not trying, to giving *in* to Grief. How bad could it really be? Taking a minute to think, with my newly acquired knowledge of wanting Love, I acknowledged how inextricably linked both Grief and Love were. Ironic, as I was chasing one and Mum was trying to escape one. Wasn't she? She *should* be, but seemed loath to let it go, allowing it to consume her instead. Life really was one big old confusing riot of strange and unforeseen circumstances, usually made by stupid people, who should know better.

Rage was also a funny thing. When it didn't overwhelm me unexpectedly, when I *felt* it coming on, it would always start as a small knot in my stomach and then spread, slowly, as if teasing, until it consumed and took over my entire being. Currently it was in the knot stage, and I tried my hardest to think calmly. Watching Mum put the sandwich to her lips, and actually have difficulty in taking a decisive bite, apparently at a loss as to whether to open or close her mouth, I had to turn away. Disgusted.

Unable *not* to look again, like watching an horrific accident in slow motion, I studied her as she pawed at the bread and inspected it, as if it were an alien thing, something she'd never encountered before and didn't know how to handle.

It wasn't surprising as I realised she was stoned off her face.

Quickly, reining in my very genuine knot of rage, I sprinted up the ill-fated staircase and into her bedroom. Went to her side of the bed. I assumed it was still her side of the bed and that she hadn't moved over to the emptiness that had been Dad's place. Opening the top drawer, I didn't even have to rummage about. There was a bottle of liquid diazepam. And a syringe. Examining the label, I noted the prescription date, and rose my eyebrows. *Interesting.*

Slipping both into my pocket, I went back down to Mum. Feeling I'd done the right thing having confiscated her right to overdose. As her son, that was the least I could do: keep her safe and breathing. That was my duty.

I was careful not to trip on the stairs, now aware of how precarious such an action could be.

'How much of this have you taken, Mum?' I waved the bottle at her, but got no response.

The sandwich with a bite out of it, lay abandoned on her chest. Opening her eyes, it took a while for her to focus. 'Leave me alone, Barney. I'm sorry. I can't do it. Not now.' She closed her eyes again, and then seemed to make a gargantuan effort to speak, and dragged open her heavy-lidded eyes to looked at me. 'It's the drugs I'm taking. I'm so sorry. Forgive me. I really can't do it.' Her voice was a mumble. 'Whatever *it* is.'

'Can't do what? Function? Live? Love? It's me, your son. You still love me, so get it together, Mum. Please.'

But her eyes were already closing again.

Putting my lips to her ear, I whispered, hoping she'd hear me, although I doubted it. 'Guess what, Mum? I had a tea party with Guilty, Furious and Calm yesterday afternoon. You'll never believe what I discovered.'

I waited, hoping she'd at least open her eyes, but there was no discernible reaction and her breathing was heavy.

Sitting back, I took her hand in mine. 'I'll tell you anyway, because I know this will make you proud. I discovered that I want to be Loved. Isn't that weird?' I waited again, politely, giving her a chance, even though I knew she was past answering. 'It's really weird and really rather wonderful. It's opened up whole new possibilities and it also fits in with my existing plan of wanting a normal life, you know, a wife, a child, a house. Isn't that great? Fortuitous, doesn't even cover it.'

Scooping her up, I carried her like a baby up the staircase and into her bedroom. Pulling back the duvet, I slipped her gently beneath the covers and kissed her on the forehead.

'Get well soon, Mum. Really. I miss you about the place. And I want you to be happy for me, because now I *know* I want to be Loved, I might be all right.'

I tucked the duvet under her chin.

'Well, as all right as can be expected, but it's definitely progress. And it's all because of you that I'm equipped, *fully* equipped, to deal with Love when it comes my way.' I bent to speak again into her ear, so used to communicating and whispering into tiny dolly ears.

'And it *is* coming my way. It's all coming together. Finally. In part, that'll be thanks to you. But in a greater part, it's because of my plan to orchestrate a real life for myself and be proactive. I'm going bravely into the unfamiliar. With people. *Real* people. With *women*. *A* woman.'

Leaning back, my rage had left me completely: testament to Intellect over Emotion and proving my mother's teachings were indeed correct. Always had been. The knot of rage had gone, and I was extraordinarily calm. Thinking had saved me.

Grinning stupidly and yes, I'd go so far as to say, *Happily*, I gave her the punchline. 'One woman. Her name's Odette. But I'm not stupid enough to suppose I Love her. Why would I? But perhaps I could. In the future. Maybe we could get married – the whole white picket fence and everything. Anything's possible.'

Patting Mum's hand, preparatory to leaving, I smiled. 'I think she might be the one to give me the life I crave. Maybe she'll need a little persuasion, but not a lot, I don't think. We had an instant affinity with each other, as if we were meant to be. Of course, she hasn't *said* anything, but I know. *She* might not even know it yet, but it's all going in the right direction.' I stood up. 'I've got a date with her tonight at eight o'clock at The Pig & Whistle. This is it, Mum. It really is.'

I laughed quietly.

'I'm getting myself a real life, with a real woman in a real relationship.' I bent and squeezed her hands in mine. 'I'm going to be normal, Mum. After all your hard work, it's time.'

Standing at the door, I waved, looking with love at my mother as she lay in her bed, all forlorn and lost-looking and her eyes shut. 'And I might even learn about Grief and how best to save you along the way. That was the starting point of all this, and I haven't forgotten you. I want you to know that.'

She'd done so much for me, and here I was, finally putting it all to the test.

'See you later, Mum. I may be off on my date tonight, but I'll never leave you. Never.'

18

—————

ADELE

I heard every word my psychopathic son uttered, and am keeping my eyes shut until I know he's gone.

It hadn't been difficult feigning a drugged sleep. Yesterday evening, Adele had taken 20mls of liquid Valium for the first time in her entire life, as given to her by the family GP months ago, who'd suggested it would be easier for her as she was so averse to taking tablets. *20mls will sedate you, you need to rest, what a nasty shock you've had, what a tragedy, I'm so sorry. Never hesitate to call me.*

She'd never cared for Dr Wright; he'd always been flirtatious, had always stood too close, and because Timothy had died, he'd been overtly over-keen to offer his sympathies, suffocating her with smarmy, meaningless condolences, all the while squeezing her hand and holding on to it for far too long. Thinking himself in with a chance. The fool.

Not caring, having avoided taking the sedation until last night, Adele had squirted the liquid into her mouth with the syringe, and unsurprisingly had gone straight to sleep.

This morning, she had immediately known this wasn't the blurred, cushioned and soft-around-the edges path she wanted to linger on. She had, however, used the Valium as an excuse to rid herself of her son, pretending she had taken it that morning, purely so he'd leave her alone. So, Barney could keep the bottle he'd taken – Adele had to be awake for this new chapter of her life.

Instinctively, she'd hidden under the cushions when she'd heard her son come bounding into the room late this morning, or early this afternoon: time had ceased to be a solid thing and had become fluid and meaningless. She hadn't the energy to deal with Barney, and had felt petty and spiteful acknowledging she was angry and upset with him for his indifference to his father's death. It wasn't Barney's fault. None of it was.

Timothy's death had been the trigger that had lit the fuse that was her son, and made him explode. With an alarming bang. All her life, she'd been waiting for this moment, and here it finally was.

He truly frightened and disturbed her.

His behaviour might, however, be the kick up the arse she needed to stop this holiday from life she'd taken. A dangerous mourning cruise, and now she wanted to get off. *Needed* to get off and get back to living.

Adele told herself she should be up and functioning now, anyway. Instead of quietly drowning and not even shouting for help.

She hadn't needed Barney telling her she looked like crap, but until this moment, she hadn't found it in herself to care. Sobbing in bed and hiding from the world for months had done little for her skin. She looked like she felt: abandoned and alone and uncared for.

But *now* she cared what she looked like. If she was to save her child, she could at least have the decency to look like a person in her own right, and not one half of a couple, bereft, bedraggled and brutalised by loss.

Listening to her son, she hadn't immediately thought Barney was having a psychotic break, or even suffering a mania. He was simply overexcited and unfamiliar as to how to react to all the new things that were apparently happening in his life. He was *not* on a murderous rampage, Adele told herself. At this stage, it was all still a novel game of discovery for him. As if he were testing very new waters and had got carried away with his own perceived prowess at existing in the strange new world in which he found himself.

Yes, Timothy was gone and Adele had nothing left.

Except Barney.

Whom she loved.

And who appeared to be ready to venture off, wandering into a life that didn't sound real except in his own head. He wasn't equipped – *at all*. Despite her happily sacrificing her own life for her beloved son, she'd failed. She'd lost him to a fantastical and deluded other-world, in which he wouldn't be welcomed by polite society. They'd see through his charade of a personality and they'd destroy him.

Or he, them.

However much Adele had lovingly nurtured him, clearly nature now had the upper hand.

But not if she could help it. *It is* not *too late. It isn't. I can do this.*

It was time to be his mother again and rescue him.

And if this Odette woman did truly exist and wasn't a warped figment of Barney's brain, which Adele didn't really believe, then Odette would need saving too.

Taking a deep breath, she got up and ran a bath. She'd have to get Barney out of the house on some pretext. In her dressing gown, allowing herself to enjoy the heat from the bath water as it ran boiling hot, she took out her mobile from her pocket. For a moment, Adele's mind was a total blank –

perhaps grief really *had* destroyed her and left her with nothing worth having. Not even her brain. Gritting her teeth, she stood still, the steam filling the room. *Get it together, Adele. Your son needs you. Timothy is gone. You're on your own. So, get to it.*

Wiping the phone screen of condensation, it dawned on her that she'd be unable to text him, sounding coherent, without him becoming suspicious of her miraculous return to an undrugged state in such a short space of time.

Despite his inability to grieve, he was not intentionally cruel.

He *was* a kind boy she told herself, even though he frightened her. Even though she thought he was teetering on the edge of something unholy. Even though she knew she was kidding herself.

Adele wondered which way he'd fall and who'd be there to catch him.

She also wondered if Barney was quietly madder than she'd ever suspected.

If so, his insanity was getting noisier by the moment.

Keeping her dressing gown on, she wandered back into her bedroom and walked slowly over to the window, where she looked out onto the front of the house. The long gravel driveway leading away into the street and beyond. She stood there, for ten minutes, in a gentle panic, trying to think. And desperately hoping. As a life-long lover of walking, Adele prayed Barney would go off for one of his daily trots to calm himself for his coming exciting evening; it was precisely the sort of thing he'd do.

Finally, *Thank God*, Barney came into view. Adele could hear his shoes crunching on the gravel, saw his head down, and fists pumping as if he was speed-walking. Lifting the sash window, she poked her head out, remembering at the last minute, to maintain a vaguely soporific look, as if she were still under the influence. 'Barney. Hey, Barney, up here. It's me.'

Swinging his head up, seeing her, he smiled and held his arm in the air in a happy greeting. 'Feeling better already, Mum?'

Shrugging, keeping her expression muted, she mumbled out words, knowing he wouldn't be able to hear.

'Can't hear you,' he shouted. 'What do you want? I'm going to the shops. Anything I can get you?'

'Flowers. Can you get me a bunch of flowers. Like Timothy always did. Please, Barney-Boo.'

Even from here, she saw his expression change as if he'd been struck with an idea of some enormity. It clearly pleased him as he smiled broadly up at her. 'No problem, Mum. Your wish is my command.'

Closing the window, Adele waited for a minute, watching Barney until he disappeared.

And then she ran, almost tripping over the cord that held her dressing gown together. Up the back stairs, then panting, she stood outside the door to Barney's rooms. *Don't let him have locked his door, he never locks his door, please God, let it be open.* Twisting the knob, her heart hammered as it refused to budge. Anxiety overwhelmed her and frantically, she jiggled the handle again. The door swung open. Almost weeping with relief, she tripped and stumbled but she knew precisely where she was headed – the small dolly room, which Barney always referred to as The Rehab.

As usual, as was normal for her son, the room was fastidiously tidy, not a hair out of place. Unfortunately, it was hair that she sought. In a curtained off alcove, Adele found what she was looking for. Some already-prepared strands were laid out, beautifully brushed and silky smooth. Adele tried to ignore the mannequins who wore the finished articles: wigs of varying colours and lengths and styles, which hung down their blank faces, in bobs, fringes, curls and waves.

Turning, Adele nearly knocked a row of dolls from the shelf with her elbow. She found the actual porcelain dolls strangely unsettling as some of them sat, watching her, in their spookily bald state with their skull caps on, waiting to be plugged, glued, and finished with new hair. Her hands shaking, she was very *very* careful not to disturb and unnecessarily move anything she didn't need to. Running her fingers over the weaves of alpaca fibre interwoven with human hair, she marvelled at their authenticity. She knew it wasn't standard to use real hair, but Barney liked it this way. It made the dolls more realistic.

Every colour was there, but she naturally concentrated her attention on the blonde and black. Perfect for what she wanted. She did *not* want to stand out by adorning her scalp in pink or red or orange tresses. She'd be wearing a beret, and would only allow a few choice but carefully selected swathes to be visible. Letting the strange hair slip through her fingers, she picked herself a couple of the largest glued strands, imagining it as a ponytail for herself. And prayed to God that Barney wouldn't notice they were missing.

Quickly, because she couldn't resist the temptation, she picked up a whole wig from a faceless mannequin. Knowing she was being silly but unable to stop herself, she put the far-too-small manufactured hairstyle on her head. Looking in the mirror, the Shirley Temple tight blonde curls perched precariously on top of her own hair like a pile of lopsided tiny golden worms. The desire to laugh almost overwhelmed her, but she sucked in air deeply and gathered herself.

As if on a mission to derail her best laid plans, Adele again dithered and delayed when she opened up the eyelashes drawer. All perfectly and neatly laid out, like sleeping bodyless spiders. *I am* not *fucking gluing lashes to my eyelids. That is a step too far. It is so grotesque and* not *normal. In* any *way whatsoever.*

Hurrying from the room, sweating now that she'd done it, hair in hand, Adele hurried back to her bathroom to take her now probably cold bath. Undressing, she tried to calm her breathing. She was finally alive again. *Forgive me, Timothy. I miss you so, but tonight we're going to help our son. Perhaps, he won't need it. Perhaps, perhaps, perhaps. But either way, you're coming with me, whether you approve of my deceit or not. What else can I do, darling Timothy? I'm carrying you in my heart wherever I go, so please feel free to advise.*

She patted her chest and closed her eyes, allowing herself to pretend Timothy was by her side. Opening her eyes, she was all back to business. She was relatively confident her disguise would be good enough, especially with sunglasses and a scarf slung casually around her neck, perhaps obscuring her chin should it be necessary. But she'd be at The Pig & Whistle early, and would wait for her son and his two women friends, however nervous she was.

As she left the house at a quarter past seven, she felt ridiculous and self-conscious in her camouflaged headgear. The fresh air hit her and she realised how long she'd been hiding away. It was good to be breathing in life, however anxious she was about her destination and indeed, completely unclear what, if anything, she would do.

Touching her beret and making sure it was sitting comfortably upon her head, hair secured firmly in place, she acknowledged to herself how truly and horrifyingly appropriate it was to be wearing dolly hair, each brushed and silky strand, heavily pinned to her own hair beneath the beret. She practised letting her new ponytail drape over her shoulder. Flicked at it, making sure it was secure. Stroked it.

Adele shuddered.

My son has always thought of himself as a doll, and now I am finally playing his game.

But I am *not* a doll. I am his mother.

It felt dangerous and very wrong and obscenely perverse.

She got into her car and drove to the pub, pretending everything in her world was completely normal.

19

—

ME

After I'd put Mum to bed and made sure she was safe, my mood changed into what I assumed might be classified as pre-date jitters – an odd sensation. I wasn't sure exactly what it entailed, but I was definitely nervous. Strangely, I had to introduce myself to a kaleidoscope of butterflies who'd taken up a fluttering residence in my stomach. Who *knew*?

So excited, I effortlessly refused to let Mum's giving-up spoil my very special day.

Anyway, I loved her and it hadn't been such a chore tending to her. Receiving her instruction from her bedroom window had been good to see and hear. At least she was vertical and finally making the effort. Flowers always cheer, that's what Dad used to say.

Mum's request for them had given me the idea of a little gift for the unsuspecting Odette, although I'd have to present them to *both* women, for how could I ignore Jodie? It would be rude and uncouth. But really, they were only for Odette. What better way to woo a woman than to turn up with a beautiful spray of colourful blooms? It was perfect.

On this point, I was taking my lead from Dad buying Mum flowers, books I had read, and films I had seen. Not a solid foundation for wooing, but what's a man to do?

Back at the house with Mum's roses and carnations, I put them in a vase for her. She was probably still too out of it to manage doing that simple task, but I hoped, again *Hoped*, she'd cheer up when she came into her kitchen and saw them arranged just so, with love.

Dumping mine in their cellophane in a bucket of water, not wanting them to wilt, I got down to the serious matter of clothes selection for the coming evening.

After much deliberation, I went for smart/casual – a red long-sleeved cotton top and a grey jacket and blue jeans. I was going for attractive but unthreatening. Trailing my fingers over my array of little dolls-to-go, I had difficulty picking one. Sexy Simon? Approachable Andy? I most definitely wasn't giving Charming Charles another outing – he'd been useless and would be changed into someone else, someone more appropriate, at a later date. Not now. Now, it was all about mentally preparing myself for the evening ahead.

I spent some time brushing my dolls' hair, caressing their eyelashes – I loved the way they tickled my cheek when I brushed my face up against them – and I gently kissed Lucky Lucy on her red cupid-bow lips – who doesn't need a little Luck now and again, after all. For a while, I allowed myself to be lost and at peace with my china sweethearts.

I checked my watch and couldn't believe how quickly time had passed. There were only two hours to go before kick-off. *Two hours*. Was it too early to get dressed now? No. No, it wasn't. Stripping and re-dressing, I stood in front of the mirror and inspected my reflection and I was pleased, thought I looked more than presentable.

When my private and separate doorbell to the main house rang out, I froze, startled into immobility. I wasn't expecting any deliveries of doll accessories, nor any new inks. Everything was in order and nothing was pending.

Nobody ever rang my doorbell. Concerned, I went downstairs and opened the door.

'Hello, Barney. It's me.' Grace stood there in a harlot-red dress and held her arms out. Did she expect me to *hug* her? Fury, real deep-down frightening rage, made me shake. My mouth worked silently, but no words came out.

Grace's laugh brought me back to her hideous and very real and unwanted presence. 'It's me, silly. I thought you might like some company.' She paused. 'As we had such a lovely lunch yesterday. I thought it would be fun to carry it on.'

Her lips spread again, and I couldn't help but notice her pink lipstick had bled out into the fine wrinkles around her mouth. When I didn't respond vocally, I wondered if my anger had made me mute. Silently, I realised I was more enraged than I had ever been before. Ever. *No one* came to my rooms, uninvited. In fact, I had never invited anyone, so her being there felt like a physical assault.

Slowly, I saw her expression falter.

She laughed nervously. 'Barney, what's wrong? Why are you so surprised to see me? Come on, let me in. I insist.'

Dismayed, my anger paralysing me, she pushed past me and walked boldly up the stairs. I watched her buttocks jiggling in a disgusting way, undulating and wobbling in her vacuum-packed dress as she went higher and higher up the staircase. It was when she reached the top, placed her hand on the interior doorknob to my private quarters, and turned to smile at me that I finally lost control. Taking the steps two at a time, I was inches from her stupid face before she had time to react. My closeness, instead of stopping her dead, made her panic and, spinning away from me, she fumbled at the handle and toppled forward through the door. She was *inside* my house full of dolls, inside my sanctuary, where no one was welcome.

I pushed her hard in the small of her back and she fell further into the sitting room. On her knees, looking up at me over her shoulder, I watched, fascinated and genuinely appalled, as her eyes rounded and filled with tears. Unable to stop myself, I bent down low and slapped her in the face. It had been intended as a punch, but as my hand neared its target, my brain screamed out, *No, no, no, don't do it*, and at the very last minute, my fist unclenched and only my palm connected with her flesh.

Standing and staggering back, my hands covered my mouth as I realised what I had done. Mum had always told me how very wrong it was to hit a woman. It was wrong and it was bad. And I had just done it. I'd never hit a woman before, although had often wanted to. The reality of it wasn't as satisfying as it was sickening. Perhaps it was Grace herself who made it so repugnant an act. I didn't move but watched with a morbid curiosity, her still form, her cheek reddened by my hand, her chest moving as she breathed.

Panting, I forced myself to stand back from her as she lay temporarily flat on her back before rallying and cupping her hand to her face. My hatred of her was like a living thing, and I wanted to vomit all over her. *How dare she?* I couldn't digest nor even comprehend her audacity. Nor her making me hit her – something I'd vowed I would never do, and now she'd made me. I wanted to kill her for that alone.

Bending forward, attempting to find Calm somewhere within me, I still shook with Fury – my two arch enemies at loggerheads once more. Surprised, I felt wetness on my chin and realised I was drooling. This was what this dreadful, outrageously awful woman had reduced me to. Wiping away my dangling spit, I closed my eyes so as not to see her. 'What the hell are you doing here, Grace? I didn't invite you. You are not welcome. Get out. Get out now.'

Finally, making myself look at her, I watched as her eyes skittered in their sockets, wild and uncontrolled. It reminded me of my dolls' eyes when I rolled them in my palm. It further enraged me when I saw her eyelashes were clogging together with her tears – making them not nice and sweeping and whispery soft as they were on my dolls. I *hated* Grace. I hated her spoiling everything.

'You hit me.' Her voice was plaintive and whining. But somewhere in there, she managed to throw in an accusatory note.

'And I'll hit you again if you don't leave now. This minute. Go on. Get up and fuck off.'

Incomprehensibly, being offered a free pass to leave, she instead sat on the floor, crossed her ankles and righted her fallen handbag. 'Why did you hit me, Barney?'

How stupid *was* this woman? I'd hit her hard, and yet here she remained, wanting to discuss it with me. Clenching my fists, I swear to God I could imagine my hands on her throat – so vividly I could actually feel the pressure – squeezing and squeezing, throttling Grace in order to stop her breathing, whilst she talked and stared endlessly at me. She was *still* asking her questions.

This was precisely why I had avoided people in the wild. They were surely madder than me.

My panting had become less, but my breathing was still ragged, as if my lungs had shrivelled in hatred. 'I hit you because I don't like you, Grace. I'm going out to meet Jodie and Odette soon, and you are not invited. You are not welcome here, nor in the pub tonight. You are not included in any part of my life. I cannot stand the sight of you. You are truly repellent to me.'

Getting to her feet in an ungainly fashion, she finally stood, her hand still attached to her cheek. *Boo-fucking-hoo.* 'You owe me, Barney Snapp, and you will be mine. I'm not going until we have a little chat.' She flashed her lipstick-stained teeth at me. 'You can't make me leave. What're you going to do if I simply refuse to go? Kill me?' Laughing loudly, the sound echoed around me and it was all I could hear.

Again, my emotion was real: completely fucking shocked. 'Aren't you frightened of me?'

'Should I be? You're nothing but an animal, but even so, you're my sort of animal. I want you. And yes, that's how bloody desperate I am.' She stamped her foot. 'I will *not* lose out again. Once Jodie has you, you'll forget me, I know you will.' Grace finally lowered her hand from her cheek and, instead, clasped it with the other in front of her, interlocking her fingers, as if she were a librarian ready to admonish someone for talking too loudly.

'I've already forgotten you, Grace. Go on, shoo.' I was confused and knew my words lacked any authority. I was out of my depth. And sinking fast.

I flapped my hands at her ineffectually, not understanding the dynamics of this union *at all*. As far as I was aware, if you hit a woman, you were in deep shit and they were scared and inept at physical confrontation and victory would belong to the male abuser. That's what I'd *thought*. But Grace was apparently very different to the average woman.

'That's quick,' she said, as she swiped at her eyes, drying them. 'Jodie interviewing you, I mean. She must think you're really special.' She laughed suddenly. 'Or, she's really bloody desperate to get you for herself. She knows about our lunch yesterday, you know. Maybe our liaison spurred her on.'

'What are you talking about?'

Grace hit her forehead with her open palm as if she were the stupidest person on earth. 'Oh, yes, of course, you're going to pretend you don't know what's going on. Come on, Barney. It's me. I know, so don't bother lying to me. There's really no point. *I know*. We *all* know.'

I didn't know what she was talking about, but kept my mouth shut. It was never a good idea to show how weak and floundering one really was. I'd wait. She'd tell me. Or I'd make her. I'd hit her once, and the heavens hadn't fallen. If I hit her again, nothing bad would happen. Mum had been wrong.

She tilted her face to the side as if she thought I might find it attractive. Circling her, keeping myself out of hitting-her range, I clenched my jaws together and waved at the sofa. 'Sit.'

Smiling, thinking she'd won something, she perched on the edge of the cushion. 'You're a liar, aren't you, Barney? Just like Jodie and Odette. And me. You *are* one of us, that's why Jodie wants to see you. To make you a member of her oh-so fucking-special club.' She caught her breath. 'But you and me, we can be in our own gang, wouldn't that be better? Wouldn't it? Just you and me? Wouldn't that be perfect?'

It took a while for me to actually hear her words and I battled to understand their meaning. Gratefully, I let my brain take over and felt Fury subside as I concentrated.

'Yes.' I sat down on an armchair, my mind going through every interpretation of her ramblings, and automatically agreed, giving myself time to catch up. 'You're right. I lied.'

They *wanted* me to lie. But I wasn't clear about what. Going through what I knew, all I'd done was join a bereavement group. That's all they knew of me. That my father had died. He'd fallen from my arms. They knew nothing else. Death was the only common denominator. It bound us. And I knew, but couldn't care less, that Grace had lied about something connected to her sister's death. So fucking what?

Putting everything into it, I twisted my face into Empathetic, Accepting, Understanding.

'Tell me your lie, Grace, and I'll tell you mine.'

Her shriek of delight made me jump as she slapped her hands on her knees, in apparent Delight. Reverting to my norm, gratefully, I welcomed my brain as it cancelled out all emotion. Like Puzzled Penelope, I sat there, non-responsive, my face a blank, my heart empty, my eyes dead.

'You know my lie already, let's not pretend.' She opened her eyes wide and waggled her head from side to side as if she were about to scold a two-year-old. 'Duh, Barney, I watched my sister drown. There. Now you officially know. I could have tried to save her, but I chose not to. So, I just watched. Bad bad me. Now tell me your lie. Fair's fair.'

I saw the time and I didn't want to be late. 'Are you going to leave now, Grace?'

Strangely, she laughed. 'No, silly. Course not. We're not finished, are we? Nowhere near finished.' She leaned forward. 'We haven't even started.'

When I moved, she wasn't expecting it. Drawing back my fist, I punched her smack in the side of her face. It knocked her out. A punch would do that, I knew. And second time around, it was definitely a lot more satisfying. Verging on the Enjoyable.

She splayed back in the chair making my furniture ugly, and quickly glancing around, I considered taking her unconscious body, and dumping her somewhere. Outside. But then, she'd tell someone I'd attacked her. I'd be arrested. Very aware I should have quizzed her further on my meeting with Jodie and Odette, I conceded that I had no time. And no time to dispose of her properly.

I *had* to keep her. There was no bloody choice. She *had* to stay here: *in* my fucking doll sanctuary. It fucking wasn't fucking fair, fuck it.

Rushing, worried that Jodie and Odette wouldn't wait for me, I flung Grace's limp body over my shoulder and, thinking it the least personal space in which I could keep her, I took her to the utility room and deposited her on the floor next to the washing machine. My flat was a maze of rooms: a warren of cubbyholes and oddly shaped spaces. This particular room was at the end of the east side, and up a few steps. Sweating and rushing, I found some sturdy clothes line and bound Grace's hands and feet. Dragging her over to the radiator, I attached her to it. There was plenty of clean laundry, which I'd recently done, nicely ironed and starched in a neat pile, so I made her comfortable with pillows and a duvet, should she get cold.

Running, I went and fetched the Valium I'd confiscated from Mum, and skidding back into the utility room, I squatted beside Grace. She came to quickly, but was confused and groggy. Squatting in front of her, I made my voice treacly soft and Concerned.

'Here you are, Grace. You've had a nasty accident, quite a bump on the head you took there. Sit up, yes, that's right. I've got some medicine that'll make you all better. Promise.' Holding her chin in my hand, I inserted the loaded syringe into her mouth and depressed the plunger. I rubbed her throat for good measure, making sure it all went down. 'There, that's it. And swallow. Good girl.'

Her eyes cleared. 'What's going on? What happened?'

Speeding around the room, I found some gaffer tape under the sink, nestling behind the washing powder. I taped her mouth up, making sure she was breathing normally through her nose. Patting her cheek, I forced myself to smile at her.

'I've told you already. You had a nasty accident, Grace. Isn't it a shame your sister wasn't here to save you. Oh, yes, you let her die. Gosh and darn it, life's a bitch, right? Now, I'm off. You just relax and I'll see you later. Sleep now, and night night. Don't let the bed bugs bite.'

There, done. *Finally*, I was ready to go. I grabbed the flowers and left the house.

There really was no excuse for being late.

20

———

ME

Standing outside the pub, I regulated my breathing and loosened my grip on the bouquet of flowers. In my haste, I'd forgotten to bring one of my to-go dolls and thought it didn't bode well for the coming evening. And that would be all Grace's fault. I was on my own and was nervous enough as it was without the added irritant of not being armed with a china ally.

I was unclear what was expected of me. But, if Grace was to be believed, I knew I'd have to lie. I was going to have to play it by ear, which was as risky as it was unstructured. Lack of formality and a prior knowledge of the game rules increased the likelihood of making a social gaffe. But, essentially clueless as to what Jodie and Odette wanted from me, I had no choice but to open the door and go in.

My ears were instantly assaulted by the noise of lots of people. The drinkers' loud grating laughter, the chinking of glasses and bottles, the smell of cheap perfume and stale tobacco, the sheer volume of people pressed together made me flinch. It was physically disgusting. The filthy masses, made dirtier by their forced proximity to me.

Dolls are my vehicle. They carry me – they are me, and I, them. I do not belong here. I do not belong in this chaos. Already I knew the very human reality that was Odette would never match up to the exciting, exhilarating fantasy I had created in my own head. I'd made a stupid mistake, carried away by the novelty of it all.

Clenching my body, I squeezed into a clearing and looked around, desperate for a seat and some space. And then I saw them. My two ladies. They were huddled together at a table, with a third and empty chair that I knew was for me. Their heads were bent together as they chatted earnestly – not a whole lot of Merriment going on as far as I could see. I braced my shoulders and sucked in air slowly.

I saw Odette glance at her watch then look up and around, scanning the crowds, seeking me out, and finally her eyes came to rest on mine. I hailed her, stupidly and belatedly realising I had waved at her with the bunch of flowers. *Smooth; smooth and classy.* Instead of a leading Hollywood actor from the silver screen, with cleft chin and steely-blue eyes, I was entering stage left as an awkward third-rate understudy. A bloody extra. Telling myself things could only improve, I approached, a false smile set in place, and a look of Excitement cemented on my face, simply *Thrilled* at seeing them again.

Really, I wasn't in the mood – what with Grace and all – she'd managed to suck the Joy right out of the evening. I hoped and prayed the Valium would have had the same effect on her as it had on Mum, and that she'd be sleeping peacefully. Initially unsure as to how I felt about what she'd told me, having reflected on her confession on the way here, I decided, on balance, I hoped her face was really sore. Painful. Throbbing. It was my punishment for what she'd done to her sister. If not murder, she was guilty of manslaughter at the very least, and that wasn't something to be as flippant about as she had been. It was fundamentally wrong on so many levels.

My confidence had been knocked by the immorality of her crime and I realised I was back to being me – and would be all sham and pretence with the ladies. The imposter had returned and I was hugely disappointed.

Already I missed the freedom I'd experienced being with Grace earlier, not having to feign my emotions – she'd managed to bring out the real me. And it had been liberating.

But probably not so fun for her.

I also wished I'd had time to ask Grace more intelligent and probing questions as to what exactly I was expected to lie about this evening. But I was pretty sure I'd get the hang of it. Jodie and Odette would hardly be as adept at subterfuge as I.

Both women stood up as I neared the table and angled their cheeks at me, whilst holding out their hands at the same time. A tricky and unnecessary manoeuvre for me to handle, whilst holding a bunch of flowers. I thrust them at Odette, and smiled and bobbed my head, and sat down. Relieved that the salutations were done with.

'We've got a bottle of wine,' Jodie shouted. 'White. A Chablis. Does that suit, or would you prefer something else?' She looked around at the bustle of people. 'This isn't the best place to talk, I'm sorry. I didn't expect it to be so busy.'

'It's not a problem, don't worry, and the wine's perfect, thank you.'

Odette poured me a glass and pushed it towards me. 'Lovely flowers. Thank you so much.' She grinned at me and I grinned back, mimicking frantically. I was frozen with it all, and the enormity of guessing what they really wanted from me, annoyed me and placed me at a disadvantage. Odette's mouth opened, ready to speak, and I automatically leant forward. She rolled her eyes. 'How did you survive your lunch with Grace?'

Thank God. An indication that I could truly say I hadn't enjoyed it. Horribly close to her, I enunciated clearly. 'It was... well, how can I put it?' I rested my chin on my hand. 'A bit much, to be honest. I don't like her.'

Four eyebrows lifted and I realised I'd been *too* honest. 'What I mean is, I'm not good at one-to-ones, and I couldn't get a word in. So, that's why I felt...' *Fuck, what would be an appropriate excuse for my blunt declaration of my dislike for Guilty Grace?* 'That's why I felt bombarded. Grace does talk a lot, doesn't she?'

Laughing as if I'd made the joke of the century, both ladies' faces relaxed as they nodded in tandem. Jodie rolled *her* eyes. 'She certainly does go on. But she didn't make you uncomfortable, did she? I mean, by anything she said?'

'No, I don't believe so.' Cautious now, treading carefully, the conversation was already slipping away from me. What did she mean, *Uncomfortable?* I took my time, picking up my glass and sipping in a Gentlemanly fashion.

'What did you talk about?' Odette asked, all Wide-Eyed Innocence.

'This and that. Mostly, Grace quizzed me about my father's death and how Awful it all must have been. She was very Sympathetic.'

Stick with the basic truth – *the truth will set me free.* And it will make it a whole lot fucking easier for myself. As Grace would attest to. She, who'd seen me for me. Lucky her.

Jodie shook her head, as if Sad, or Embarrassed by her friend, Grace's behaviour. 'I'm sorry, Barney. Grace can be a bit much, sometimes. I hope you weren't too upset?'

Lifting my shoulders in an up and down motion, I also shook my head. 'No, really, it was absolutely Fine.'

Odette leant forward and gently touched my arm. Her caress didn't last long but it made me shrivel up and die a little. *I can't do this. I don't like people. I don't like making conversation and pretending to be friendly. I cannot do this. Who had I been kidding? Odette wasn't the one. No one was the one. Mum was right – I shouldn't be allowed out on my own.*

'Did she mention Jodie or me? You know, in general.' Odette laughed. 'Or in any juicy detail?'

The crowns of all our heads were bent in together, too close for comfort, nearly touching, but it was the only position to assume, to make conversation possible above the chaotic noise. 'No. Nothing. We just talked about Dad and the whole death thing. I mean, him falling down the stairs, how I felt and stuff. Nothing much else. She didn't mention either of you.'

Jodie frowned. 'Grace isn't the most tactful person on the planet. She shouldn't have bombarded you like that. Really, that's not fair.' She paused. 'In our little group, we pride ourselves on being fair.'

Fair and Just. Just Jodie, Objectionable Odette and Bonkers Barney.

Why did I *ever* think I could do this? The whole thing was absurd. I would have got up and left, but a tiny part of me wanted to know about the lies. Plus, I had Grace as a hostage. And she was connected to Jodie and Odette. What to do with her? What to do, full stop?

I hated all this inane chatter. What did it matter how anyone bloody *Felt* anyway? Emotions were overrated, I was discovering, and only made things worse. The whole thing made me want to lash out and stop pretending, I wanted to tell them I didn't really miss Dad, but was sorry for Mum. Nothing more complicated than that. Of course, them being all Sensitive, it would naturally be much *much* more complicated than that.

Playing the game, I pulled back and stared at Jodie, then hunkered forward again. 'What do you mean, Fair? Fair, like how?'

For a moment, Jodie seemed startled, but gathered herself quickly. 'I mean, no one should ever be forced into speaking about their own individual traumas. We've all experienced them, and the idea is that we support each other.'

Already bored and getting more bored by the minute, I drank some wine. 'Yes, you said that before, when I met you all properly the other day. Support. That's important. I understand. But what makes this group different from all the other bereavement groups? You make it *sound* different.'

'Because it is, Barney. Believe me, I know about Grief. I really do.'

'Why not tell me *your* story, Jodie? The whole truth of it? Get me into the swing of it all. I'm a bit Nervous still.' Masking myself in a Little-Boy-Lost persona, I pressed my lips together as if in apology. 'What happened to Tom, your husband? How did you Feel and Cope with it all? It must have been Dreadful. A car accident, you said?'

Boom. Take that, bitch. Do not *fuck with me. I, too, can play games.*

Nodding, Jodie turned her eyes to her glass and rotated the stem of it with her hand. 'You remember I told you on Zoom that I was a victim of abuse, that my husband was a drunk and took pleasure in beating me...?' She paused and I wrinkled up my eyebrows in a Compassionate way. Nodding, I gestured for her to carry on.

'Well, when he died...' She sipped at her drink. 'I found him.' She looked me in the eye. 'And thank God it was me who came across him and not one of my daughters.'

'Yes, that would have been Unthinkable. Too Awful to even contemplate.' I waited before continuing, purely for my own Delight and Amusement. 'But how did you *Feel?*' The last word was stressed and gave her no opportunity to avoid answering it.

Jodie pressed her body against the table as someone behind

bumped into her. The movement made the bottle and glasses topple when her weight hit it, and steadying it, she took my hand. What was it with these bloody women? So much *touching*. 'My feeling at the time was, of course, primarily a very deep and profound shock, but as the weeks turned into months and we had his funeral, do you know how I felt?'

This was one of those questions that was so loaded, it might as well have been a bullet – aimed straight at me. I knew I had to get it right, or it would be the end of this particular group for me. This was a *test*. I sat and gave it some real thought, weighed up Grace's earlier testimony, Jodie's overuse of the words Fair and Support, the covertness of this small, tight, *secret*-feeling group, and finally came up with my answer. It was hardly difficult. It must be something that would be considered Wrong or Inappropriate by most people, or something that you might feel, but would never say out loud in polite company.

'You felt Happy and Relieved. Relieved that he was gone.' I kept my face blank. 'You were full of Joy.'

Jodie looked at Odette and in turn, they both looked at me. Their faces were momentarily shocked, open and then relieved. No lying going on – I was looking at honest faces.

Odette moved the bunch of flowers to the centre of the table, and played with one of the petals before speaking. 'Do you think that's bad, Barney, for Jodie to feel happy about the death of Tom? Full of joy, like you said.'

'No.'

Odette waited a beat, as if surprised I had nothing further to add. And then simply nodded. Biting down on my mounting Fury as it knotted in my stomach, only at the Rage stage now – not fully developed – but threatening, I tried to mentally detach from them both.

A smile played around Odette's lips, and she sat quickly back in her seat, flattened the hair at the sides of her head, and made her bun even tighter as she pulled and rearranged it. 'Can you relate to that feeling of joy?'

I looked at her, flat-eyed. No acting required – *what is she talking about?* Jodie said, 'I think what Odette meant, was, is there anything about your father's death that was... that made you feel alone and confused or maybe something others would have been surprised about, had they known? Or perhaps you may have lied a little? Which would be completely understandable, you know. Strange and unexpected things happen all the time, and we all must accept them as we can. Sometimes, lying a bit helps. Fabricating a little, here and there, can often make things go so much more smoothly. Bad grief can be turned into good grief, if you allow it.'

Good grief, what pretence. But I *had* lied about Dad. We hadn't been standing together at the top of the stairs, and he hadn't fallen from my arms, and I hadn't tried to catch him. That was my lie – and they'd obviously picked up on it. If I confessed, would that make me one of them? Did I *want* to be one of them?

Grace had done much more than lie. She'd played an active part in her sister's death, by doing nothing. I certainly didn't want to be a part of *that*.

But would they want more than the admission it had simply been a stupid, panicked fabrication on my part? It couldn't be that simple. There *had* to be more. I didn't have any more. But I certainly wanted to *know* more.

I had nothing to lose and something to gain. They'd obviously all done *some*thing and I wanted to know what they were guilty of. Instead of understanding Grief, and here's the big joke, I was, instead, going to be a good upstanding member of the psychopathic community and save the day and make Mum proud of me. Really proud.

Because I recognised badness when I saw it.

So, I decided to admit my lie, but give them a little more. Just because I could.

'Yes, I lied about how my father died.' I waited a breath and whispered, 'I pushed him.'

And like two children, neither could hide their great big stupid Relief and what appeared to be *Happy*. That shouldn't be. They both sagged in the middle as if all the air had been expelled from their chest cavities, and their stomachs collapsed. Neither could help show a hint of a smile.

Odette squeezed my hand. 'Oh, Barney, that's all right, don't worry. You can talk about why when you're ready. I'm so so sorry, but we all lie. It's how we survive.'

I lie. But not like they do. I definitely lie. To survive. I never said I didn't. But I wasn't aware there was a specific club for it. The rules for enrolment: lie and keep secret about committing bad and very wrong deeds. That isn't me.

It was all too confusing to find myself in the midst of two women, make that three if I were to include Grace, who, it turned out, were liars of the highest order. And Odette was an assumption at this point – but I'd bet on it. They made me sick with their pretend caring and disgusting secrets. They made the whole of life, and wanting to be a part of it, a travesty.

Zoning them out, leaning back into my chair – distancing myself from the monsters – I allowed myself to look around. It didn't take me long to spot something so familiar my heart flipped in my chest.

It was the hair I saw first. I recognised it instantly – it was so familiar to me, I'd have spotted it anywhere. That particular colour and hybrid mix of alpaca fibre and human hair; *I* had created it. It was the hair for one of my dolls. A lock of it, arranged like a ponytail, brushed and gleaming, fell from the side of a beret – sitting on the head of a woman, slithering along the wall, her back to me. My breath caught in my throat and far away, I could hear Jodie saying something inane. Calling my name. Wanting me back in the fold.

Ignoring Jodie, I stood, and pushing past people, I laid my hand on the shoulder of the woman who was attempting to hide, her back to the room. At my touch, she turned, and I found myself staring into the startled eyes of my mother.

21

ADELE

From her stool at the bar, Adele saw her son as he entered the pub. Bearing blooms. It was just the sort of thoughtful thing he was capable of after years of tuition on how to behave nicely, but how appropriate it was, she didn't know.

Having checked out all the customers before he'd arrived, Adele had been unable to spot who Barney might be meeting, and had sat back and tried to relax. It would all become clear now that he'd arrived. Partially hiding behind a large man, Adele peeked around his elbow, keeping Barney in her sights.

Her son was obviously not enjoying the crowds, and she couldn't blame him. Already looking defeated, dejected and discouraged, Barney made his way over to a table where two women greeted him. Adele saw him go through the motions, after awkwardly exchanging pleasantries. As his mother, it was plain that his polite charm was only superficial, and he was clearly tamping down his irritation and dislike of the whole situation. His previous excitement for the occasion was lost. She wondered what had happened to so crush him.

She waved her glass at the barman. 'Another water, please.'

Adele tried to ignore the heartbreak that was Barney and sipped from her glass.

It was, of course, impossible to hear any of the conversation her son was having with the two women. Adele vaguely tried to guess which one was Odette, but knowing it didn't matter, that Barney's courtship of her was already floundering, she instead attempted to get a feel for what they might be speaking so seriously about.

It didn't have the look of a fun, social evening: there was very little laughter, nor much happiness on show. The nature and subject of their conversation eluded her, but the longer it went on, the more she feared for Barney. The meeting appeared strained but that, of course, could merely be the very presence of her son.

He had the natural ability to depress anything remotely light, without even being aware of it. He gave off ripples of *odd* to those more naïve and unworldly, or conversely, to those more attuned to the subtleties of life. He often made shopkeepers nervous, or unintentionally upset the postman when he was delivering letters if he wasn't consciously concentrating on being *Acceptable*. A wrong look, a misplaced word, a blank face: Barney unsettled people. He had to make a concerted effort to keep it all together and appear, in his terms, normal.

Even from beneath the smelly armpits of a trio of young men behind whom she now sat, the crowd an ever-changing beast, the bodies around her forever shifting, Adele saw Barney's barely contained anger and worried he'd lose his temper. Both women crowded him in a predatory fashion, and Adele could see her son's body tense, but was pleased to see he was still in control and managing to hide his fragility. This wasn't an environment he'd be used to – this place, on a Friday night, would completely unsettle him.

Studying him and his companions, Adele still couldn't

really believe how easily he could take people in with his mimicry and fakery and trickery – to her, his pretend personality rang out as loud as a church bell. Impossible to miss.

Sadly, she watched him and wondered if she could save him. She must. That had been the purpose of her entire life, and now, without Timothy, it was all she had left.

Before she'd even finished her second glass of water, Adele felt more confident in her doll's hair, beret and sunglasses. Eventually, knowing she had to actually *do* something, she left her stool, gently pushing and elbowing customers out of her way: they were standing five deep at the bar, and it was like walking through something solid but sweaty. Keeping her back to Barney, inching her way through the mass of bodies, moving and swaying as one, she held her mobile to her ear, as if in deep conversation with a friend. Ridiculous, bearing in mind the noise, but it was a prop and she gladly hid behind it.

Finding herself having to physically strain against the direction of the tide of men and women going in the opposite direction, she finally found relief in reaching the wall: something solid and reassuring. If she were to help her son in any way, she had to at least know a little of the conversation going on between him and the women. Otherwise, what was the point of being here? *I only want to find out the purpose of Barney's sudden alliance with these people. Because he doesn't do* just-for-fun. He would most certainly have a very definite agenda going on and, in order to help him, she needed to know what his plans were.

She ran her fingers through her doll's hair and adjusted her beret and glasses, all the time concentrating on keeping her back to the room and carrying on her fake deep conversation with no one on her mobile. Head down, one hand on the wall, she slithered along, ignoring the bumping from others as she made her way down the room. Of course, it wasn't long before she realised she'd completely lost track of where she actually was, how far down she had progressed and she was now completely disoriented.

Adele needed to turn and get a feel for where she was, but was afraid that should she turn her face, Barney would see her. For all she knew, she was only feet from him, instead of at a more healthy and safe vantage point of several yards, which was what she'd been aiming for. Feeling ridiculous at being lost, she stopped and tried to gather herself mentally. The sunglasses reinforced her feeling of blindness.

If Barney saw her, she couldn't think of any logical reason for being here. There was no excuse for being so ill-prepared, and she was mortified that she hadn't come armed with more of a plan. If she carried on, she'd be at the door. And that would be as far away from Barney as the bar had been, and at least there on her stool, she'd been hidden.

Taking a deep breath, she dipped her head, pressed random keys on her mobile, and gave herself thinking time.

Someone's hand touched her shoulder and she automatically turned.

'Hello, Mum. What're you doing here?'

Barney's eyes were bright, his cheeks red, and for a moment, Adele was genuinely frightened, thinking he might strike her. He was unable to fully rein in the fury that wanted escape, and his grip on her shoulder tightened.

Leaning his face closer to hers, she could smell alcohol on his breath and felt his body shaking with anger. 'Take the hair off. Take it off, *now*.' He raised his hand as if to rip the hair from her head, and Adele grabbed his fingers, instinctively.

'No, Barney. Calm down. I apologise.'

'You've been in my Rehab. You stole my hair. You *stole* from me.'

'Remember who you're talking to. I'm your mother, Barney.

Your mother who loves you. I'm deeply sorry I went into your private dolls' room, but I had to make sure you were okay. Do you understand? I stole from you and I followed you, because I love you.'

Adele was shaking, her voice was shaking and her mind was skittering about, unable to think clearly. It had been wrong to use the doll's hair – she hadn't thought it through properly.

'Just what the bloody hell are you doing here, Mum? Go away. Fucking go away and leave me alone.' He sneered at her. 'But leave the hair.'

'That's not happening. And really, I'm so sorry, darling. Please forgive me. I just couldn't bear to let you come here without knowing you were all right and–'

'How dare you? I don't want Jodie and Odette seeing you, I won't allow it. You'll spoil everything. You are *not* my mother, okay?'

Adele didn't dare move or speak, but waited for him to finish. She put her hand on his arm but he brushed her aside.

'Do not touch me. Ever again. *And take the fucking hair off.* It's not yours.'

'I'm not taking it off here, don't be silly. But I am sorry. I'm so sorry. I wanted to make sure you were all right, that's all. I'll go. Right now. Don't tell them who I am. They don't need to know. I didn't mean to embarrass you.'

Barney laughed. '*Don't tell them who I am.*' He mimicked her voice, his falsetto strained and cruel sounding. 'No chance of that happening, *Mum.*' Still gripping her arm, she watched him as his brows furrowed and he tried to think himself out of the situation she'd placed him in. Gently, he tightened his grip on her and she saw his white teeth as his lips curled back in rage. 'How can I explain you, to *them?*' He jerked his head backwards, indicating the two women. His face flushed a deeper crimson. 'You've ruined everything. Why are you here?'

'Tell them I'm an old friend. I'm in trouble. My mother is ill. I've just been on the phone and I'm on my way to the hospital. I was here having a drink, on my own, and I've just got the call. They'll believe that. Tell them you saw me, and came to ask if I was all right, that sounds realistic. Barney, really, please, you're hurting me, stop hurting me, please.'

He loosened his grip.

And looked at her with his see-nothing stare. Her insides curdled and she wanted to vomit. 'It's all right, Barney, I promise you. I'll wait here and you can go and tell your friends you're escorting me to my car. It'll be fine. Okay? Please, calm down.'

She wanted to kiss him and ask for forgiveness, but his body language demanded her silence. And so, she waited to see what he'd do.

Barney closed his eyes and took some breaths. He didn't move. Adele didn't move. She awaited his instruction. It was all she could do; she owed him that. She'd contaminated his very private space and couldn't believe she'd had the nerve. In his mind, she'd defiled and violated him. Adele wasn't stupid, but she'd behaved as if she was.

Barney opened his eyes, and Adele saw a calmness had settled in her son. He put his mouth to her ear. 'I've had enough anyway. I'll say I'm going with you, an old friend, to go to the hospital. I can always see them later. They'll keep. Leave now and wait for me. I'll come and find you in the car park.' Turning his back to her, he pushed someone out of his way, and then he stopped and came back to her. 'I've just decided. I'm going to ask them over for drinks this week. Won't that be fun?' He laughed and this time he really did leave her standing on her own, surrounded by people.

Her heart pounding, Adele nodded and nodded again, and finally got her legs moving.

Drinks? He was inviting them over for drinks? Jesus Christ. What was he playing at? It wasn't what he did and he wouldn't know how to do it. The thought of it quickened Adele's stride and the beat of her heart.

His drinks invitation changed everything. It wasn't over after all, as she'd hoped, but only just beginning.

It wasn't often that Barney surprised her. She'd assumed the night hadn't gone well. His whole demeanour had screamed out his pain and difficulty and yes, his dislike of the women, so why the drinks invite?

He rarely bothered even dipping his toe into society, aware that he found people unfathomable and usually unpleasant. They never came up to his very high standards and he was always disappointed. If anything, presuming Adele was right, his meeting with Jodie and Odette had only reinforced his notion that the world was indeed a bad place and he didn't want to play in it.

So why was he prolonging his friendship with them by inviting them into his flat? His sanctuary, as he called it. His safe place.

It didn't make sense and, aware she was on the verge of tears, Adele stared at the floor, left the pub, and waited for her son in the car.

Confident she knew Barney inside out, she sat behind the steering wheel and wondered what he'd tell her. He'd always talked to her, he couldn't help himself – Adele had always been his sounding board, for he had no one else. She was pretty sure she would hear the truth of everything tonight.

She wasn't *as* sure she'd be able to handle it.

22

—

ME

Sliding into the seat next to Mum, I was in a *much* better frame of mind, having briefly shapeshifted into a Functional Social Man again. I'd said my goodbyes to the Grieving Girls, asking them to come for drinks at my flat. Reluctantly, I'd had to give them my address, which was a first, and to tell them I'd contact Grace so she wouldn't miss out on the fun.

I had been rewarded with an enthusiastic double *Yes* from both women – achieved sans Charming Charles anywhere about my person. I slammed the car door. 'Jodie and Odette will be attending a drinks party, hosted by yours truly, on Monday. Seven o'clock sharp.'

Mum didn't answer, she just turned the engine on. I placed my hand over hers on the gearstick. 'And I think you'll find, I never, and will never, give you permission to touch my dolls, are we clear on that? I won't tell you again – take the hair off.'

She turned to look at me. 'Do *not* speak to me like that, using that tone of voice as if I'm an imbecilic juvenile. Who do you think you are? Who do you think *I* am? I deserve some respect from you. I've apologised. Here...' Grabbing wildly at her head, as if she suddenly didn't like the stupid hat, nor the hair and wanted to rid herself of it as quickly as possible, she ripped the beret off and unpinned the ponytail. 'There, it's yours and, as I said earlier, I'm sorry I took it. It won't happen again.'

'No, it won't.' Looking at her, I relented. 'And *I'm* sorry. I know you love me, as I love you, and I shouldn't speak to you like that. It's Rude and Uncalled for.'

'Are you taking the piss, Barney? Initialising automatically inside your head, because that's what it sounds like. Don't give me one of your performances, because frankly, I'm not in the mood. I've been sitting here, worrying, upset by your show of temper to me inside the pub, and I've been shaking, do you know that? Shaking with fear, because I thought you might hit me. *Shaking with fear*. Because of you. And that's not fair.'

I adjusted my seat belt, mortified that Mum had thought I might hit her. I would never do that. I knew I owed her everything – she'd created me, and with her help, I'd fashioned myself into a version of a doll, and together, we'd made me whole. I wouldn't dream of hurting the person who had shaped me, and made me the man I was today.

I apologised again and saw Mum's face relax. Slightly. She started the engine and pulled out onto the main road. Keeping her eyes straight ahead, she said, 'Who did you take with you this evening? Which to-go doll?'

Shaking my head, I didn't answer for a while, for my omission of going doll-less into the big bad world was unheard of. 'I didn't take one. I forgot.'

Mum's head whipped round to stare at me. 'You *forgot*? You never forget. What were you doing that was so important you forgot?'

'Hurrying, preparing, choosing the right wardrobe, not wanting to be late. I forgot, that's all.'

Neither of us spoke for a bit. She quickly glanced at me

again. 'How did it feel, having nothing to rely on other than yourself? No doll to reassure you.'

'Okay, I suppose. I just ended up being myself, let loose into life and struggling – Bonkers Barney. Not that *they* noticed: too wrapped up in their own lies.'

Changing gears, Mum slowed down. 'Why are you asking them over to your flat, anyway? It's always been off-limits to everyone except me.' She turned a corner. 'I mean, I'm pleased but puzzled. You don't like company, especially in your private rooms. You might find it...' She squinted as she scrabbled for the right word. 'Too *intimate*. They'll be in your space and I don't want you feeling hemmed in. Think about it carefully, Barney. It could be a mistake.'

'I have no choice, Mum. These women are different. I *have* to have them round. I can't do a pub again.' I shuddered theatrically, but really, I didn't have to work hard at it. I'd hated every minute being in the crowds, and had been bewildered and appalled by the women. It had been a dreadful combination. 'I have to see them again, in a setting more conducive to conversation. I haven't finished with them, and it needs finishing, believe me. They need to explain, in detail, what they have all done, and if that means having to invite them to my flat, then so be it.'

'What do they need to explain?'

'All three of the women from the bereavement group are sick and their behaviour is obscene and deviant. None of them behaves as you taught me, nor in the way the world is supposed to operate, not even in a way that would be accepted by our criminal system. They have all done bad things, and I'm going to fix it.'

I leant over and kissed her on the cheek. 'Don't worry,' I whispered and seeing a small, tight smile flicker on her lips, I relaxed. 'So, I'm assuming you want to know who Jodie and

Odette are, and what the bloody hell I'm playing at?' I laughed to make it all better and she nodded and bit her lip. Then she risked another peek at me.

'You said all *three* of the women. There were only two. Where was the third woman?'

'She couldn't come. But I'm sure she'll be up for my drinks soiree. She's called Grace.'

'Is she the one who texted you, and you were disappointed it wasn't one of the other two?'

'For God's sake, Mum, it's not important. All three women will be coming for drinks. Stop trying to confuse me. What I need you to know is, I think I've been accepted into some sort of weird, special club. For the morally reprehensible. They bill themselves as a group for the bereaved, but really, they're much more than that. Can you believe it?'

Stroking the doll's hair flat on my thigh, the movement soothed me and a real sense of calm took hold, even though my mind was still grappling with the complexities and indeed shock at being a member of a group that wasn't quite right. Even by my own standards.

'What do you mean, Barney? What bad things have they done?'

'I'm not entirely sure, but they're all lying about the deaths of their loved ones. To fit in, I lied about Dad. A silly lie, completely meaningless, but that's why they've accepted me. Don't you think that's odd? I mean, really strange? It's like some weird sort of cult or something. Not anything I'm familiar with.'

'You're not overly familiar with life in general. Specifically, people. I don't want to sound harsh, but you know I'm speaking the truth. You don't *understand* people. You haven't had enough experience of them, and maybe that's my fault. I should have encouraged you more in that respect.'

'You don't need to apologise for anything, Mum. Really, not.'

'Anyway, what makes you think they were lying?'

'They told me they were. They were proud of it. Odette hasn't said anything about her mother's death yet, but I'm sure she won't break the pattern.'

After turning into our driveway, parking the car outside the house, and putting the handbrake on, Mum turned fully in her seat and took my face by my chin in her thumb and index finger. 'What lie did you tell about Timothy? What did you say?'

'Don't panic, Mum, I swear it was nothing. All I said was, I'd been standing beside him at the top of the stairs when he fell. Instead of next to you, both of us looking up at him. See? Nothing.'

'I don't understand. What does the lie mean?'

'No idea.' *I have some idea, but don't think Mum needs to hear it.* 'I told you, it's meaningless. I just lied because that seemed to be the prerequisite for membership. Reveal a fabrication of your choice. I'm of the opinion they think it means *some*thing, but as you know, it means nothing. After all, what could it *possibly* mean?'

Mum didn't say anything and I waited, impatience beginning to niggle away at me. I had Grace to tend to, and Mum wanting an extra-long conversation now we were home wasn't ideal. She put her hand on my knee. 'I don't want you seeing them again. Cancel the drinks. Stop all contact. It doesn't sound like the sort of group nor the type of people you should be mixing with. If I'm to believe everything you've said.'

'Don't be silly. What have I lied about? Absolutely nothing. Apart from standing next to Dad, that's all. You know I can't lie to you. I just wanted you to know what was happening, bring you up to speed as it were. And what my plans are. And as to my intentions, otherwise known as my plan...' I smiled engagingly at her. '...I aim to find out exactly what crimes or atrocities the women may or may not have committed, and make amends on their behalf. Right is Good, and Wrong is Bad. You taught me that, Mum, so really, I'm only carrying out your wishes.'

'I wish you'd stop seeing them. All of them. Please, Barney, it doesn't sound like something you want to get mixed up in, leave it, move on, find new friends. These ones aren't suitable.'

She got out of the car and walked towards the house.

'Mum?'

Turning back to me, she paused on the driveway. Slamming the door, I stayed by the car. 'Is that it? No "Goodnight, darling", no nothing?'

'I'm tired, Barney. Do what I ask, please.'

'Mum?'

I watched her shoulders tense up with frustration.

'How did you freshen up so fast from the Valium? You were semi-comatose earlier today, and now you're as bright as a button. How did you manage it?'

'I was awake enough to hear you were meeting someone at eight o'clock, and where, although that's about it in terms of anything I can remember specifically. I felt better after a long sleep, a cold bath, lots of coffee, theft of your doll's hair out of a place from which I'm banned, and the subsequent fear from that, a long walk, and lots of water at the bar.' She paused for breath. 'And then, I had to endure more fear, Barney. From you. From your behaviour tonight. Fear is a real slap in the face – it certainly perked me up.' She shrugged her shoulders. 'And all for the want of protecting you.'

Even from this distance, I could see her smile in the dark.

'And that, m'lud, is my confession in full. Now, I'm going to bed. Goodnight, darling.'

A lot of confessions tonight, and overall, Mum's answer sounded *good enough. But of course, I knew she'd lied.*

She disappeared into the house, leaving me on my own.

Mum should really consider herself extremely lucky. I'd never really lied to her before – I found it difficult, as she knew me so well. When I attempted a falsehood, it was as if I were a sheet of clear glass and she could see straight through me. So, right now, I felt pretty proud of myself. She'd lied and I'd caught her out. But I'd lied by omission.

The third woman, also-known-as Grace, remained my secret.

And Grace would need checking on right about now. Having told Mum the truth of the ladies' lies, I definitely wasn't telling her I had captured Grace and was holding her hostage against her will. Tied to a radiator. I was pretty certain Mum wouldn't approve and it might very well be the thing that really ruined her evening.

It was a lie too many and if I'd told, Mum wouldn't leave it alone.

She wouldn't let me keep Grace.

And Grace, the odious Grace, was the one thing I had on my side, and Jodie and Odette had no idea about it.

That was my one huge advantage I had over the ladies.

It put me in the lead.

Caressing the doll's hair, letting it trail softly through my fingers and whisper against the flesh of my arm, I slowly made my way around the side of the house, to my woman-in-waiting. I already had a fairly good idea of what I was going to do to her.

And to both Jodie and Odette.

The ball was most definitely in my court.

23

JODIE

Odette had gone home on her own after they had left the pub, and Jodie now sat in her sitting room with a relatively large shot of vodka. As a treat. A stupid treat, bearing in mind her past relationship with alcohol, but bugger it, one wouldn't do any harm.

She couldn't help but hum a tiny bit, under her breath. Strangely, the sound frightened her – it brought back memories of Tom. Humming louder, Jodie attempted to delete her husband's image from her head. She should never have allowed him access to either her body or her mind in the first place. *How can I have been* so *stupid?* Smiling, she put the glass to her lips again. *Who's the stupid one now, Tom?*

The children were in bed, the babysitter had gone, and Jodie relaxed into the sofa, embracing her drink as if it were some sort of treasure. Perhaps it was. She took another little sip, needing to eke it out and determined to enjoy every bit of it. It was a large shot, so she could take her time with it. She held it up in the air, toasting her late, lamented husband. *Cheers, Tom. This one's on you.*

Laughing quietly, Jodie leant back on a cushion and thought about Barney. He really was a strange man – one minute so soft and polite; the next, remote and impossible to reach. Something harsh and cold would creep over him and, fleetingly, he'd seem a different man. The next minute, he'd return, all smiles and bashful, as if he'd been there all the while.

In an odd way, Jodie found him more than a little intriguing; she liked his unpredictability, and his apparent inability to maintain an entire conversation without temporarily abandoning whoever he was with and briefly disappearing inside his own head. As if he were regrouping.

Like a very young child left alone without his mother for the first time – unsure of how to behave properly, but trying very hard to be liked.

Most of all, she felt sorry for him, and instinctively wanted to save him – in whatever way she could. Everyone needed something different, a very bespoke type of love to take away all the hurt that was specific to only them. It was clear to her that Barney was full to bursting with hurt. His oddness and his naivete were strangely endearing, and Jodie found herself fascinated by him. With him.

All she had to do was prove to herself he was deserving.

Three years ago, Jodie had liberated her own children, freeing herself in the process. And she'd come alive, brightly and colourfully, bursting into life again, astonished at the newfound power she'd acquired with the death of her husband. Until she'd been pushed to the very limit, she'd never really understood the strength of motherhood. It was her calling. She had saved her children, for what else could she do? She should have done it earlier, though.

Naturally and seamlessly, she'd offered up a variety of that same mother-love to Odette – it had been an easy gift to give: a cushioning, buffering love to protect Odette. Grace had been a harder person to give supportive love to, but still, Jodie had managed it. Grace lacked the class and elegance to ever be grateful for anything, but Jodie didn't want gratitude. She wanted to give people freedom and absolution from their actions.

It's what good people did. They *forgave*.

Taking a drink of the vodka, Jodie's thoughts about Barney lingered in her head. After Tom had died, as time had passed, she'd better understood her ever-growing role as protector and had fully embraced it. It didn't need overthinking. In simple terms, Jodie was the guardian and defender of the damaged and the flawed. *If* their actions had merit. If they ticked that box, her intervention and subsequent release from their misdeeds would follow, all things being equal.

Barney fit her profile. For who other than a recklessly trusting man would admit to pushing his own father down the stairs to two relative strangers? It was as if he were screaming out for help, and she had heard him. She would be there for him. It was her duty.

His confession had shocked both her and Odette. However unexpected it had been, Jodie had immediately wanted to fix his angst, his guilt, his grief – had wanted to make him whole again. She cast herself as the storybook repairer-of-all-things-broken – protector of the good and the misunderstood. As Jodie envisaged being Barney's saviour and giving him peace, her cheeks warmed at the thought.

Drinks at his place on Monday would be an opportunity to really dissect Barney on an emotional level – if he allowed it. She wondered if Barney's mother knew her son was guilty of patricide. On an immediate level, murdering one's own father was an unthinkable thing to do. Unforgivable. But he must have had his reasons for such an atrocity. Jodie was prepared to give him the opportunity to explain himself.

And if he was worthy, she would concentrate her efforts on protecting him from himself, and set him free.

She was excited at the thought of drinks at Barney's flat. It would be good for the women to stand in solidarity again, all three reunited in her cause, the club's cause. Focused on their new group member, helping him through his very own personal nightmare. Jodie conceded she had to include Grace, however irritating she could be, for she was still one of them.

All in all, Jodie felt everything was falling into place.

It went without saying, Jodie's children would always be her priority. They kept her breathing and smiling and alive. Never again would she allow anyone to threaten their safety. As the mother of Katie and Emily, she'd die for them.

She'd kill for them.

And now her mission was to protect and rescue others. For the greater good.

Her life was perfect, happy and content with her two children. That simple. It didn't make her a bad person, but it did mean she understood those that murdered in order to be as happy as she.

With no warning, thirteen-year-old Katie was suddenly there, standing at her mother's side, wearing her pink jim-jams with painted-on darker pink lobsters sidling across the material. Jodie startled and almost spilled her vodka. 'Hello, you. It's late. Why aren't you in bed? Anything wrong?'

The girl shrugged a teenagerish shrug, able to convey volumes using no words. It had become 'a thing' – Katie rarely expressed herself in anything other than monosyllables and weight on one hip. Her daughter made a making-a-supreme-effort-here body movement, and deigned to smile at Jodie. 'What're *you* doing? I heard you humming from the kitchen.'

This was tantamount to a long speech, and Jodie bent forward and placed her hand on her daughter's soft cheek.

'That's because I *was* humming. No great mystery.' A silence lengthened between them – not an uncomfortable one, but an easy familiar one.

Katie threw herself onto an armchair. 'You don't hum anymore.' She twizzled a piece of her hair, wrapped it around her finger, and then sucked the end of it. 'Not since Dad. Humming means Dad.'

Shocked, Jodie put down her drink, already shaking her head. 'No, it most definitely doesn't, Katie. Promise. It was more of a happy hum. People do happy humming all the time.'

'You weren't doing it like most people. Your humming means you're feeling the opposite. It was unhappy humming.'

'If it sounded like unhappy humming, I'm sorry, but honest, Katie, I was just sitting here feeling very happy, and started humming without even knowing it.'

'You always do it when you're thinking of Dad.'

The statement was like a splash of iced water in the face and made Jodie cringe as she conceded the truth of her daughter's words. 'When did you grow up? Did I miss it?'

Shrug. Big hair twizzle. Major eye roll. 'Prolly.'

'Yeah, well, you're right, darling. Bang on, as you'd say. I *was* thinking about your father.' Automatically, before she could stop herself, Jodie reached for her vodka. And Katie's pretend-not-to-notice glance made Jodie sit back and leave the glass on the table, untouched. Her oldest child was and always had been very emotionally mature for her age. With guilt, Jodie remembered her own unwelcome role in the particular fiasco that had been her marriage to the bastard that had been Tom.

And the effect it had had on Katie. And on Emily. Nothing drastic, nothing that Jodie hadn't been able to help and soothe them through, but still, they had both been stained by the ugliness that had been their shit of a father.

Patting the seat next to her on the sofa, Jodie waited. 'Come on, Katie. Come and sit with your wrinkled old bag of a mother. I'm feeling all lonely over here with you over there. Come on.'

Katie shook her head. 'Nah, I'm all right.'

'You might be, but I'm not. Please. I want a cuddle and to squeeze you to death.'

'Oh God, *Mum!*' But it was said with an embarrassed smile, and hanging her head in mock shamed-to-death-by-a-parent, Katie lolloped across the room and collapsed into a heap of gangly bony limbs next to Jodie. Pretending great distress at being handled, Katie gave nothing back to the hug, simply allowing herself to be enveloped by her mother's arm.

Jodie sniffed loudly. 'Pooo-*eee*, you stink, Katie. Have you been smoking again?'

Laughing guiltily, Katie turned her face up to Jodie's and pecked her on the cheek. 'Yeah, I'm on about fifty a day now. Fucking lungs are killing me. But it's not as bad as puffing on my pipe. Wow, that *really* stinks.'

They both giggled, the thought of Katie sucking on a pipe like an old man, created a shared visual picture that amused them. Both of them doubled up, roaring and howling with giggles, which was a much bigger reaction than the joke warranted. Before hysteria set in, Jodie actively relished in the laughter that consumed them both – this was really what it was all about.

Putting on her adult head, she became a real grown-up of the maternal variety. 'Really, Katie, I know I'm laughing, but you shouldn't be smoking. You'll regret it later when you can't run for a bus without turning purple. Your eyeballs will pop from your eye sockets like bursting balloons, you'll start gasping like an old geezer, and keel over dead from a heart attack. Not pretty.'

'God, you're gross, Mum.'

'Thanks.'

Jodie took hold of her daughter's hand and held it. 'This makes a change, doesn't it? Us two, sitting here, having a nice chat.'

'A *nice chat*?' Katie couldn't help the smile that played on her lips, although she was desperately trying to keep the teasing of her mother going. 'Old ladies have *nice chats*.'

'Well, excuse me for being so ancient. How about this.' Jodie straightened out both her arms, and dropping her wrists, letting them dangle, extended each thumb, forefinger and little finger on each hand. 'How bloody hip am I? And, Katie, you are totally *slaying* those lobster jim-jams, true that.'

Squealing, Katie clapped her hands to her ears. 'Stop, Mum. Wow, you are *so* uncool.'

'Back atcha. Chill, baby, chill.'

They both dissolved into peals of laughter and Jodie would have been happy to stay here, in this embrace, forever. It made her world worth loving. Her children were her entire life.

'You crack me up, Mum.'

'I meant it about the smoking, though. Stop it, because you *will* regret it.'

'I'll stop smoking, if you stop humming.'

Jodie had no answer for that, and the vodka forgotten on the table, she held Katie, who'd scrunched up in a ball and leant into her.

'Do you miss Dad?'

No, darling, not in the slightest.

'Of course I do, darling. Lots and lots.'

'But he was mean. To you.' Katie turned her face upwards in Jodie's lap, and gazed at her mother. 'And to us.'

'He's gone now, Katie. You're allowed to feel however you want to feel. There's no right or wrong way – just your way, and I'll support you whatever.'

Katie closed her eyes, a small, relieved smile on her lips.

This was true contentment, Jodie knew. It didn't get any better.

Her children were her world.

They were her whole reason for being.

They were the whole reason for Tom not being.

24

ME & GRACE

The evening had been so packed full of events, I was surprised it was only eleven o'clock in the evening. Drained, it felt much much later, and I still had things to do.

The first thing I did upon entering my flat by the side entrance, was to hurry through the sitting room and lock the door that led into the main house. I'd never bothered before, but now I knew Mum had the capacity to creep up and enter, I thought it wise to keep her out.

And then onwards, to the utility room, unsure of what I might find. Hopefully, Grace would still be asleep and there'd be nothing for me to physically *do*. I wanted no further altercation with the woman. Opening the door, I popped my head around the frame. Grace hadn't moved and looked more than comfortable, lying under the duvet on her side, her head propped on the pillow, facing away from the radiator – exactly as I'd left her. Even from the door, I could hear the faint but unmistakable sound of her snoring through her nose. It turned my stomach. Far too personal a sound to have to listen to.

But on looking at her, I thought perhaps one might argue that her shoulders looked awkward and potentially painful as they were turned at an unlikely angle, her hands bound to the radiator as they were. Ditto, the position of her feet. An interesting note: Grace was the length of one radiator. A perfect, if useless fact. On reflection, I thought I was being a little loose with the truth when I'd labelled her as *comfortable*.

I quietly crossed the room. Obviously, my intent was not to kill her. But she remained, and would do until Monday night, as my guest. Whether she wanted to stay or not. She'd invaded my space and would now suffer the consequences of her behaviour.

My plan, although not entirely formulated yet into anything that could be described as either concrete or definitive, was, however, slowly coalescing into something really rather wondrous. I was yet to work out the finer details, for all the women, not only Grace, and my idea, even in its infancy, filled me with great anticipation and excitement. My emotions were neither forced nor false, and were certainly very real. Perhaps my capacity for feeling had been kick-started with my sudden association with people, however unpleasant and unfathomable it was all proving.

It was strange that along with Mum, whom I loved and therefore had no need to internally initialise my emotions with, Grace also freed me from that often-tiresome burden, but because I *hated* her. The more I encountered the emotions of strangers, the more confused I became.

Maybe Mum should have encouraged me into the world sooner, before I'd become so entrenched and shut-down in my ways. We'd see how it panned out though – I was loath to blame my mother as she'd always acted in what she thought were my best interests. It wasn't as if there'd ever been a handy local creche for baby psychos where she could have dumped me, to familiarise myself and play with other little weirdos. Mum had done everything she could.

Now I was, too – with what I had at my disposal. A very

good brain and, unexpectedly, a bound and gagged woman. The ripple of distaste and anger I felt for Grace was unenjoyable and brought me absolutely no pleasure at all.

But despite the presence of the third woman, as I was coming to think of her, I was careful not to allow myself to get carried away with my ever-blossoming plan and my own perceived success at its imagined culmination. Emotions were actually overrated I decided – I'd survived tonight with Jodie and Odette, but I'd been cut off from them by the end, and they hadn't even noticed. Nothing diabolical had happened. It was fine being me after all. Survivable.

What disturbed me was the realisation everyone had lied, and that knowledge sat like a worm in my gut. Twisting and turning and making me feel sick. Even Mum had lied to me. That wasn't what I'd expected and I didn't like it. It made me nervous. It wasn't right, it wasn't what Mum had taught me. It wasn't how I'd anticipated life being.

The real test would be Monday night, and we'd see just how adept I was at feigning my emotions, because deep down, I still recognised everything that was people was beyond me.

So, until Monday evening, I'd be marking time.

Tamping down what I could only articulate as the beginnings of a thrill, or what most definitely felt like a very physical pulse of genuine eagerness, I almost giggled at the whole concept I was dreaming up. Unable to stop plucking away at any loose threads still present in my great plot, I knew it needed finessing. And that was really something to look forward to. If I could pull it off successfully, it would be my biggest achievement to date.

Leaving Grace, I went and got her handbag and returned, smiling – in control. Sitting cross-legged on the floor, I unclasped the bag and rootled through it, grimacing, perplexed at its feminine contents: tissues, lipstick, powder compact, more tissues, chewing gum, a trashy romance book, and her mobile. Turning it on, I was relieved she had no password set in order to access her WhatsApp, and I scrolled through her messages, reading the haughty-toned one from Jodie:

> What are you doing, Grace? Why are you meeting Barney on your own? Txt me back. J.

That made me smile. It seemed I was in great demand. Going to Sent messages, I checked Grace's reply, but there was none. What a rebel our red-haired girl was.

But I *was* worried. I remembered Grace telling me she'd been on her lunch hour on our disastrous date. Did she work on Saturdays? That was the question. I didn't want her not being somewhere she should be and consequently, anyone missing her. Which meant I had to speak to the bloody woman. Giving it some thought, I went to my kitchen and knocked up a cheese and cucumber sandwich – who could resist? En route, I picked up and filled the syringe again, only 10mls this time – I thought of it as a top-up – and returned to the tied-up woman, who was mine for a while. I wasn't convinced I really wanted her, but I'd do my best.

Back with the washing machine, squatting once more next to my sleeping redhead, I gently peeled away the tape from her mouth and shook her shoulder. And then again, a little harder. Finally, there was a response, and her tongue flicked out from between her lips, attempting to lick them. Perhaps they were dry, but it was something I didn't need to see, so I glanced away, vaguely sickened by the sight of something anatomical that should have remained internal. It was not for public show, in my opinion.

I shook her again. 'Wakey-wakey, Grace. I'm home.'

Slowly, her eyes opened and took some time before they

focused. Finally, her eyes met mine, although hers appeared slightly blurred as if she were seeing the world through a haze.

'It's me, Barney. How are you feeling? Here, I've brought you food. Come on, sit up.'

Today, I'd already tried to hand-feed my mother, and now was having to hand-feed my intruder, romancing both with delights for their stomachs. A cheese and cucumber sandwich never went amiss in my book, although I'd yet to have a serious taker today. 'Wake up, Grace. And keep your eyes open.' I shook her harder and slapped her face. Not hard, but hard enough. It seemed to do the trick.

'Barney, hello. What are you doing here?'

'I've brought you food. Let me prop you up, there, no, this way, turn towards the radiator more, that's it. Bend your elbows. Perfect. I hope you enjoy.'

It took some time for her to realise her hands were tied and a look of utter confusion crossed her face. But not alarm. Not yet. Just pure incomprehension at the physical inability to take the offered sandwich herself and put it in her mouth. I held it to her lips, and she opened her mouth like a small bird, without question, and bit, chewed and swallowed. She performed this task successfully three times, before she turned her head away. 'Enough. Not hungry.'

'Do you normally work on Saturdays, Grace?'

'Saturdays? No. Weekends are off. Weekends are mine. I like them. It's my time for myself. No bookshop. Sandra opens up on Saturdays. Sandy Saturdays. Why do you ask?'

I didn't think I had anything to worry about, but to be sure, I said, 'Any plans for this weekend, Grace? Meeting friends, wild parties, anything exciting? A family get-together, any social activities?'

'No. Nothing. Just me and my books and my cat at home. I like being on my own.'

Thank God for small mercies. Slowly, the more she spoke, the more her speech improved and she seemed a bit more alert and aware of her surroundings. 'Why can't I move?' Her face showed puzzlement. 'Am I paralysed?' Giggling, her head fell forward and sort of rolled around on her shoulders.

'Don't you worry about that, Grace. I'm here with you. We're together, that's what you wanted, wasn't it? Could I tempt you with more cheese and cucumber?'

Shaking her head, she appeared to take my explanation at being together, as entirely normal. I waited for her to come around properly, and held the syringe tighter to my thigh. Checking the time on my watch, I decided it wasn't too late to text Just Jodie on Grace's mobile. Scrolling down the contacts, I found Jodie's number, and texted:

> See you on Monday at Barney's for drinks.
> 7pm!

I dithered as to whether I should add a kiss before pressing Send. I quickly read other messages between the two women – and discovered a stark lack of XXs. I also noted there were very few messages to and from Odette and Grace, so not including her, I pressed Send, turned the mobile off, put it in my pocket and sat back to study my catch in more depth.

Although her eyes continually closed for longer than it took to blink, when she did open them, Grace started to slowly take in her surroundings, me, and at last, her gaze settled on her tied hands. 'Who tied me up?'

'I can't imagine. Here, let me help.'

I pretended to struggle with an impossible knot and eventually sat back, defeated. 'Sorry, but you're well and truly stuck. What a calamity. What to do now? Any suggestions?'

'I want to go home, please.' But she laughed and there was no real desire shown. It was simply mindless babbling.

'Believe me, Grace, going-home time has well and truly passed. You had the opportunity, but you squandered it. So, here you sit, my permanent and uninvited guest, with the guilt you carry, for all the wrong reasons. I know you haven't been entirely honest with me, but you will be. Just you wait and see.'

She opened and shut her mouth, seemingly at a loss. Then her heavy lids began to close. Jabbing her gently on the shoulder, her eyes found mine again. 'See, Grace, there really are consequences to actions. Mum always told me that. And I took note.' I closed my eyes briefly. 'Even though Mum is a liar, like the rest of them. Like you. But you must do the same and check yourself before embarking on any action as rash as insinuating yourself into places where you are not welcome.' I smiled at her. 'Wouldn't you agree that would be sensible?'

Back to confused, Grace smiled sleepily. 'Yeah, I suppose you're right. But why am I so tired? Nice tired. All warm and cosy tired. I like it. I'm all fuzzy.'

I didn't care about her stupid ramblings; I was only happy we hadn't come to blows.

Having already read the recommended dosage on the bottle, I knew the maximum per day was 40mls. Manually opening her mouth, I gave her the Valium, purely so I could get a good night's sleep without having to worry about her waking up while being safe in the knowledge that it wouldn't kill her.

Or, maybe it would. Unsettled, the worm had unpacked and was staying. Along with doubts. So many self-doubts. I did my best to cheer myself up, remembering my plan, and reminded myself, if Grace died, it wouldn't be the end of the world.

Hers, yes. But not mine.

I was in so deep now, I'd almost forgotten who I really was, and my entire life had turned rickety and definitely not something upon which I could rely. Everything had changed. I found myself contemplating undertaking some freestyle risky exploits with my redhead in order to rid myself of my quickly disappearing intellect. If my mind left me, what would I be left with? Somewhere along the line, since Dad had died and I'd joined the bereavement group, I'd lost myself.

To get myself back on track, I vowed that tomorrow, Grace and I would definitely play a game or two together to pass the time. She was too out of it currently for it to be any fun at all for me, and I certainly wasn't about to take advantage of that fact. Because that would *not* be fun. Not in my book. I'd been brought up to be a gentleman, and liked my interactions with people when they were *not* semi-conscious.

I needed the practice, after all.

That was my intellect talking. I didn't like my interactions with people when they were *conscious*. My grip was loosening on all that I'd been taught. *All the women were liars* – that had been so unexpected and unfair. And Grace, who now lay at my feet, did annoy me so. Even asleep. I wanted to tease her a little, scare her a little, hurt her a little. Purely because I could.

Bending over her, I prised her eyelids apart and stared into her eyes. Not as clear and as perfect as my dolls' eyes – not even close. They lacked the shine and the glint and the light. It would have been so easy to poke them clean out of Grace's stupid face, but of course I didn't. That wouldn't be right, but it seemed I was the only one not lying and attempting to follow the rules.

It crossed my mind that I was teetering on the edge of giving in to childish desires, something I thought I'd put behind me. I was enjoying the thought of bullying Grace. As a young child, bullying had got me into trouble. Mum had been horribly upset when the school had informed her I had a penchant for belittling, humiliating, embarrassing, hurting and terrifying weaker children. And all the children had been weaker than I.

After Mum's bespoke style of homeschooling, hand in hand with the dolls, I honestly did understand the unfairness and the cruelty of tormenting others. My intellect told me this was true, but in times of stress, which would be now, it seemed I'd reverted to the idea of that specific tactic, at which I'd been so unnaturally talented. I was ready to be really mean to Grace.

That thought sobered me. I wasn't one for needless mental torture – I'd outgrown that. *Hadn't I?* Feeling as if I'd lost all perspective, I tried to remember that I was a well-brought up adult man, who knew good from bad.

Tomorrow, with no bullying tactics, I'd think of something to do that would warm Grace up for Monday night's festivities. Something gentle and kind and *Socially Acceptable*.

It was apparent I might very well need a session with my dolls to re-evaluate my current mental state. The least I could do was try to live up to Mum's best expectations of me. I owed her that much.

Even though the bitch had lied to me. *Mum had lied to me*. I couldn't really forgive her. It made me feel sick. And unsettled, rattled and unsure of myself. It made me giddy and tearful. Frightened, it made me stop and question everything. I found myself in a previously unvisited place, where all was new and strange and alien. Nothing was in my control and I realised, perhaps it never had been.

For if the world was full of liars, as it seemed it was, where did that leave me? I, myself, was the biggest falsehood walking, and now with my discovery that the world was full of deceit, I found I had nowhere I could call my own. It left me desolate. Having always been the imposter, it was a shock to discover that all this time, everyone *else* had been faking it. Which left me with no label, no comprehension of my role, no identity.

My mind floundering, I tiptoed from the room, feeling very un-me, which wasn't nice at all. Not understanding why I was teetering on the brink of something, I was struck with a nauseous surge of vertigo. The floor beneath me seemed to slip and slide and shift. My mind reeled. My armpits prickled with sweat. By the time I reached the door and had closed it quietly behind me, I had to stop myself from running to my room. My legs trembled with the routine action of maintaining a steady pace, and not breaking into a sprint.

Wanting to cry, and not knowing why, I went to bed and curled up into a ball under the duvet, and concentrated on not unravelling, as I attempted to sleep the sleep of the chaotic.

25

GRACE

Grace opened her eyes and it took her a moment, a very quick moment, to realise all was not as it should be. For some inexplicable reason, her hands and feet were bound to a radiator, and her mouth covered with tape. A vague memory danced on the edge of her brain, but she couldn't quite grasp it fully.

Trying not to panic, she ran her mind back to the last solid, real thing she *did* remember. She knew she'd visited Barney, and they'd been chatting in his sitting room the previous evening. She *thought* it was the previous evening, but couldn't be sure. After that, it all became blurred and she had no clear recollection of exactly what had happened, her mind unable to hold on to anything with any firmness. *I know it's morning, because my watch tells me so. It's nine o'clock. I'm groggy, as if I had too much to drink last night, but that doesn't feel right. I haven't got a headache and I'm sure I didn't have a drink. I feel strangely sleepy but awake, as if I've been unconscious for a long time.*

Her shoulders and hips hurt and she was frightened. It was impossible to ignore the fear that slammed in her chest, as if her heart was having some type of cardiac event. Her mouth was dry and her tongue felt thick, as if coated in something arid and sandpapery. More frightening, she couldn't open her mouth, and for a moment, she wondered what it would be like to choke on her own tongue.

Attempting to get her mouth near enough to her hands that she might be able to free herself of the tape that bound her lips, she quickly discovered it would be an impossible physical feat. She was no contortionist and couldn't stretch her neck anywhere near enough to her tied hands as her legs prevented any more movement along the radiator. After a panicky ten minutes, tears of frustration running down her cheeks, she lay awkwardly back onto her hip on the duvet. Trying to keep her breathing from becoming a gasping hysteria, horribly aware that her ability to inhale and exhale was seriously compromised by the tape on her mouth, she successfully willed herself to stop crying.

Breathing slowly, Grace tried to regain some form of calmness before attempting to remember *anything* from the previous evening. As far as she knew, it was still Saturday, but how could she be sure? If it was Saturday, Sandra would have opened the bookshop. Grace hadn't made any plans for the weekend, and had been looking forward to reading alone and relaxing. She'd had no plans to see anyone.

Which means, no one will know that I'm here, tied up to a radiator.

Something in Grace's mind jumped in recognition, as if the telling of her weekend plans had been told. To Barney? Had she told him that? *What else did I tell him?*

Did he rape me? She didn't feel physically hurt, other than what felt like a bruise on her face, and she was still partially covered with a duvet, her head on a pillow, were she to relax enough to place it there. Would he bother attempting to make her comfortable if he'd raped her? She didn't think so. Anyway, he didn't seem the type. She didn't think he was sexual in any way.

Is he going to kill me?

No. Well, not yet anyway.

More importantly, *why* was she tied up? What had she done to Barney that had made him kidnap her and hold her prisoner? *Was* it only Saturday, or had days and days gone by? Was it even Barney who'd captured her? Perhaps her abductor was someone else entirely and Barney wasn't involved at all. She cried again, unsure of anything, becoming more frightened as her tears fell – risking suffocation. *I can't breathe if I cry. Not through my nose, which is getting bunged up. Stop crying.*

When the door opened slightly, she stopped breathing entirely and didn't move. Her eyes stretched wide. After a few seconds, she had to expel the air in her lungs, and felt two whooshes of hot breath escape her nostrils. Trying not to panic, she made herself regain a more regulated breathing pattern and she waited as the door was slowly, oh-so fucking-slowly, opened, as if the person entering was stretching out the horror, delaying revealing his identity.

Barney entered the room and, not bothering to look at her, walked over, squatted down and placed a tray on the floor in front of her. Grace automatically tried to speak, but of course her voice only came out as a muffled incomprehensible mumble behind the tape. Still, keeping his eyes on the food, Barney deliberately ignored her. She didn't know what to say, even if she could.

Without any warning his head came up and their eyes locked together. Except they didn't, as he seemed to look straight through her, as if she wasn't really there. Unceremoniously he ripped the tape from her mouth. She gasped at the pain and felt her eyes well up with tears.

Her voice, when it came, was hoarse and raspy. 'Why am I here? What have I done to deserve this?' Pleased she'd said something sensible under these unthinkable circumstances, she felt slightly emboldened by her own courage. 'Barney, it's me, Grace. I thought we liked each other, you know, *understood* each other.' She attempted a smile but found herself talking to the top of his head. 'Barney, please. Let me go. I won't tell anyone, I promise.'

The silence wasn't a nice one and all Grace heard was her own breathing and a whining tone to her voice. Watching Barney, she decided to keep quiet. His whole body was tense, his movements jerky, as if he wasn't quite in control. *He looks frightened,* she thought. Feeling perplexed, she decided the safest thing was to keep quiet. If he wasn't speaking, then neither would she. That would show him. Bravado was all she had.

There was an egg in a blue and white striped eggcup on the tray, some toast cut into triangles with a knob of butter and a knife on the side, and a bunch of grapes. Barney picked up the teaspoon and cracked it against the top of the egg. Peeling the shell from the top, he broke the perfect white globe with the spoon and scooping some out, he'd gone just deep enough that he'd got some yolk as well as the white. Grace realised she was starving, and was mesmerised by the food, but angry that she had to succumb to being hand-fed. Like a baby.

Everyone had always thought her a fool her entire life, especially Polly. And now, of course, Jodie, who'd made herself bloody ink monitor of the club. Well, Grace wasn't stupid enough to refuse food. Who knew when barmy Barney would feed her again? Feeling like a child, she opened her mouth and he roughly pushed a spoonful into it, the metal spoon knocking against her teeth. Chewing and swallowing, she opened her mouth again. *Fuck him, I'll show him he doesn't frighten me.*

The egg finished, he quietly but very quickly buttered some toast and held it up for her, dangling it in front of her mouth. Mentally and physically unable to be aggressive, Grace went with malleable and accepting. No trouble at all. The perfect house guest. 'Have you any marmalade, Barney, please?'

The toast stayed in position, hovering in the air in front of her face, so close she could smell that burnt toasty smell. Barney kept his expression neutral and his eyes continued to stare blankly at her. Politely, she accepted there would be no marmalade coming. Obediently, she opened her mouth and bit down, chewing and repeating the action until it was all gone.

If he's feeding me, he's not going to kill me. And I don't know when he'll feed me again, so I'll eat the grapes as well. She opened her mouth and from further away than was necessary, Barney threw one grape into it. It was such an unexpected way to be fed a grape, Grace almost choked as it hit the back of her throat. Closing her eyes, refusing to acknowledge the terror she felt, she instead concentrated on savouring the sweet juice as she bit down on it. It burst, filling her mouth and making her salivate.

To her shame, a little dribble escaped her lips and she felt it slide down her chin. Grace could hardly miss Barney's look of total disgust. Blushing, she brought her shoulder up to her face and made a pathetic and failed attempt at wiping it away.

Apart from the dribbling, faking that she wasn't frightened was working. Up to a point. She was good at pretending and she had no choice but to play his game. And she was keeping it together – not wailing and beseeching him to let her go. It wouldn't achieve anything.

I need my strength to deal with this situation, so I bloody well will finish eating what's on offer. I'm not that stupid to starve myself to make some idiotic point.

She got through eight grapes and, feeling better, Grace

smiled at him and decided the only way to play this was to go along with it, as if it were all utterly normal. She coughed in a ladylike fashion, and using her most charming voice, said, 'Thank you very much. That was lovely. You really do know how to make a good breakfast. I'm very grateful. Are we going to lunch together as well?'

When the fingers of his left hand suddenly clamped themselves around her jaws, for just a minute, Grace thought he might kiss her. Taken by surprise, she clamped her lips together. Instinct made her body pull back from the lunatic and, without thinking, she tried to bite him.

It took a minute to realise he was trying to *open* her mouth, had no intention of kissing her. His fingers pressed into her face, forcing her jaws apart. Panicking, she tried to wrench her neck back, out of his reach, but his hand held her face in a vice-of-fingers. Her jaws were released, unable to stay closed with the pressure he exerted. Barney inserted a large plastic thing into her mouth. Liquid filled the back of her throat. He flattened one hand over her lips, holding her neck in place with his other. Her throat betraying her, Grace swallowed.

Barney sat back and looked at her. Actually focused on her face as if seeing her for the first time.

'What have you given me?' Grace looked at the floor and saw the syringe Barney had dropped. 'What was in that? Is it poison?'

She heard her own voice, shrill with panic, tears falling already. If only she could stick her fingers down her throat and make herself vomit, but she couldn't. Grace heard Barney's flat voice. 'It's a sedative. It won't kill you.'

'I don't want to be sedated. Why are you doing this?'

'It's for two days. Today and tomorrow, Sunday.'

Not bothering to really take in what he'd said, Grace wasn't sure whether she was already feeling the effects of whatever he'd given her, but knew she had to pee. 'I need to go to the loo.'

'Jesus *Christ*.'

Barney, clearly furious, stood up, cut the ties that bound her, and pulled her roughly to her feet. 'You can go now, and again at lunch and dinner. If you need to relieve yourself in between those times, I'd suggest you don't.' Pulling her by her wrist, she stumbled behind him, her legs not working properly, pins and needles numbing them and then hurting as the blood flowed back into her limbs.

The lavatory was next door. Turning the handle, Barney walked into the small room, dragging her behind him, and pointed at the toilet. 'There you go. Do your stuff. I won't watch.'

He turned his back and folded his arms. Weeping quietly, deeply ashamed, Grace sat and couldn't stop herself peeing immediately. It sounded so loud as it splashed against the basin and she felt her cheeks redden. 'Can't you leave me to it?'

Barney didn't bother answering, so she finished, wiped herself and thanked God she hadn't needed a poo. And at least he'd kept his word and not looked. As she pulled up her knickers, Grace was suddenly aware of a strange softness that seemed to envelop her, starting in her head, and gently creeping around her body. It had to be the drugs. They must be working. It wasn't unpleasant, but she didn't want to be unconscious again.

Having to lean on Barney's arm, he led her back to the radiator. 'Please, tie me up in a different position. I'm really sore and stiff. Please.'

'Can't.'

And that was his only answer. She could tell he was hurrying now, wanting to go, as if the sight of her made him sick. Trying to keep her voice from sounding like she was begging, she said, 'I want another duvet to lie on, and another pillow to rest my arms on.' Again, he made no reply. 'It's the least you can do, Barney, bloody hell, please. Pretty please?'

She could tell he was really anxious to go now, as he hastily doubled the duvet over and got another pillow, threw her down and retied her hands and feet with fresh cord. His tone was flat and he flicked at his hair, jiggling his foot, wanting to run. 'See you at lunch, Grace.'

It was with relief that Grace gave in to the gentle warmth of the sedative as it wrapped its arms around her, dragging her away from this room and this man. Finding herself smiling up at him from her exceedingly comfortable bed, Grace smiled. 'See you later, Barney.'

She heard the door as it closed and couldn't care less.

26

————

ADELE

It was ten o'clock on Saturday morning, and Adele was pottering about the kitchen, fretting.

Barney's invitation to the women for drinks on Monday wasn't right. It felt decidedly wrong. Knowing her son as she did, Adele was deeply concerned for him. He'd seemed so brittle and on edge and quietly angry last night in the car, although pretending all was fine and dandy, happy that his invite had been accepted. But he was upset by something. She could tell, and it scared her. *He* scared her. There was definitely something very wrong with him – in a new and different way.

On a practical level, Barney did *not* know how to host a drinks party – the idea was ludicrous. The possibilities, all bad, as far as she could see, were many and varied. She wished it wasn't so, but it was.

Startled, she heard Barney's heavy tread on the stairs and automatically she braced herself. Turned a smiling face to her son as he entered the kitchen.

His face was white and taut and pinched. Barney's expression was so tight it might as well have been cast in marble. He didn't attempt a smile. That in itself was out of character.

Barney always liked to please her, but his eyes skittered about and seemed loath to settle.

'What's wrong, Barney-Boo?'

'Nothing, Mum. Why do you always think there's something wrong? There's nothing wrong at all, okay?'

'Coffee?'

'No.' He shook his head, then relented and said, 'Sorry, Mum. No, thank you.' He perched on the edge of a kitchen stool and she kept her silence. Waited. Knowing he was working himself up to asking for something.

'I need some more of that liquid Valium, Mum. Okay? Ring up Dr Wright and ask him. Tell him you need some more. He's an old family friend, he'll do it if you ask him.' He looked at his watch. 'He'll do it for you because that's his bloody job. You could get a Saturday morning appointment – they won't be full yet. Tell him you've run out. Because you should have.' He grinned at her, showing all his teeth. 'You're overdue for a refill, despite your lies about taking it regularly. The prescription date is on the label – it was given to you just after Dad died, so why pretend you've been taking it since then? It's nearly full. Why lie? Why is everyone fucking lying?'

'What have you done with the stuff you confiscated? Why do you want more?'

'Because I do, okay? I just fucking do. I can't sleep. I had loads last night, and then I spilt the rest. I can't sleep. Please, Mum, I need some help here.' He stared angrily at her. 'And I need an explanation for your lie. Why would you lie to *me*?'

'I pretended I'd been taking it regularly because I couldn't cope with having to be with you. That's the brutal truth. I wanted to be alone, so I could remember Timothy – without interruption. And now *you're* lying to *me*. You don't look like you had any last night. You're as bright-eyed as you could be. Although, you're struggling with something, that I do know.'

When Barney sprang up, Adele automatically stepped back, holding her hand up between them, as if that would stop his advance.

'I need to sleep. That's it. I shouldn't have to explain any more than that.'

'Do you need to talk? You can always talk to me, you know that.'

He stamped his foot like a child. 'Ring up bloody Dr Wright. Do it now.'

Adele weighed up her options. Of course she could flatly refuse his request, but really, what she needed to know, was *why* he needed more liquid diazepam. There was no way in the world he'd taken any last night. It was early, and he'd still be showing the effects if he was anything like her, and there was no way in the world, he'd taken 'loads' as he'd said.

'Why do you really need it, Barney? Tell me and I might help you.' She waited a beat. 'Trust me. You know you can. You need help, and I might be more willing than you expect, to make things easier for you, so tell me the truth and we'll take it from there.'

Adele watched her son as he let his head fall into his hands. Cradling his face, his fingers splayed over his cheekbones, his eyes visible through his knuckles as he stared at her, he moaned. 'I can't do it, Mum. All this bollocks, this *life*. I hate it. Why are people so wrapped up in their own sense of entitlement? As if they're owed something. I don't understand it. I can't do it, I really can't. Why is everyone lying?'

She slowly approached him and took him in her arms. Shh-ing him like a baby, Adele rocked him back and forth, both of them standing with their heads touching – Barney making a strange keening noise; she, keeping quiet. Keeping her fear of him silent.

'How bad is it, Barney? Tell me.'

Feeling him tense, she knew she'd said the wrong thing as he both mentally and physically pulled away from her. He managed a self-deprecatory fake laugh, as if he were teasing himself. 'Christ, I'm so tired, I don't know what's wrong with me, I swear to God, Mum. Go on, ring Dr Wright.' Barney's smile wasn't convincing, and didn't match his obvious emotional turmoil.

They faced each other, and Adele wanted to cry for her broken son. She could understand how disappointed he'd be if he felt everyone was lying. *Were* the women lying? Adele didn't know. She held her arms out again, wanting to hold him to her.

'I don't want a cuddle, Mum. It's too late.'

'Maybe *I* want one.' He didn't move and she didn't want to force him into a hug, so she shrugged her shoulders. 'Why not cancel your drinks evening? You don't have to go through with it. Look how the women have upset you already. Don't see them again. Call it a day.'

'Yes, I do have to host the party. I've got a plan and I have to follow it through. But I need to sleep, to calm down. I'm going to go off pop, Mum. I'm fucking losing it. Please, help me.'

'Do you want to talk properly?'

'Not with you, no. Not with a liar.'

She sighed. 'I had to lie, Barney, for my own sanity. For your sanity, I suggest you talk to the dolls. They always help.'

'Do you think they can? I'm desperate. I don't know what to do. Everything seems so bloody complicated. You haven't taught me enough. I don't have *enough*. I'm not bloody equipped for all this. It's all too much, I'm barely keeping it all together, okay? *Do you understand what I'm saying?*'

Hurt, Adele turned away. 'Yes, I understand. But I don't know how to help you if you won't talk to me. I'll ring Dr Wright now.'

Picking up her mobile, she pressed the number and waited.

Barney also waited until she'd got through to the receptionist, before saying, 'Thank you, Mum. Please leave the drugs outside my interior door. You'll find it's locked now. No liars allowed.'

Adele managed to get through and sorted out a new prescription.

And wondered what she was enabling her son to do by giving him what he'd asked for.

Disturbingly, Adele realised she'd somehow become part of something he was planning, to use his own words. He had a plan – that on its own sounded ominous. A plan involving the women, she was sure. And he'd also admitted to being out of control. Going off pop.

She was in cahoots with Barney, and didn't know what she'd got herself involved in.

Calling after him, she said, 'Talk to the dolls. And, Barney, please try to relax. Talk to them.' But he'd already gone.

She wondered if he was having some sort of psychotic break. Should she help and support him? Do whatever he asked of her?

Or should she talk to the doctor about him?

Or simply pray she was wrong, and hope for the best?

Hoping for the best wasn't really Adele's style.

With Timothy gone, she had no one to talk to, no one to ask for advice.

Closing her eyes, so weary with it all, she knew she'd help Barney.

He was her son and was all she had left.

She had no choice.

She'd made him. She'd save him. She'd put him back together again.

It's what she'd always tried to do.

27

ME

It was eleven o'clock, Saturday morning, and Grace had been taken to the lavatory, and served and fed a proper breakfast of toast, eggs, and fruit. Having to feed her with a spoon, or worse, having to put the food directly into her mouth with my fingers, had been a revolting task; somehow it was a physically intimate interaction, intimate in a particularly repellent way, but it had to be done.

Wanting and needing to hurry, I had kept my interaction with her to a minimum and ignored her endless questions. She had been much more on the ball this morning and was only slightly groggy. Nothing that another 10mls hadn't sorted out. I couldn't escape her presence quickly enough.

I was unsafe and didn't trust myself, and I didn't like that.

Mum had been talked to, had been lied to, in order to guarantee more supplies of sedative, and I might have got her onside – time would tell. I'd only lied about the drugs – nothing else, so I felt no guilt. And I might need her assistance in the immediate future. Or I might not. I was willing to be flexible and not scupper myself by being too rigid.

It had been a busy and productive morning, but now the

need for speed was all-consuming and I hurried into the sitting room where I set up my dolls. Desperate to talk with them, I felt like weeping with need. And this morning would be nothing as sweet and charming as a dolls' tea party. Today would be more brutal – the school playground with Bully Bertie, Miserable Mona, and Victim Victor. I had always been exceptionally proud of Victim Victor's name: obviously the alliteration was a never-changed requirement, but the notion that a victim was so at odds with being victorious, always made me laugh.

It wasn't so bloody laughable now as I questioned my own grip on reality. Perhaps *I* would turn out to be the victorious victim if things continued on their current path. Unsure as to what I was even thinking, I concentrated on assembling the tableau so it was absolutely right.

Fury spurred me on. But I didn't need Furious Phil to actually put in a physical appearance – he sat in my mind and heart and body, uncalled for. There. Waiting for the slightest thing to set him off.

I'd temporarily forgotten who I was and was desperate for clarification from my dolls, who needed not to let me down. Not knowing what had brought on this desertion of myself, I put it all down to the unprecedented pressure and angst I had been under, the interminable pretending to be someone I wasn't, the sheer fucking difficulty of being alive amongst people.

Sweating from all the rushing, the dolls were finally in position and set to go. Inhaling deeply, I sat on the floor, hugging my knees, and waited for them to start.

'Hey there, Victor. I'm back.'

Victor's whole demeanour was pathetic and fragile, and he'd already given up. Before it had even started. He made me tremble with anger. But, telling Fury to fuck off out of my mind, I made Bertie do his thing whilst Miserable Mona, Moaner to her friends, watched on, like the pathetic article she was. I had to force me and Fury to sit this one out and only be part of the audience. This wasn't meant to be interactive – it was a performance – a lesson in life from the dolls.

Bertie's voice was brash and coarse, and he repeated his greeting, raising his voice, his body advancing on the ever-shrinking Victim. 'I said, hey there, Victor. I'm back. Remember me?'

Victim could only nod, having no words strong enough to rise to the challenge of Bertie. Moaner predictably moaned, sensing trouble, but nevertheless, she piped up, 'Leave Victim alone, Bertie. You're really *really* horrid and mean. Nobody likes you, you know. No one at all. I know how that feels, because I'm so miserable all the time, I only have one friend.'

Bertie laughed and I could hear the cruelty in his voice. 'What, am I supposed to care? Do you think I need friends? Look at the pair of you, you and Victim. Neither of you *deserves* a friend, because you're both so weak. Weak as water disappearing down the drain – no interest to anyone. Keep out of it, Misery.'

Victim covered his eyes with his hands. 'Please don't hurt me, Bertie. I haven't done anything wrong. Why do you always seek me out? I've never hurt you. Why do you hate me so much?'

'Because you're weaker than even water. You're nothing, and nothing deserves nothing. Nothing needs rooting out and made into something. Anything is better than nothing. At least I make you frightened. That's something. If not for me, you'd sit there on your own, and nobody would even notice you. You'd cease to exist. You need me to make you, you.'

'If Victim needs you, that means you need him,' Moaner said. 'Not that anyone cares what I think. They never do. All they hear is me moaning and being miserable, and nobody really listens.'

I jumped up, unable to keep quiet, Fury inside me. 'Well, fucking stand up Miserable, be happy, be jolly, stop being so fucking wet.' I swung around, hunched to get down to doll level. 'And you, Victim. Why don't you stand up for yourself? What is wrong with you? Do you have no bloody spine at all? No fucking backbone? What is *wrong* with you? How can you be so useless? Who wants to be a fucking Victim when they grow up? It's not a good thing; it's a thing to be avoided at all costs. You stupid loser. I *hate* you.'

Punching Victim, I felt his face crack as my knuckles grazed and bloodied on his fractured cheekbone. I heard Fury laugh in my head. And heard myself laugh out loud with him.

Bertie shouted, 'Whoa, fucking whoa, you two. Tell Fury to fuck off. *I'm* in control here, this is my party – you two aren't invited to this game. It's between me and Victim. Wanna guess the winner?' His braying laughter made my head hurt.

Sitting again on my heels, my hands at my temples, as if making sure my head wouldn't fall off, I said, 'Fury's always here at the moment. He won't go, however much I ask him.' I had a headache. 'But tell me, Bully Bertie, how do you actually *feel* when you're bullying Victim? He's no match for you, it's game-over before it's even started, so where's the pleasure in that? Where's the victory? What makes bullying so great?'

Puzzled, Bully glanced at me as if I were something he'd tried to avoid stepping on when he'd come into the room out of uncharacteristic courtesy. 'I could stamp on you right this minute,' he said. 'I could flatten you, because that's what I'm about. And you would suffer. That would be fun, don't you think?'

'But I'd fight back, so you'd never pick me to trample on. Because I'm a worthy opponent. It would be a fair fight, and that's not what you're about.'

Miserable's soft voice interrupted me and Bully. 'Even a

moaning minnie like me, has some worth, you know. My parents love me. And I have friends as well.' She blushed and shook her head, her clip-on gold hooped earrings swinging, her pink lips pursed and down-turned, her woe-is-me eyes, tragic. '*One* friend. Kind Carol. *She* likes me, she's my best friend, and that means even I'm worth being nice to. Everyone's worth it. You're the stupid one.' She hung her head. 'Even though I know you'll all ignore me because no one really notices me. I'm not bright and shiny enough. That's why I'm always so miserable.'

Fury screamed at her. 'Count yourself fucking lucky you have Kind Carol. Everyone knows Misery likes company, so what are you moaning about? You should be more like Grateful Gertie, but you're not. You're just a Miserable stupid cow.'

Fury had taken over, and his words had come out in a shower of spit as he sprayed his venom all over Miserable. Bully put his hands on his hips, and Victor shook his head slowly, as if in defeat, although so far, he'd escaped anything seriously tortuous.

Apart from his broken face. But I felt no Guilt. Why should I?

Bully's gruff old voice – it had always been so much older than his years – said, 'Well, what a pity party this is turning out to be. Look, Barney, I'll talk bluntly and openly to you, boy to man, as you and Fury have gate-crashed my party and leave me no choice.' He took time out to flex his muscles. 'Bullying is good because it gives you power. But as a child, it is only ever basic, primal and crude.'

Bully Bertie opened his mouth as he smiled at me, and I could see his teeny white milk teeth. 'On the other hand, if your desire is to cause mental torment and distress in adulthood, well, you're talking a whole new subject. You still want, as any decent self-respecting bully, the ultimate prize, dependent upon your needs. You want *some*thing from the poor abused soul whom you are mentally and/or physically annihilating. But *now*, as a grown man or woman, the avenues open to you are immense. Do you know why?'

'Tell me, Bully,' I said, enraptured by his lecture, my breathing coming out as gasping panting, so eager was I to hear the answer.

'Because, all things being equal, you now have a far superior and functioning mind, which can be used creatively and with malice aforethought. And *subtle* bullying is even more fun, because for that, you have to be clever. You no longer need physical violence, any swearing, nor threats, but instead, quiet innuendos and subtle insinuations; they work really well and are a powerful tool. You can get great results that way. To undermine others, to get under their skin, to make them doubt themselves – *that's* especially satisfying.'

This argument for the defence quietened Fury, and I waved at Bully for him to carry on.

'It's actually an art, bullying. If you do it correctly. It gets you what you want, and people don't even realise they have become your Victim. They follow along, being all Polite Petra about it all, and they make themselves Vulnerable Veras – open to gentle goading, prodding, teasing, open to *suggestion* – all camouflaged as Humour or Patronising Concern. You should try it. It works like a charm.'

Nodding quietly, my mind digested this.

Bully spoke again. 'But that's what you call sophisticated bullying – it's a step above just being a total shit simply because you can. And it is totally wasted and ineffective on useless twats like Victim Victor. So, take my advice, Barney. Choose your Victims carefully, and you too could be as successful as me.'

Smiling, feeling calmed and reassured, I realised the session had come to an end. Thanking my beloved poppets, I bowed gratefully and took my leave, as they took theirs – back to their allocated spaces behind cupboard doors. Kissing my fingertips, I transferred my touch to the wood and whispered, 'Thank you, my perfect china people. What would I do without you?'

In reply, there came a faint rustling of noise, perhaps it was the murmur of clapping dolly hands, thanking *me*. I liked to think that was it. I stood there and applauded them back, immensely happy with our liaison. My relationship with my dolls was a forever thing, and I was at one with all of them.

Their collective wisdom had given me the strength to carry on the charade that was human life.

I was back to being Barney Snapp, your friendly neighbourhood psychopath.

All clear thinking and logical reasoning and nothing else.

Perfect on the outside, and dead and empty on the inside.

I was proud to be able to walk amongst people and play their game, and they would never even guessed who I really was.

Giggling out loud, I most definitely heard the sweet sound of their shared mirth as the dollies joined me, laughing and rocking their beautiful china heads, their mouths open gaily, and clapping all the while.

Barney, Barney, Barney, stay and play. Please, don't leave us, Barney. We love you.

'I love you too, my precious babies, and don't you worry. I'll be back soon. Promise.'

28

ODETTE

Saturday and Sunday had dragged for Odette, as they always did. During the weekdays, she'd occasionally pop in to see Jodie, but every weekend Odette was limited to visiting her mother's graveside, having no friends other than Jodie. Jodie's weekends were taken up with fun-filled kid stuff and Odette didn't like to intrude. She envied Jodie's love and commitment and life with her children, and knew she shouldn't rely on her so much. It was pathetic and sad and juvenile.

The sun was still shining but was losing its warmth quickly as it dipped on the horizon. Odette sat by her mother's tombstone, still haunted by her death, but strangely at peace at this moment in time. *Hey, Mum. How are you? Guess what I'm doing tonight? I'm having drinks with a nutter.* She laughed. *Impressed?*

Odette imagined Mum laughing with her. But thinking about tonight, the smile slipped from Odette's face. Jodie had got this whole Barney thing very wrong. Odette was pretty sure he wasn't all that he claimed to be. Or he was more. Either way, both versions were bad. The way Barney had just admitted, *I pushed him.* Who bloody said a thing like that? Openly and with no fear. No subterfuge or finesse – only the stark truth. And if not the truth, what the hell was he playing at?

Odette reckoned Barney was more than a little spooky. He wasn't all there – he was missing something. Like *substance*. He didn't behave like a normal person; he was too measured and careful and rehearsed. *What should I do, Mum? There's something about him I don't trust one bit. You always told me, never trust a man who makes you feel nervous or stupid, for whatever reason. Always go with your instincts. Leave immediately.*

The sun slowly started to die in the sky. Odette didn't want to leave her mother, she never did. At least here, however sad it was, Odette was safe and loved and loving. Tonight, she'd be on edge and wasn't sure what to expect.

Fuck it. I'm always up for a challenge. I always was. *Bring it on.*

Odette gathered her belongings, blew her Mum a kiss, and got up. She was expecting an awkward evening at best, and at worst... well, she didn't really know. But whatever did or didn't happen, Odette was up for the fight. No one messed with her. Especially not some loony-tunes whack-job who'd apparently pushed his father down the stairs. What was bloody Jodie thinking? Barney didn't belong in their Club. He wasn't struggling with guilt and remorse and grief. Odette didn't know how she knew that, she just did. However skilfully Barney had faked it so far, she'd never been truly convinced by him. Nearly, but not quite.

She decided to flush him out tonight. Naturally, she'd be polite and listen to his story. And she was sure he'd have one, and it would be a belter. He'd had plenty of time and enough clues dropped by Jodie to know the sort of thing he was expected to come out with. Barney wasn't stupid. Neither was she. *Fucking bring it on.*

Suddenly, Odette couldn't wait for the confrontation. She'd had enough of being on her own, wallowing and drowning and sinking. Jodie was all she had in this world, and Odette would make sure her friend wasn't making the biggest fuck-off mistake of her life. The protector needed protecting, and Odette was ready to fight for her friend.

Getting ready at home, she chose something simple to wear and was buggered if she was going to go to great lengths to look overly attractive, or even as if she'd made any discernible effort at all. *Presentable* was as exciting as Odette was prepared to go. A red top and tight black jeans. A black jacket, white scarf. Sorted. Dressed to kill, in a polite, demure, nothing-to-frighten-anyone-here way, Odette got on the bus and sat on the top deck, looking out of the window.

When she got off at the bus stop, she glanced again at the directions on her mobile, and started walking. It was a fifteen-minute trek and by the time she got to Barney's house, Odette was sweating. Annoyed, she checked the details he'd given her and Jodie. *Go to the side door on the right.* The house was vast and beautiful and was worthy of a gasp, had Odette been the gasping type. She wasn't, and she walked briskly down the side of the house and rang the bell to the door. Hearing footsteps coming down the stairs, for a moment, her nerve deserted her and she wondered if this really was a very bad idea. *We know nothing about him. Nothing at all. He could be* anyone.

'Odette. How lovely to see you. Thank you so much for coming, do come up.'

Barney beamed at her and, sidling up the stairs in front of her, he checked she was following.

'Am I the first one here?' she asked, feeling stupidly and unexpectedly unsure. *Not so bloody cocky now*, she thought.

'You are indeed. It's just you and I. We'll get the party started, don't you worry.'

'I wasn't worrying.'

He stopped at the top of the stairs, placed his hand on the door handle. 'Good, I'm glad to hear it. Because there's nothing to worry about, is there? Come on in and let me take your jacket and scarf. Here.' Inside the flat, he held his hand out and, reluctantly, Odette unwound her scarf and gave it to him. 'I'm keeping my jacket on for the moment, thanks.'

'No problem. Take a seat. Pick a chair, any chair.'

Grimacing at him, disguising her distaste and concern as best she could by allowing a passing smile to flutter briefly on her lips, Odette took the nearest chair available. Manoeuvring a cushion so it sat in the small of her back, she glanced around the large sitting room with its grand sash windows. There was a lot of artwork on the walls and a soft light that was warm and welcoming. It was more than comfortable, and she felt a little better. As if bad things couldn't possibly happen in lovely rooms.

'Drink? I've wine – white, red or rosé. Champagne, or beer, or maybe you'd prefer a spirit?'

'Champagne, please. That would be lovely,' she said politely and wondered why she felt so nervous. Jittery, like a teenager on her first date. Alone with a boy for the first time. She clasped her hands together and got a grip on herself. Barney disappeared into what she assumed was the kitchen, and she heard the pop of a champagne cork. Taking advantage of his absence, she stood up and walked over to the nearest wall, looked closer at one of the drawings. It was really good. Remembering he'd said he was an illustrator, embarrassed and shyly admitting he drew pictures of this and that, she studied it closely. And was staggered.

'That's one of my drawings I told you about.'

Despite herself, Odette jumped as Barney appeared at her shoulder, but managed to carry on peering at the picture, as if she hadn't nearly wet herself. 'Yeah, I remember you saying.

You said you spend your days drawing, but this is so much more than that. This is beautiful. You're a real artist. I'm blown away.' She bent her head nearer the drawing. 'The expression on the face is incredible. You've really captured her tragedy. Her whole face screams out heartbreak. I love it.'

'Thank you very much.'

Ignoring him, excited by the splendour of his work, Odette moved around the room, going from wall to wall, looking at each framed piece. There were six in total. Returning to the first one, she accepted the glass of champagne Barney offered her and studied the artwork again. 'It's truly amazing. How did you get that expression so right? It's perfect. Incredible.'

When Barney didn't immediately speak, Odette turned to him. His face was rigid but suddenly it came alive. As if he'd momentarily been turned off, and then power had been resumed. She wasn't sure of the reason for the pause in his expression, why it had gone blank – perhaps he'd been surprised by her praise.

'You're quite right, Odette. It is an expression of heartache. I drew it from memory.'

Odette wasn't sure what to say but, thankfully, Barney seemed to have warmed to his subject. 'It's a picture I created of my little sister, Sarah. She was always so sickly as a child. Sickly Sarah. She died when she was twelve. I'll never forget her, and I carry her here.' He tapped his chest.

Bowing his head for a moment, he then raised it sharply, appearing surprised to find Odette's gaze still on him. 'I'm so sorry, Barney, I had no idea. What did she die of?'

She watched as his body stiffened again, and conceded it had been an overly intimate question. Too pushy. 'You don't have to say, I shouldn't have asked.'

'Leukaemia. And I don't mind you asking, how could you have known? It was a dreadful time for the family, and Sarah was in and out of hospital so many times, more in than out towards the end, but she managed to make friends on her ward. Good friends. Everyone loved her.'

Odette wasn't sure how to respond, so she shook her head and tightened her lips in sympathy. Barney seemed to be remembering, so out of respect, she didn't move, not wanting to disturb nor interrupt his memories.

'I always remember the little girl in the next bed to Sarah. When they were both really ill. Dying. At the same time. It was unthinkably awful. But this little girl was such a sad thing. So young. It was the most tortuous and worst thing to ever have to witness. The child's name was Mona. What a miserable death for a child; she was younger than Sarah, only eight, and she always wore these tiny hooped clip-on earrings like she was a real grown-up. She was really something.'

Embarrassed at the unnecessary details, Odette muttered something unintelligible but hopefully something that sounded sincere. Of course it was too tragic to truly comprehend, but she wasn't comfortable hearing about the specifics of a child's death. Not his sister, but a friend. *Slightly weird.*

He clapped. 'But enough of this melancholy chitchat – hardly suitable for an evening of drinks. Anyway, I don't like to talk about it. But I'm glad you like my work. I'm very proud of it.'

Relieved that the conversation had moved on, Odette thought his anecdote misplaced and inappropriate, and wasn't convinced it rang true. *I'm overthinking it,* she thought, and threw herself gratefully into the change of subject. 'So you should be proud. I've never seen drawings like these before. I'm wildly impressed.'

'Good, I'm so pleased.'

Standing together as they were, in the middle of the room, an awkward pause settled over them. Odette shifted uncomfortably, and he mirrored her, finally settling on staring at his feet. After what seemed an eternity, his head rose and he beamed at her. 'Could I tempt you with some food, or would you prefer to wait for Jodie and Grace to arrive? Nothing fancy, but I hope I've catered for your every whim. As the host with the most, I've done my best.'

Odette was surprised. 'I wasn't expecting food. You shouldn't have gone to the trouble.'

'Oh, it's not a sit-down formal thing, more of a buffet.'

'You're a cook as well?' Odette smiled stiffly and wished Jodie would arrive.

'Believe me, Odette, I *could* lie and say I'd prepared everything myself, but it's wrong to fib, don't you think?' Barney spluttered out a laugh, which threatened to turn into uncontrollable giggling. It took Odette by surprise and she simply stood and watched him as he snorted out his hilarity, his hand cupping his mouth. She was relieved when the laughter stopped, coming to a halt before it became full-on hysteria. Wiping his eyes, gathering himself, he flicked his hair back, his expression returning to bland. 'My mother helped with the canapés. And when I say "helped" I mean she prepared them all. Lots and lots of them, so I'm sure you'll find something that appeals.'

A leftover titter leaked out, before he wiped his face with his hand and fully regained his composure. Odette had missed the joke. His uncontrollable laughter had been disproportionate to his words – she couldn't even see the connection. She laughed briefly to show willing, but was unable to get any real oomph into the sound. Maybe he was nervous, she decided, giving him the benefit of the doubt and unable to think of anything else. She waved her glass at him. 'Let's wait for the others to get here, but you can top my glass up. That'll do me.'

Please, give me a minute on my own. You're too much. Much

too much. And I still think you're bonkers. More so now than when I arrived. You have not put my mind at ease.

'Of course. I'll bring the bottle in, shall I? With the ice bucket, obviously.'

'Obviously.'

Sitting again, Odette was no longer interested in the artwork on the walls, nor the soft and warm lighting, nor the alcohol and food in the lovely room. There was an edge to Barney that made her very uncomfortable and as she waited for her drink, she realised she was beginning to experience more than an awkward unease. Verging on a flood of anxiety, she managed to calm herself before being overwhelmed with panic. She was *not* enjoying being alone with him, nor did she really know exactly what she was nervous of. Not him, physically. She wasn't afraid that he'd suddenly leap up and attack her. It was something far more subtle and unknowable than that, but whatever risk he posed, it made her flesh creep.

Perhaps it was everything: Barney, Jodie and Grace, the coming evening with the stories that were going to be told. She didn't want to know anything more personal about her host – he'd already said too much, and some of it hadn't sat too well with Odette. He had no reason to lie to her, but she rather thought he had. And had done it purely because he could.

This a very stupid game to be playing with the wrong man.

29

———

ME

So far, as I fetched the bottle of champagne on ice, I thought the evening was going very well. Odette and I eagerly awaited the arrival of Jodie, and I thought my first *ever* guest and I were getting along famously. However false it all was.

I did *not* count Grace as a guest. She'd been more of a pest who'd snuck in, uninvited. She'd been contained for the moment – awaiting her release, and subsequent big entrance.

After talking to Bully, I'd decided to leave my captive alone for the rest of Saturday and Sunday, other than feeding, watering, maintaining her drug regimen and allowing her to relieve herself. As discussed with Bully, there was no sport to be had in mentally torturing someone who was so clearly weaker than oneself. It was a waste of time and had promised no fun whatsoever. Being left on her own for such an extended time would have been enough for Grace to conjure up all sorts of hideous scenarios, with no input needed from me.

And I was surprised Odette had believed my ludicrous story about Sickly Sarah – but why wouldn't she? It had been so credible, I almost believed it myself.

I'd made the sitting room as cosy and comfortable as

possible before my guests arrived – all my dolls were locked away from prying eyes, safe and settled in their cupboards. I'd gone to the trouble of fixing small padlocks on the handles, to deny any unwanted and intrusive access. The large dining table had been brought into the sitting room, upon which I could lay out the food, and hopefully, later, around which we would all sit.

But that seating arrangement might very well change – the key was all about being flexible and going with the flow. I'd be playing a lot of it pretty much by ear, until the denouement, but my plan was fully prepared and had only to be executed. No small feat, but I was confident. And excited.

All playpens, doll accoutrements, toys and accessories had been secured inside the dolls' cupboards. There'd been a lot of scuffling noises and giggling from behind closed doors when I'd secreted the dolls away. It was a very recent thing, the dolls taking the time and effort to speak so openly to me – we all enjoyed it, and it made for a much less lonely existence for all concerned.

Mum had indeed come up trumps on the food front, and had obediently left more Valium outside the interior door on Saturday afternoon. We'd texted back and forth about the food and what she should prepare, but I knew she was only trying to curry favour with me, intent on getting back in my good books again.

And, of course, I'd let her. Because I loved her and we all make mistakes. Even Mum.

The doorbell rang. I could hardly contain myself. Jodie was here. I patted both of my pockets, my mobile, on, and Grace's mobile, off. No doll-to-go about my person, I was going commando. Rushing back into the sitting room, I placed the ice bucket on the table. 'Help yourself, Odette. That must be Jodie. Do excuse me.'

Walking down the stairs in what I thought was a steady and restrained Host-Like way, I opened the door. Jodie immediately stepped forward and, grabbing my hand, pulled me in for a kiss on the cheek. Faintly taken aback, I reciprocated by giving my cheek, but my lips never made contact with her skin.

'Lovely to see you, Barney, and thanks so much for organising this. Very kind.'

'My Pleasure, Jodie. Odette's already here, please come up.'

Jodie chattered all the way up the flight of stairs, but I wasn't listening. I was concentrating on making sure I presented myself Correctly and Appropriately. Hopefully, my intellect well to the fore, I could carry this off for as long as was necessary before I allowed them to meet the real me. Smiling Politely, I opened the door to the sitting room and watched, with interest, Jodie and Odette welcome and embrace each other. And Very Sweet and Heart-Warming it was too. Remembering my duties as host, I dipped my head towards Jodie and took her coat. She was wearing a red dress, which clung to her body – quite clearly she'd made more effort than Odette in the wardrobe department. I made my face choreograph an Open and Honest expression, raised my eyebrows, and asked a question. 'Odette's on champagne. The same for you, Jodie?'

'Thank you, Barney. Super. What a lovely room.'

Hurrying into the kitchen, I realised how much speed was required to be a good host. Making sure both women had what they wanted, Stressed already, I calmed myself with an internal stern talking-to. Walking back into the sitting room, my Welcome Beam on my face preceding me, I brought Jodie her drink. 'Do sit down, both of you. I'll pour myself a drink and we'll all sit. Get to know each other properly. Much better than that simply Dreadful pub. So noisy. Unbelievable.' I shook my head, and both women mimicked me, Jodie saying, 'Yes, wasn't it awful. That was my fault – completely the wrong choice of venue. I certainly won't be returning there.'

Laughing Gaily, I returned with my drink and sat opposite the women who'd both chosen armchairs. Pushing aside an assortment of cushions, I sat on the sofa and immediately felt like I was about to be interviewed as their two faces turned towards me. Standing, I moved to a third armchair and angled it more towards my audience. There, much Cosier and more conducive to sharing social niceties and secret-telling.

Unsure as to how to start proceedings, Jodie did it for me, regaling Odette and I with tales of her Much-Loved children, and I was only required to nod and make vague responses. I was pleased as it gave me a chance to calm down, and by the time she'd stopped with her inane prattling, the champagne had kicked in and I felt a lot more relaxed and in control. This would be easier than I'd anticipated. *Do not worry, Barney. Your mind is your weapon. Use it wisely.*

'Isn't Grace here yet?' Jodie asked. 'I'm surprised. I'd have expected her to be the first to arrive.'

Holding my hands out to the side, I furrowed my brows – Puzzled. 'No, not yet. So far, it's just us three, I'm afraid. I'm sure she'll turn up soon.'

'I'll text her.' I watched Objectionable Odette as she extricated her phone from her back pocket and quickly tapped out a message on her mobile. A silence fell, as if we all expected an immediate response from the Missing Grace. Getting up from my chair, I Smoothly and Casually moved towards the kitchen. 'I'll get another bottle, this one's nearly finished anyway, so there's one on ice for when Grace arrives.'

In the kitchen, I turned on Grace's mobile and put it on silent. Finally, Odette's text came through.

Where are you? You're late. We're all waiting for
you. O

A bit Blunt, I thought, not much Love lost there, but having acquainted myself with Grace's texting style, I quickly replied.

Bit of an emergency at bookshop. Burst water
pipe. With Sandra now. Running late but I'm
coming. I'll text Barney to apologise and see
you when I can. G

Still using her mobile, I texted myself, turned hers off and returned to My Ladies.

On cue, my phone beeped out its received message sound, as did Odette's. Placing another bottle in the ice bucket, I read mine and Odette read hers. We looked at each other. 'Burst water pipe?' I asked.

Odette nodded. Shrugging but looking a bit Disappointed, I finished pouring Odette another glass and topped up my own. Jodie waved my offer away, and I said, 'Well, that's a shame about Grace, but at least she'll be coming as soon as she's able. It doesn't matter if she's late as we're in no hurry as far as I'm aware, are we? We have all the time in the world.'

Jodie crossed her legs. 'Yes, she'll turn up sooner or later, I'm sure. What a beautiful flat, Barney. Big.' She glanced around. 'It's much bigger inside than I'd imagined.'

'Yes, there are lots of rooms. I rattle around in it, but I Love it. It's my home.'

Odette sipped from her glass and with her other hand, adjusted her up-tight bun. 'It must be nice being home again.'

What? For a moment, I was non-plussed. And then I remembered my lie about moving back to comfort Mum in her Hour of Need.

'Yes, it is. Mum kept my rooms pretty much as I left them, so no having to bring back furniture and beds and stuff. It was all here waiting for me, as if I'd never left. It *is* nice being back in the family home. With Mum.'

Odette seemed on an attack-mission of some type, as her unsmiling face said, 'How is she? Your mother?'

'Bearing up. Considering. I do what I can.'

Her expression screamed out *I just bet you do*, her face full of Disbelief and Scorn. I rather thought I had made an enemy of the tight-bunned Odette, and made adjustments in my head as to how best to address this unforeseen problem. Silly bitch. How dare she wilfully antagonise me, in my own flat, drinking my champagne and about to stuff her stupid greedy face with culinary delights? Pressing my lips together, I noticed Jodie was also aware of the growing tension between Odette and I, and I sought to make Jodie my ally. That would seriously piss off Odette.

Steepling my fingers together with my elbows on the table, I managed to paste on Slightly Dejected. 'I'm sorry Grace isn't here yet, but would you like something to eat while we wait? There's everything you could desire, and plenty of it.' My smile felt brittle, and I was increasingly annoyed with Odette, but Jodie made it easy for me.

'Oh, food. How marvellous, I could eat a horse.' She tittered, as if she were a fool. 'I didn't leave myself enough time before I left, what with sorting out the children. I'd love a little something.'

'You may have a very large something, Jodie. Do excuse me, while I bring it in.'

Mum had given me strict instructions as to what to serve up first, so, carefully, I arranged a clutch of fresh lobster claws on ice – and thought it splendid enough looking to be presented on their own. I added a sprig of parsley for colour, and mayonnaise for those so inclined, and took the platter through with some ceremony – Proud of my offering and hoping it would get the praise it warranted. Both women came to the table and sat on dining chairs.

Jodie actually gasped. 'How splendid. Lobster – my very favourite.'

Odette held her hand in the air apologetically. 'Sorry, I don't eat lobster, but that's fine. Sorry, Barney.'

'Not at all, Odette. Think nothing of it. Perhaps you'd like some smoked salmon instead? Lemon and pepper suit you?'

Her smile was as tight as a stretched rubber band. 'Great.'

'Good.'

Hating Odette for spoiling my *pièce de résistance*, I threw together some salmon and some buttered brown bread in the kitchen. I assumed Odette was woman enough to assemble the two together herself without a bloody map, and heavy with tray, I re-entered the stage, ready to carry on my Performance.

To show Willing and to be All-Inclusive in the festivities, I placed claws, a lemon wedge and some mayonnaise in front of Jodie, and helped myself to a couple of lobster claws, enjoying cracking them open and finding the treasure inside that was the firm white flesh.

Jodie was getting stuck in and was clearly Enjoying and was Impressed by the spread so far. 'Delicious, Barney. God, I'm ravenous and the lobster is simply delicious. I can taste the sea. Just the thing, thanks very much.'

Just the thing for Just Jodie.

Her voice pitched in again, clogged by the food still sitting in the back of her throat, waiting to be swallowed. 'This really is a treat.'

Miss Tight-Bun was playing with her food, pushing it around her plate like an ungrateful child. Gritting my teeth, I had to look away. I was pretty sure she was pretending not to like the salmon. Wanting to slap the Haughty expression from her face, I found it easier to ignore her entirely. Tune her out completely. She'd keep, after all. I had all evening with the Liar. With both Liars.

Eating Politely, I wasn't sure how to broach the subject for which we were all gathered.

Again, Just Jodie to the rescue.

'How did you feel after Friday night at the pub, Barney? I'm so sorry we didn't really have time to properly react and talk your story through. It was unfortunate, the noise, your friend turning up and needing your help, it was impossible. I couldn't help but feel you were left hanging after your Brave Admission. And for that, I truly apologise.' Wiping a lobstery lemony drip from her lips with the back of her hand, although napkins were provided, she gave me a Worried and Concerned glance. 'I'm assuming tonight we can all tell our stories.'

Pretending Relief and Gratitude, I patted my mouth with a napkin, making a subtle but important point that they should be used. 'Shouldn't we wait for Grace?'

'That would be fair,' Miss Tight-Arse commented. 'I'm sure she wouldn't want to miss what you have to say, Barney. I think you have a fan.'

I don't think Grace is a fan anymore. I must remember to ask her when I go and collect her later.

As if the thought had just occurred to me, I made a suggestion with oodles of Embarrassed Temerity, as if I were overstepping the mark, taking leadership away from Jodie.

'I admitted... you know, what I said in the pub, because I felt I could Trust you both. But now, I find myself Nervous at the thought of Revealing All. Perhaps you could start, Jodie. Tell me your story, all of it, and I'm sure that will arm me with the required Courage I need, in order to bare my soul to you both. Properly and missing nothing out.' I shrugged my shoulders.

'That way, Grace won't miss anything, as I'm sure she's heard both of your stories.'

Jodie nodded Warmly. 'She has indeed. I don't mind starting, if that would make you more comfortable?'

'It would. And worry not, Jodie, there's plenty more food, which I shall keep on coming so it will make the Telling that much Easier and Comfortable for you. As if we're all Eating and Chatting and none of it is Anything Out of the Ordinary. Just shooting the breeze amongst friends with nothing to be Shocked about.'

'There *is* nothing to be shocked about,' Odette said, her tone Flat but oddly Menacing. 'Not as shocking as your revelation.'

Jodie pushed her plate away. '*Odette*. Really, what is wrong with you?' Turning to me, she said, 'Ignore Odette, Barney. She has her own story and some would find it most definitely shocking and out of the ordinary, but as you say, we are amongst friends, and we all support each other. That's the main thing.'

Jodie pushed her chair back, folded her napkin and held on to it in her lap. 'Shall I start?'

'Please do,' I said, genuinely relieved. 'But first, let's make ourselves comfortable. Would you prefer to sit in the armchairs, and I shall bring refreshments when needed? There's plenty of alcohol to whet the whistle, so where's more comfortable for you, Jodie?'

'I'm fine right here.' She licked her lips. 'And thank you for doing your best to make it easy for me, Barney, you're a kind man.'

You have no idea.

I tilted my head and, listening very carefully, I heard the soft sound of the dolls' limbs intertwining and rubbing against each other, and then a muted cheer from them all.

Astonished, I even heard Mona's voice. Discreetly listening hard and tuning out any external noise from Jodie and Odette, I heard her say, 'Even *I* don't feel miserable now. Well done, Barney. What fun! Hip hip hooray.' There was much snickering from the dolls but her voice was the most distinctive of them all. I swore she was laughing with glee, and I imagined her earrings swaying as her face moved with hilarity and unexpected happiness. *I've cured Misery.* I concentrated on not joining her in her praise of me.

The two lying women in front of me were extraordinarily easy to manipulate *and* I'd cheered up Miserable Mona. She was proud of me.

I was pretty proud of me, myself.

30

JODIE

Odette had sat back in her chair, obviously having heard Jodie's truth before, but Jodie checked to see how truly receptive Barney was – her new listener. His face appeared genuinely interested and open, and so far his expression had shown no pre-judgement of her at all, nor displayed any sign that he might be disapproving. Of course, he hadn't heard her story yet, but Jodie was confident he'd accept it and not be appalled by the brutality of it. He sat in a neutral fashion, face blank, presumably not wanting to appear too eager to hear her secret, but his eyes were alight and aware – not wanting to miss anything, Jodie thought.

The only thing that threatened to spoil her telling, was the very obvious tension between Odette and Barney. When their host had been in the kitchen, Odette had whispered, 'We don't have to go through with this, Jodie. I don't like him.'

'*I* like him, and it's my choice. And you'll support me by telling him your story as well. I'm sorry you don't like him, but I have the right to share my tale with whoever I think is safe. Barney's safe. *We're* safe.' She'd waited a beat. 'And he's included because I want to share my secret again. With him.

Rightly or wrongly. Confession always makes me feel so free. It reminds me of who I am.'

Odette had shaken her head, but reluctantly agreed she'd tell her story when the time came. Because she was a good and true friend. 'But to be clear, Jodie, I'm only doing this for you. To support you. No other reason. And I *am* right about him, and you're wrong. He's not safe.'

Jodie felt guilty she'd so easily coerced Odette into something she wasn't comfortable with, and it upset her.

But that's life, Jodie thought. *Never bloody comfortable.*

Seated at the table, with her audience of two, Jodie now concentrated her mind, wanting to be lucid in her confession, and leave no room for misinterpretation. She crossed her legs and wiped her fingers on her napkin.

'As you know, my husband, Tom, was a shit. That's not news to anyone. But I can't explain how truly impossible he made my life, how he was systematically destroying me, night after night after night. Me and both my children. Our lives were at risk as well as our sanity. But it was Katie and Emily who tipped the balance.' She momentarily closed her eyes as a picture of her children popped into her head. *I did* do the right thing, there is no question. She opened her eyes. 'It was our anniversary, and as my husband beat me, and I kept my screams silent to protect my babies, I vowed to myself, I must do something, anything, to make it stop. To change it forever.'

Barney didn't press her prematurely, wanting to know the details of that moment. Jodie would tell it as it happened, and he would not interrupt her – of that, she was certain. Odette sat quietly, looking forlorn, but Jodie knew she had Odette's full support and love. Never did she doubt that.

Jodie picked up her glass of champagne and took a long swallow.

'Twenty years we'd been together, and Tom had bought me

a new black dress for the occasion. But instead of admiring how I looked, and telling me how beautiful I was, he weaponised the stupid dress – used it to tease and demean me. He beat me. I accepted the punches, as I did most nights, and kept on trying to tell myself it was all my fault, it had to be.' She drank greedily and Barney refilled all their glasses. 'But later that night, standing over my sleeping children, I realised, someone had to protect *them*. For it was patently obvious the violence would spill over and touch them in some way. I was Tom's punchbag, but I would not allow him to touch my children.'

She stopped speaking and, as always when remembering, she could taste and smell and hear that night as if it were yesterday. Blinking, she brought herself back to Barney's sitting room.

'Having lived with Tom for so long, I knew his habits. I knew them well, and his routine had become predictable. Him and his stupid fucking sports car – I hated it. I also hated that he was a drunk, and because I was as weak as he was a bully, I dallied on the outskirts of alcoholism myself, but I never let it really take hold. That night, although I'd certainly had a few shots, I made a decision. A very sober decision, which would change everything.'

Jodie remembered the sheer excitement that had filled her, making her laugh out loud as a very silly thought became a very real idea.

'Tom hated the children. He didn't mind showing them off when he was being Mr Wouldn't-Hurt-A-Fly, out in the real world, going about his fatherly duties, but deep down, he resented their presence. He'd taken to avoiding them. Not speaking to them. Completely ignoring them – to Tom, if he couldn't see the children, he could pretend he was a happily single fatherless man, with not a care in the world.'

Barney dared to speak. 'He sounds a brute. I'm so sorry.'

Jodie shrugged. 'I was used to it. Our marriage was more like an arrangement. But Tom made a stupid error. He stopped thinking, forgot how to be fun, stopped being natural and spontaneous, as he had been when we'd first met and I'd fallen in love with him. He'd become boringly predictable, and I knew his every move before he even made it.' She paused. 'However much I'd had to drink.'

Picking up her glass, Jodie noticed it was empty. Barney jumped up and disappeared into the kitchen. The noise of the cork seemed to galvanise Odette. 'Are you sure you're okay, Jodie? You seem angrier than normal.'

'I *am* angrier than normal. I don't know why, but just the thought of Tom makes me so bloody furious.'

Barney came back in, filled her glass, and popped the bottle in the bucket. Almost deferential, clearly not wanting to break the mood, he faced Jodie. 'Is there anything else you'd like?'

'Not at the moment, no.' She waved the now-full glass in her hand. 'This will do me. But we really must eat later. After all the trouble you've gone to.'

'Plenty of time to eat, no worries there.' Seeming pleased with everything, Barney settled back on his chair and loosely crossed his arms. Smiling at her, he included Odette in his expression, as if they were all a team. Serious faced, he looked her in the eye. 'Let's carry on, shall we, if you're happy to, and you have everything you need.'

Not needing his permission, Jodie dived straight back into the revisiting of her old life. 'Tom had taken to not sitting with us after dinner, and would escape to the garage where his precious car was. Instead of coming to bed, he'd hide away with his alcohol and his fucking car.' She took another sip and thought, *I really mustn't get drunk.* 'I knew he couldn't resist hunkering down in the driving seat of his sleek, shiny toy – his very own erection on wheels, pathetic fool that he was. I hated

Tom and I hated his car. He'd sit behind the steering wheel with a bottle of whisky, and God knows what fantasy he played in his head, but he'd always turn on the engine, and sit there, revving it. Vroom, vroom, like a child playing at being an adult.'

She felt her own face twist in dislike as she pictured her husband, behaving like a complete... idiot was too kind a word. Behaving like an utter knobhead, there, that was a much better description.

'More often than not, he'd pass out at the wheel and, being a good wife, I'd turn the engine off, cover him with a blanket and there he'd remain, unconscious, until the following morning. He was always so careful to keep the door from the kitchen to the garage open; it had become automatic – however drunk he was. He always remembered to do that.'

For a second, Jodie stopped and was pleased at the utter silence that surrounded her. Nothing got in the way of her memory, and she revelled in it. 'That particular night, he had the added incentive of getting into his car, as I'd given him some ludicrously expensive handmade leather driving gloves as an anniversary gift. I knew he'd be unable to resist putting them on that evening. And as I kissed each of my children's sleeping cheeks goodnight, I realised, *I've got the bastard. The stupid bastard – I've got him.*'

Odette was staring at her oddly and Jodie acknowledged she might be more than a little bit pissed. Pushing aside her drink for the moment, she was plagued by a rare anger – one Jodie thought she'd got rid of years ago. Not understanding her current fury, she edged her glass to within touching distance again and said, 'I'm sorry. I don't know why I'm so bloody furious. God knows why. It was long enough ago that you'd assume I'd be over it by now. Three years and counting.'

Shaking his head, Barney's expression was unreadable, and

he licked his lips. 'If I may be so bold, that's no time all. Not in the grand scheme of things.'

Irritated, Jodie picked up her glass. 'Am I being blamed for something here? Have I not followed the correct protocol?'

Odette made shh-ing gestures with her arms, pushing her hands palm down in the air, as if Jodie were a child having a tantrum. Jodie felt like stamping her foot but knew that would make her seem more out of control, and what... *insensitive?* She sucked air in deeply to her lungs, trying to calm herself. Perhaps it was the stress, the retelling of it for only the third time to a new person, maybe it was Barney himself – for all she knew, it could be real anger at what she'd been forced to do on her anniversary. Whatever the reason, Jodie sucked it up and stared at both Odette and Barney, and carried on regardless.

'It was late, around midnight, and I could hear the car in the garage with its motor running. The kitchen door was open and I sat there on a stool, quite calmly but knowing exactly what I was going to do.'

She couldn't hide the smile as it kissed her lips. Not caring what her host thought of her, Jodie let the smile become a grin. 'I waited and waited until I couldn't wait any longer. I admit to being excited.' She held her hands up, as if she were guilty of something, but her happy face said otherwise. There had been absolutely no guilt then or now. Why should there be?

'Eventually, sure he must be completely out for the count by this time, I tiptoed into the garage and right up to his side of the car. A mindless tune was playing on the radio and Tom was out cold. The stupid bastard had his new gloves on – British Racing Green, with holes in the leather over the knuckles, as if he were a real driver. I remember thinking what a complete tosser. And then I laughed. I recall that quite clearly – laughing and knowing I was about to finally take back control of my life from him. I stood there for ages, watching him, making sure he was passed out from alcohol and unlikely to waken.'

Now she lifted her glass and took a deserved swallow of champagne. 'All that abuse I'd suffered, the fear I'd endured, trying and failing to protect my children from Tom, his presence, the poison he oozed all over my babies just by breathing, that's when I knew I was doing the right thing.'

Catching the eye of Barney, ignoring what she knew would be disapproval that she had allowed herself to get a little tipsy, Jodie politely enquired, 'Barney, I hope all this isn't too shocking for your sensitive sensibilities, is it? Because if it is, tough shit and ex*cuuuse* my language.'

He held his hand in the air and then not knowing quite what to do with it, he let it fall again into his lap. 'No, not at all, Jodie. You carry on. Please.'

'There's not much more to tell. I left the engine on, and I closed and locked the car door. Running, I went to the open door to the kitchen and closed it. Me on the kitchen side, obviously. I took some sheets out of the washing machine and rolled them in a neat tight roll, tucked it tight up against the bottom of the door frame. Made quite sure none of the build-up of carbon monoxide would seep into the house. I didn't care how long it took and sat down to wait. Hot chocolate warmed me and made it all seem how a normal family time at home should feel. So, I made a lovely big sausage sandwich and had a nice relaxing bubble bath. Hours and hours passed. It was summer and the sun came up early, all bright and yellow and glowing and I finally opened the door to the garage.'

'You killed him,' Barney said.

'Oh, yeah, I killed the bastard. Damn right I killed him and I'd kill him again if it were possible. I went in, with a teacloth over my mouth, to check Tom had stopped breathing, and then I stood back to see if his chest was rising and falling. He was definitely dead. And I can*not* tell you how happy that made me feel.'

She closed her eyes at the relief of that moment and sighed, then was quiet for a minute.

'You're humming, Jodie,' said Odette. 'Stop humming.'

Jodie hadn't realised she had been humming. *How drunk am I? But so bloody what if I am humming? Or drunk?* What was a bit of humming between friends? It was hardly a criminal offence and nothing to get worked up about.

Unlike murder.

Steadying herself, stopping the humming, she finished up tidily. 'I woke the children at eight o'clock and put the offending sheet in the washing machine, I rang the police at about half past eight – a more reasonable time for the discovery of one's husband. It was recorded as an accidental death, another foolish drunk under the influence of alcohol who'd made a fatal mistake. It was all very painful.' She laughed. 'For about one fucking minute. And it was the best thing I've ever done. I'd killed him and the very bad man was dead forever. I and my children were free. And I felt no guilt – then or now.'

The end of her story brought no applause. Barney's reaction was minimal. 'You killed in order to save your children.' He nodded. 'That's fair.' He gave it more thought. 'You murdered your husband to free yourself.'

'It wasn't murder. It was justice.'

The telling of her story had liberated Jodie once again, and she luxuriated in her triumph. 'Got a sausage on a stick, Barney, or a handy vol au vent at your disposal? Anything, really. I'm suddenly ravenous all over again.'

She threw back her head and roared with delight. 'Isn't this fun? It's always so exhilarating to get the truth out there to others who understand. I feel so much better now. Thank you for listening. Every time I speak it out, it cleanses my soul.

Hence this group. It's my mission to release others from the guilt of their acts, and to reintroduce them to a blame-free existence.' She dipped her head. 'Welcome to our club, Barney.'

Barney remained quiet, his lips pursed together, his arms crossed and his feet neatly tucked together. It irritated Jodie. 'For God's sake, Barney. You didn't really still think this was a bereavement group, did you? By now, you must have cottoned on to that misnomer. It was never that. You've joined a Murder Club. Sit back and enjoy.'

31

ME

'That's fair,' I'd said. *That's fucking outrageous*, I'd thought.

Was the entire world made up of secret murder clubs, or had I just been incredibly unlucky stumbling across this one?

Not being stupid, I knew I wasn't surrounded by killers when out in public, but equally, it reinforced my growing belief that it had been a dreadful mistake stepping into what was laughingly called *the real world*. It wasn't for me. It was full of mad people, doing mad things. I didn't fit in and didn't want to.

On a more pedestrian level, I wasn't entirely sure as to how best to proceed. Jodie's method of murder had been mildly interesting, verging on the not-interesting. Fairly mundane, if I were being truthful.

And if I were being truthful, I was the only one in the room being that.

But it was her lying about it for all these years that really offended me. I'd managed to exit the room, hiding my fury. I wanted to strangle her, but of course, that would make me no better than she, and for the first time, I truly realised my own worth. I *was* better than the women.

And my world, where I truly belonged, was also better.

The complete and utter *sham* of a life Jodie had led with her beloved children. The deceit she'd carried out – all in the name of love for her daughters – I couldn't grasp the enormity of her falsehood, the wickedness of her actions.

According to the rules of this particular club, it seemed one could disguise and camouflage any indiscretion, as long as you did it for all the right reasons. Indiscretion was an extremely polite word for murder in this context. But the moral of the story was, if I'd understood correctly, it was perfectly acceptable to *kill* another human being, if you could argue your case well enough. It seemed being an abusive man warranted whatever was thrown at him. Personally, I thought murder was wrong – that simple. Irrespective of how bad Tom had been, he hadn't deserved that.

My concept of the world as I'd perceived it from the sidelines for years and years was, as it turned out, sadly inaccurate. Knowing I was better than this, I felt superior to the women and if only they really looked, they'd see me for the good man I was. Instinctively, I knew I would no longer internally initialise any emotions from here on in. Because I didn't care and had no desire to be like these people. I didn't need to mimic them, they weren't worthy and I wasn't anything like them. I didn't want to be.

And that didn't bode well for my guests. But it certainly reinforced the brilliance of my plan.

The strict belief system by which I lived was most assuredly shaken and upset, and from an etiquette point of view, I wasn't convinced I knew how to politely move on from the admission of murder, to food. Nor how I'd carry on my soiree, without showing how truly disgusted I was by Jodie's story. Although I wasn't a religious man, I knew taking the life of someone was considered a sin. And I, for one, wasn't one for forgiveness. Murder went against all my teachings and values.

But I needed to hear Odette's story too. To make life whole and right again.

To make it come full circle.

The game had to continue, as much as I loathed the sight of the two women soiling my clean and perfect living space, their falsehoods scattered willy-nilly, messing up the place.

Only by completing the night's activities would I achieve my purpose, so remembering the plaudits and support of my dolls, I allowed myself to be spurred on by their adoration of me. I would make everything all right. For us all. Me and them.

That's all I really had left, after all.

And Mum. I still had Mum.

I did wonder when they'd both start worrying about Grace's absence. Sooner rather than later, I thought, even though I was aware Grace wasn't the most popular of women in this gang. Because she'd told me how she'd always hovered on the perimeter, pathetically knocking on the door, begging to be let in, but had always been ignored by the two mean girls in charge. But I knew Jodie and Odette would have to mention her soon.

Sticking my head around the door, I said, 'Would you like some cold meats, and cheese and salady stuff, Jodie? Odette?'

'Super,' said Jodie.

'Yeah, lovely,' said Odette, her voice deliberately flat and bored-sounding.

'Coming right up.'

First of all, I texted Mum, as arranged, and told her to ring me in precisely two minutes. Waited for her *OK* and once received, careful not to hurry, I slid a folded red and white chequered tablecloth under my arm, and walked into the sitting room and opened one of the un-padlocked cupboards.

Taking out four beanbags and moving the armchairs back, I cleared a space, and placed the beanbags neatly on the floor. Knowing both women were watching me from the dining table,

I stood back as if to admire my own handiwork, and then turned to them both. 'It's time for a picnic, ladies. More informal and cosy than having to sit at the table. More comfortable too.' I feigned surprise as my mobile rang. 'Do excuse me for a minute.' I looked down at the phone, and then back at the women. 'It's Grace.' As I was virtually on the floor already, I hunkered down and sat on my heels. 'Hello?'

'Why am I really ringing you?' Mum said.

I waited a beat as if listening. 'I'm sorry to hear that, Grace. How long do you think you'll be?'

'I hope you know what you're doing, Barney.'

'Okay, no, no really, don't worry. I'm so sorry, how awful. We're not going anywhere, so don't panic. What?'

I held my hand to my ear as if the reception were bad. 'Hello, Grace? Are you there?'

'What are you playing at, Barney? Do you want me to come up?'

'No, absolutely not. No. No problem at all. Hang on. What?'

'Barney, I'm hanging up now. I haven't the time for this.'

'No, of course, that's fine. We'll see you when we see you. Good luck, bye, yes, bye bye.'

Pretending to be dismayed and disappointed, I looked at the women. 'That was Grace. Obviously.'

'You surprise me,' Odette said, her voice heavy with sarcasm.

'What's happened? Is she still coming?' Jodie at least pretended concern, although she seemed more intrigued by the appearance of the tablecloth as I laid it out flat on the carpet, pocketing my mobile as I did so. She was less obviously drunk now, which was a good thing. Easier to manage.

'Grace is trying her best. She's had to go to some DIY place, apparently. She kept on cutting out, but as far as I can gather,

her shop's flooded and she's having to clean up. Doesn't want to leave it like that, so she might be some time, but she's definitely still coming.'

I saw Jodie's feet appear in my eyeline. Her sensible black shoes were only inches from my fingers as I concentrated on creating the perfect picnic tableau, pulling the creases out of the cloth. Standing, I swerved, not wanting to come too close to Just Jodie, and I arranged the beanbags in a large semi-circle. 'There. Perfect. I'll bring in the food. What fun.' I clapped my hands and was wide-eyed with excitement. 'There are no rules to say you can't have a picnic anytime, anywhere – that's what I say, anyway. Sit, Jodie, please sit. You'll find the beanbags most comfortable. You just have to squish around a bit, and then they swallow you up whole. I love them.'

Smiling with real delight, she collapsed into a beanbag and giggled. 'Ooh, lovely. Come on, Odette. Come and join the party.'

'I'm coming.' Odette got up slowly and we passed each other, each of us giving a wide berth to the other, but both still playing the superficial courteous game of host and guest. Nodding and smiling and feeling almost feverish with eagerness, I dashed back into the kitchen and started putting out food onto my best china.

Mum had done a great job and it required little work to make the food feast-like and sumptuous. It would take several trips but it was worth doing properly. You couldn't hurry perfection, even if that perfection was only a thin veneer, covering something other. Something clever but bad. Not as bad as Jodie's past brutal behaviour, but still bad – because it would all be a lie – as far as they were concerned. I'd discovered this was how people in the real world, behaved.

Hello, real world. Here I come. But I come with no lies, only my truth. And you all might find that a whole lot worse.

When I laid the plates on the cloth, Jodie actually squealed. Even Odette couldn't keep her eyebrows rising in surprise. At last the spread was laid out in all its finery.

'Wow, that's some picnic,' Odette said as she managed to extricate herself from the beanbag that had consumed her, and knelt in front of the food.

I adopted a bashful pose but was genuinely pleased. Finally, I joined the women down on the floor. 'Who wants to be Mother?'

'I rather think that's my job by default. This really looks delicious, Barney. Don't you agree, Odette?'

'It really does. Again, I'm impressed. It's as captivating as your artwork, and that's saying something. Thank you, Barney.'

Nodding, I wondered if Jodie had told Odette to play the game and be more bloody grateful and stop being so rude and aggressive. Perhaps. Either way, I was relieved not to have to deal with a bad-tempered Objectionable Odette. There was too much to think about and my head was aching again with all the unfamiliar stimuli. I wasn't used to it and had to fight down panic. For a minute, my vision blurred and I lost all sense of spatial awareness, as if I were falling down a deep hole. The two alternate realities were merging – mine and theirs, confusing me, pulling me in two directions simultaneously – their world, brash and harsh and false – my world, soft and gentle and welcoming.

Jodie reached over the food, supporting herself with one arm, and touched my knee. 'Are you all right? Why not sit in one of your beanbags, get off the floor and relax back, it's right behind you. You've gone white.'

Closing my eyes, I forced my mind to think of the dolls in the cupboard. How I wished I was playing with them instead of these two dreadful women. Slowly, very slowly, picturing Bully Bertie and his confident milk-toothed grin, my breathing returned to normal. For a frightening minute there, my mind, my great intellect upon which I relied, had threatened to abandon me, and I'd had to grasp frantically at it, keeping it with me. Relieved I'd retrieved my great gift, I managed to speak, the pain in my head receding.

'I'm so sorry, I don't know what came over me. Please, help yourself to the food.' I fell back into the beanbag as suggested. Knowing I had to hold on to this harsh reality and finish this game, I forced out a smile. 'See, all better now. And please, this is most important...' Holding a beat, feeling the thump of my heart as it slammed in my chest, I smiled gently at them. Four eyes stared at me, waiting on my every word. *Fools*.

'You *must* leave room for a very special après-dinner drink – it's a family tradition of ours, a celebration of life, a toast to the future, and a coming-together of new friends. It's quite a belter of a shot, and so tart it'll make your lips pucker, but absolutely delicious. It should be downed in one, but I won't force you.' The dipping of my head, the brief novelty discovered at Dad's funeral, now bored me, so I didn't bother, and instead, held my gaze with each woman. 'It would mean a lot if you'd have that drink with me after we've listened to Odette's story. In way of celebration. Before I tell you what I am guilty of.'

'Of course, Barney. It would be my pleasure. Thank you for the offer, and I'll do my best to down it in one,' Just Jodie said, up for the offer of more alcohol for any old reason.

Odette nodded, already eating. 'Yeah, I'm up for that, count me in.'

'Go on, Odette. Tell your story.' Jodie looked at me, one hand holding a huge chunk of cheese and smoked turkey. 'I never tire of hearing it, Barney. It's a beautiful story but you must open your heart to be able to see and appreciate that beauty. To see past the tragedy. I want you to be receptive to her, not judgemental.'

'I don't judge. I'm happy and privileged to hear your story, Odette.'

Whenever you're ready, Odette, I'm ready – for your lies and admissions of wrong-doings, all dressed up prettily to disguise, will not take me in. Believe me, if you're ready, I'm ready.

Burrowing into my beanbag, I settled down, remembering to keep fury buried. Discreetly I moved my head, in a nod of respect, directing it towards the dolls' cupboard. *I'm coming, dolls, your God is coming. Just a little while longer and we'll all be together. Hold on to your hats, the new world order is nearly upon us.*

32

ODETTE

'Just so you know, Barney, I'm telling this story for Jodie's benefit. Not yours. I don't like you, and I don't trust you. You make me uncomfortable, but I'm here, and I'll play the game. Normally I'd leave – my mother always told me, if a man makes you feel nervous, leave. But Jodie wants me to go through with this charade, so for her, I'll do it. Not for you.'

She watched Barney's face – it didn't show shock or anger or anything in particular. He shrugged. 'I don't know what to say to that, Odette. An unnecessary and misplaced character assassination which I could have done without.' He lifted his shoulders up and down. 'But for the record, I'm actually incredibly boringly and fantastically normal, as it turns out, so your discomfort belongs to you.'

In mid-swallow, a crust of bread between her lips, Jodie sputtered and coughed. 'Jesus Christ, Odette. What are you saying? If you don't want to tell your story, don't fucking bother. This is not the spirit in which it's meant to be shared. Either tell it nicely, or don't tell it at all.' She swallowed. 'Or you can leave, but I'm staying.'

Stupid Jodie. So caught up with her eagerness to protect,

committed to her cause, Jodie was blind to the mistake she'd made by selecting Barney. Other than getting up and leaving her here, Odette felt compelled to stay and speak of what really happened to her mother. Keeping her gaze on Jodie, as if Barney wasn't there, Odette nodded solemnly at her friend. 'No, I'll stay with you.'

Wedging herself deep into the beanbag, Odette planted her feet on the floor.

'Jodie, this story is told again, for you. Because you understand it and see what I *hoped* I'd see when it happened, but as you know, it didn't really work out like that. I'll start it like I always do. Like a tradition.' Odette wanted to cry already. She picked up her glass and drank from it, hoping it would give her courage, but knowing it wouldn't.

'I have something of an admission to make.'

'Tell me, Odette,' Jodie whispered, her hands folded calmly in her lap. 'Tell me and know I'll help you.'

Sucking in a deep breath, hating to say it in front of Barney, Odette closed her eyes, wishing herself somewhere else. 'I took my mother's life. She told me to. *I want you to kill me, Odette.* That's what she said and, of course, how could I say no? It was her dying wish and I could never refuse Mum anything. She was my mother, had brought me up on her own, and I adored her. Without her, life for me would be, and still is, completely and utterly pointless.'

Every time Odette admitted this, said it out loud, she'd cry. And the tears always surprised her – by now she'd expected to be able to get the words out without weeping, but it was always the same. Perhaps she'd cry forever.

Odette was very aware that the people in the room, one her best and only friend, the other, a man who frightened her, were both completely still – it felt as though if they moved, they'd break some weird invisible spell that Odette had inadvertently cast. She turned her head and looked Barney dead in the eye. 'The fact that I facilitated my mother's death isn't a thing to get sidetracked by: it is merely a tragic fact. I shall tell you of it in a concise and unemotional way, because I can't even begin to convey the fullness of emotion that was involved. And you would never in a million years understand how I felt then, nor how I feel now.'

Upset that Barney's presence was tainting her love story, she closed her eyes again and spoke in her head to Jodie only, imagining Barney not there.

'It was an assisted dying, which sounds more palatable for the overly sensitive – which I know you're not, Barney. I think you're very cut and dried, black and white, with no shades in between, nuance and subtlety pass you by, so I very much doubt you'll understand my and my mother's choice to release her from life – but whatever your disinterest and inability to comprehend, whichever words I use, I can't avoid the truth of my actions.'

'Odette, if you must, pretend it's you and me, alone.' Jodie's voice was gentle and soothing. 'Tell *me*.'

'I stopped my mother's pulse from pulsing.

'I stopped her heart from beating.

'I stopped her blood from flowing, and I stopped her heart from loving.

'Mum asked me to kill her and I owed her that much. I had to do it, and at the time it had felt so right. I didn't feel guilt. Not then. Only a terrible sense of loss. Now, I can hardly move for guilt. And the shame. Shame I didn't know was possible.' Odette looked desperately at Jodie, needing her kindness, and saw tears sitting on the lower lids of her friend's eyes. They hadn't fallen yet, but like a dam, the tears blossomed up in a watery bubble, until they burst and overflowed, running down Jodie's cheeks. Odette wanted to hold Jodie's hand, but felt incapable of moving. Stuck in her story.

'I brought death to Mum and released her from this life – at her insistence – with all my love. I know you don't blame me, Jodie, because I know you understand I did the right thing. If I asked you to kill me, in the same circumstances, you'd do the same. You would. I know you would. Because you're thoughtful and kind and understand the ways of the world. I don't worry about your moral judgement of me, because there is none. It used to be you were the only one who knew my secret.' Odette stopped speaking. Glared at Barney. 'But not anymore.'

'And I'm listening to your tale, Odette,' Barney murmured. 'And thus far, I feel only sympathy.'

Yeah, right. Lying twat, Odette thought.

'Carry on,' Jodie said. 'Focus. You'll feel better afterwards, I promise.'

Odette glanced at Jodie, and smiled. 'You've sobered up.'

'Practice makes perfect, I'm an expert at regaining sobriety when required.'

Grateful Jodie was back to being fully compos mentis, Odette deleted Barney from her world and said, 'The actual mechanics of it are almost by-the-way. But to make it clear, it was ridiculously easy in the practical sense. Being end of life with primary breast cancer is a relatively swift death sentence. But it didn't feel like that. It was protracted, as if time was stretching out, eking out every minute – purely out of spite – and the hands of the clock never moved forward. Mum and I were living in limbo. Neither here nor there.'

Her words, her confession, were met by silence and Odette didn't want to break her mood by engaging with either Jodie, or Bonkers Barney. She picked up her glass and realising it was empty, put it down. Immediately, Barney jumped up and got yet another bottle, the third Odette thought, from the kitchen and topped her glass up. Odette automatically nodded her thanks and gratefully took a large sip.

'The cancer had spread from Mum's breast and into her lungs and bones. She made the choice to have end-of-life care in her own little home where she could be herself. With me. Just her and me, as it always was when I was a child growing up after Dad had left us. And of course, Oscar, who sat curled, purring and sleeping, on Mum's bed. It was like the cat knew.'

Odette could never forget Oscar being there, so sweet and furry and unknowing. But knowing. He *had* known, Odette was sure.

'Apart from the intrusion of the community nurses who administered the drugs, the social care team who bathed and dressed her and generally got in the way, Mum and I wanted to be on our own, with Oscar, waiting for death.

'We thought of death as a means of release; not a tangible thing but more of a concept. We all know that death comes to us all. Mum simply invited death to visit earlier than it might have otherwise done. She wanted the advantage of dying precisely when she wanted. To cut out the waiting. Mum queue-jumped and there is nothing wrong with that.'

Odette waited to see if Barney would argue the point, but of course he didn't – he was playing his understanding-sympathising-all-accepting role, the man who pretended he was impossible to dislike. She didn't believe it. Not even a tiny bit. He was a hard-wired bastard who faked his way through life. Odette was astonished Jodie had fallen for his act.

For Jodie alone, beyond caring what the frightening man thought, Odette returned to her confession. The fact she still thought of it as that, meant she was nowhere near feeling blameless about it. Secretly, she suspected she never would.

'It wasn't difficult to get an extra bottle of morphine. Although Mum was on a morphine drip – which was of minimal help in terms of relieving her pain – we always had a bottle to hand for when the pain became unbearable and Mum would take a spoonful as and when needed. It sat on her swivel table at the side of her bed, cap perched on the top, so she didn't have to grapple with the twist-down lock. My mother told the nurses she'd spilt the entire contents of a full bottle on the floor. I even made sure there was a wet sticky patch on the carpet, which I was dutifully cleaning as the fat jolly nurse turned up.'

Odette's words were falling over themselves now – she was eager to explain what had happened and was past caring who her audience was.

'Of course, the kindly GP had prescribed another 500mls. How could he not? You don't refuse a dying woman's last cry for help, and Mum had never been suicidal. She'd managed to remain upbeat and had made a point of always presenting herself as a fighter with a will to live. She had also been very restrained in how much Oramorph she took daily. Never too much, because she'd been planning her overdose ever since being diagnosed as terminal, and was keen to set the scene well in advance. She didn't want it to ever appear as if she'd been forever teetering on the brink of taking a lethal dose. Mum wasn't a giver-upper-er, so it was an easy game to play. And after all, I was looking after her. Where could be the harm?'

She sighed as the heartbreak the memory always and without fail triggered, assaulted her like a punch in the gut. Breathing slowly, Odette forced herself to carry on. 'It was important to Mum that I shouldn't come under any suspicion for helping her. And really, my only help had been holding her hand and not physically stopping her from drinking it.' She breathed deeply, sucking air in from the room, before admitting, 'Although I'd held the bottle to her lips.'

Odette stopped and wet her lips with champagne. She hated this part, all the parts of her story, but this part she hated the most. It played over and over in her head, on a nightmarish loop and was a frame-by-frame replay that she could never rid herself of. However hard she tried to forget, it would flash through her brain, teasing her, taunting her, tainting her – it was if she was transported back to the little bedroom every time she thought of Mum.

As if she'd done something truly wicked and wrong.

Whatever Jodie said.

Both her listeners were completely silent, as if they, too, were sitting beside Mum's bed.

Except, of course, they hadn't been. It had only been Odette, doing the unthinkable, all alone and dead inside.

'As I'd watched her slowly swallow the Oramorph, we'd held each other's hand, my other arm around her, supporting her weight as I propped her up so she could drink. She didn't have to finish the bottle – a little more than half was enough. Too weak, she was easy pickings for death.

'Oscar had watched quietly. Blinking slowly. Mum had taken his paw in her other hand. And although Mum had asked me to kill her, neither of us thought of her desire to die as suicidal. It was more of an attempt to regain a tiny morsel of control over her own death. She did the choosing and she'd selected the time and the day she'd had enough of the pain and the suffering and the waiting. It was her decision and her right.'

'That *was* her right,' said Barney. 'We can choose how we live; we should choose how we die.'

Jodie tried to lean forward further, as if to be nearer Odette, but couldn't gain a solid enough purchase on the stupid beanbag, and she struggled like a toddler in an impossible chair. Giving up, she sank backwards again. 'Exactly, Barney. That's it exactly.'

Odette was pissed off by Barney's comment, finding it intrusive and too familiar and intimate a statement to make.

What the fuck did he know about it? About anything. *I hate him*, she thought, and again, tried to wish him gone from her life. Permanently.

'But you have to understand, the problem with Mum's death is that it didn't *feel* right. It veered from the path that we'd so carefully planned. Both she and I had expected her to languidly drift off into some other welcoming world, but just before she'd died, she'd opened her eyes, and I'd seen fear. Pure unadulterated terror. Her eyes rounded as they skittered in their sockets, scanning the room, not focusing on me, but seemingly staring at something just over my shoulder. Something only she could see. It was only a fleeting thing, but it was a horrifying thing to behold.'

Still, after all this time, her mother's expression wouldn't leave her, and the memory made Odette feel sick. That's when she'd really questioned her and her mother's decision to end her life. It had all gone horribly wrong and Odette couldn't change it, however hard she tried.

'I can only describe her expression as naked, feral fear of the unknown. An unsureness of where she was going. An uncertainty that she'd brought death upon herself. It was that brief hanging on to life that broke my heart. In that split second, I'd seen her uncertainty.

'It was a snap-of-the-fingers moment, and it made me question forever Mum's decision to hasten her own death in such a way. Perhaps another method of dying would have been better. Gentler, more all-consuming in a softer way – without any of the terror that she experienced.'

Odette shuddered and Barney muttered something, it sounded like an empty apology at her distress. Jodie rolled herself out of the stupid fucking beanbag and slid over to Odette and hugged her. 'It's all right, baby. You *did* do the right thing, it was what your mother wanted, so never doubt yourself. It only brings you pain and gives you the wrong answer. Your mother *wanted* to die, and you helped her and that makes you the bravest person I know.'

Odette cried and didn't bother wiping her face dry. 'But I shall never know what Mum saw. What happened to her in those last seconds that so ruined her chosen way out? Why wasn't she allowed the peace she craved, without that fear?' Odette sniffed and tried to regulate her breathing. 'After she was dead, all I could do was pray that now, having lived through that fear, she was truly at peace. As was deserved. She deserved *that* at least.'

Barney spoke softly. 'It sounds painful beyond comprehension. I can't say how sorry I am, but Jodie's right. You shouldn't, *mustn't* blame yourself. All you did was carry out your mother's wishes. I'm sure she's grateful for that.'

Odette allowed herself to sink into the bosom of her friend, and welcomed the warmth. Her voice, when she spoke, was as tremulous as a child, and she hiccupped as she tried to stop crying.

'It feels so unfair. All we'd wanted was for her death to be a perfect calm, silent thing. But it hadn't been. When I'd put my cheek to her face, I felt the moment her breath stopped. It caught in her throat for a minute and she'd gurgled and gasped. It was the last sound she made and it sounded so awful. It made her death ugly. She didn't go gently – death snatched her. I don't know how she felt, but I knew it wasn't anything we'd anticipated. There had been an extra fearful something waiting for her that wasn't asked for, nor expected.

'But Mum closed her eyes and kept her secret to her herself.

'The secret of dying.'

33

ME

I knew I had to play this very carefully. Odette's story was indeed a superficially tragic one, and I concentrated on keeping my expression crinkled in empathy. The one emotion that had always eluded me. Frankly, I thought it overrated. But that's how I was wired.

The secret of dying. There *was* no secret of dying, as far as I was aware. You lived; you died. Where was the secret?

Most annoyingly, having nearly got through this endless bloody evening – I was careful not to preempt the finale, but it was so near I could smell it – I had to concentrate on focusing on the game at hand.

I was still no closer to knowing or understanding the meaning of grief – where all this had started. Bereavement left me as cold as it always had. Neither Jodie nor Odette's stories had been about grief – so in that respect, I had learnt precisely nothing about that particular emotion. Which meant I was unable to help Mum because I still didn't really comprehend the devastation death brought to an abandoned living loved one.

Why couldn't people simply accept death, get over it, shut up and move on? Really, how bloody hard could it be? Both my current in-house resident liars were ridiculously stupid and misinformed and should have a very serious word with Grieving Gregory – he'd put them right in a jiffy, or at least would steer them in the right direction.

After a decent period of respectful silence following Odette's ode to her dead mother, tuning out Jodie as she comforted Objectionable, I made a quiet and slinky move to the kitchen, creeping so as not to shatter the silence the two women wallowed in – bar a few snivelling sobs from Objectionable, and sweet murmurings from Just. Dear God, I'd never heard such sentimental tripe – the melodrama of it all – it was self-indulgent and meaningless.

I thought it time to really get this party started, and I went about preparing my very special elixir of life. Family-style. But of course, the famous traditional family celebratory drink had been a fabrication – if I couldn't beat the ladies with truth, I was prepared to sink to their level with a lie. It didn't matter. I would beat all three women using truth, lies or Valium – or a combination of all three. Whatever worked. The sedative was merely a useful and unmessy aid to my victory.

I had borrowed some shot glasses from Dad's drinks cabinet, and squirted 30mls of Valium into two of them, using my trusty syringe. Adding approximately another 30mls, ish, by eye, of tequila, I swilled the contents about with a straw and inspected it. I'd rather over-pitched this alcoholic shot to my guests as something new and exotic, but of course it would be instantly recognisable as the liqueur it was. So be it. They only had to drink it; they were not required to leave a detailed taste review on the subject. Salt cellar in hand, and a plate of three lemon wedges jauntily arranged, I proceeded into the sitting room.

Carrying the two sedated tequilas in one hand, I solemnly handed a glass each to the girls, and put the plate of lemon segments on the picnic cloth. 'Wait for me, I'll get mine. It's time to toast our new friendship and then I shall reveal all about my own actions.'

Nipping in and out of the kitchen, my large tequila-on-its-tod shot now in hand, I squatted down in front of Just and Objectionable, and held my glass up high. 'To my father and mother, and to my two new friends, Jodie and Odette. May the future bring us happiness and a guilt-free existence. We all deserve that. And, ladies, as previously stated, the family way, please. Back in one. Cheers to us all. Pour a little salt along the base of your index finger and thumb, and lick, sip, and then suck on the lemon. On the count of three. One, two, three.'

Happily, I watched the idiot liars blindly lick their hand and knock back their drinks. They both sucked on their lemons, and sucked in their cheeks. 'Tart,' said Just.

'Tequila,' said Objectionable.

'Correct on both counts,' I said and stood, taking the glasses from them. 'And thank you both for indulging me. It means more to me because my father is no longer with us, but I know he'd have approved of me continuing this ritual.'

'No problem,' said Objectionable. 'Always keen to be kind.' Grinning falsely at me, making a point of overstretching her mouth, not bothering to hide her dislike of me, I bounced it right back at her. All pretence gone.

After all, now they were mine I had little reason to carry on this façade, but better safe than sorry, I reined it in, in case Objectional was somehow immune to the effects of Valium. Nothing would surprise me and it would be just like her.

'It was a lovely toast, Barney.' Just Jodie looked at the picnic remnants on the picnic cloth. 'Shall I clear some of these plates away?'

Inwardly tutting at the fucking responsibility of hosting full-fucking-time, I leapt to my feet. 'Certainly not. I am the host. I'll be a minute, then shall come and speak my truth to you.'

I glanced at my watch. I expected the effects of the Valium to kick in, in about thirty minutes or so. I appreciated everyone would react differently. Take Grace. *Somebody, please take Grace.* I tittered as I stacked the plates on the kitchen worktop. Grace had turned out to be a very cheap date on the drug, and had come to look forward to her daily dose. It had made her a nicer person actually – less bloody chatty and more mellow. An improvement all round.

I killed ten minutes in the kitchen, scraping leftover food into the bin and washing the plates. Washing the worktops. Washing my hands. Unable to put off my re-entry into the world of untruths any longer, sighing, I ambled back into the sitting room. Prepared, though, most definitely prepared – I'd donned a light jacket with pockets, which housed another unmessy aid. I wasn't one for mess.

'I'm back. Miss me, ladies?'

Manoeuvring into my beanbag, I stared at my feet, sick of playing at normal. Totally fed up with mimicking emotions I didn't feel. Angry at the women cluttering up my dolly space. I untied my shoelaces, and then did them up again, aware I was the centre of attention, the focal point for the women. Lifting my head, I smiled. 'Do you want me to start now, or should we talk through Odette's harrowing tale first? I don't want to take over the conversation out of turn, and it seems slightly crass for me to bang on about myself after hearing such a tragic account.'

O-for-Objectionable glared at me. 'Are you taking the piss?'

I put my hand to my chest. 'How could you even think such a thing? I simply meant I was loath to trample all over your pity party, that's all. I thought your story and the riddle of the secret of death deserved a moment of contemplation.'

The silence that followed my words delighted me, and the atmosphere in the room was heavy and weighty. Like a shroud. Both women seemed rooted in place, unable to either move or speak. It was an unexpected spectacle and I waited for something to give.

Just's forehead crinkled in confusion and O was stunned. I'd proven her suspicion of me right, and all she had was *stunned*. It was a little disappointing. I held up my hand, stopping either of them from speaking – as easy as that. Not entirely sure what exactly I was conveying to the women, whatever it was appeared to be working. Perhaps it was the joyous suggestion of lunacy that I experienced as it licked around my mind and caressed my body in all its deliciousness. I welcomed it with open arms.

Finally, O remembered how to work her mouth. 'I knew it. I fucking *knew* it.'

Gleeful, knowing I was truly liberated, I could finally speak as me, Barney Snapp, misinformed psychopath. 'What did you *know*, O? That I lied to you both?' I laughed. '*Correct!* I did *not* push my father down the stairs, why would I? He was a nice man.' I held a moment's silence. 'Now he's Dead Dad. But back to the point. Lying *is* the entire premise of your Murder Club. Lying is its very foundation.'

For the first time in public, I was having an absolute fucking ball. Being honest gave me such freedom it was as though I was flying. There was no censoring of my words or thoughts – I was me. Unfortunately, this came with the realisation that Mum had lied to me about lying. Apparently, everyone did it, it was all the rage.

And all this time, I'd been stifled by Mum's instruction that an untruth was a very bad thing. These fucking women *thrived* on lies – their whole lives were complete untruths – the irony was that I'd wasted my whole life trying to conform to what I now discovered was a lie. People weren't good and right and true. They fucking *lied*.

Jodie surprised me, I'll give her that, when she sprang from her beanbag and stood up next to me. 'If that's what you think, you understood nothing, Barney, and believe this – *no one* fucks with me, not anymore. Odette and I are going now, and in case you were ever in any doubt, I never want to see you again. I made a terrible mistake inviting you to join our group, but you will not humiliate my friend, or me, you fucking shit.'

She slapped me and the sting of her hand fizzed on my skin. Naturally, I slapped her back and, tottering, she stumbled and fell. Squatting, holding her in place on her squishy seat, with my hand on her chest, I spoke to O. 'Don't even bother getting up. As you both enjoy the melodramatic, I'll speak in terms that will titillate and tantalise.' I theatrically cleared my throat with an announcing sort of cough. 'If either of you move, the bitch gets it.'

Laughing, and I do mean really gut-wrenching, belly laughing, the sound I produced bellowed out and seemed to reverberate around me. I positively *boomed* with hilarity. Someone had tweaked my audio settings and I patted my earlobe, trying to tune back into reality again, shaking my head to reconfigure my sound waves that had gone awry. *Oops.*

Silence finally regained, J and O stared at me with horror and bewilderment and fear. There, see, I hadn't lost my skill at identifying the meaningless emotions of real people. But were they lying? It was all very confusing. I coughed properly, clearing throat and mind.

And breathe.

'I have your friend, Grace, in one of my rooms. If either of you tries to leave, Grace will never get out of my flat because I'll kill her, and it will be all your fault. Perhaps that doesn't matter to you as you're both so adept at the taking of life, but it *should* matter. It should be a fucking priority, in my humble opinion. What say you both?'

Just was the first to get her shit together. 'You do not have Grace. You're lying.'

'Tut tut, Just Jodie. Lying is *your* thing; I'm a beginner only. I speak the truth. Here, look.' I took out Grace's mobile from my pocket and turned it on. 'See, I kid you not. She invited herself to stay, and she's never left. Since Friday. That's a long time to get through with Grace. But I assure you, she is not hurt in any way whatsoever, because inflicting pain is really not my bag at all.'

Neither of them spoke and I recognised their situation for the tricky one it was. Nodding sagely but with no sympathy, I said, 'Isn't it a bitch when you just can't tell when a person's telling the truth or not? It's a real head-scratcher, isn't it? For what it's worth, I could conceivably bring her in, for, now let me see, I need to get this expression right, oh, yes, I could bring her in for your *proof of life*. I believe that is the phrase most commonly used in this scenario. Would you both like that? To see one of your own, alive and well? Although I get the distinct impression, neither of you particularly likes the woman. And frankly, who could fucking blame you – she's simply frightful.'

Just Jodie kept her face remarkably still, the only sign she hadn't lost the use of it for expression was the very slight pinching in and out of her nostrils as she breathed. Maybe *panted* would be more accurate a term, as I still held my hand on her chest.

Objectionable raised her hand, like a child tentatively thinking of answering a particularly dastardly question from the school teacher. Realising what she'd done, O instantly dropped her arm and directed her words to Just, as if by not looking at me, I'd magically disappear. 'Bring her in, then. Prove it. Bring in Grace.'

Sighing, I sat back down again. 'No. No, I've changed my

mind. Maybe later. Definitely later, but not now, this minute. It's not time. Far too soon.'

O snorted and Just Jo huffed out air from her lips. 'You haven't got her at all, have you? Let's go, Odette. I'm not staying here a moment longer.'

But she didn't move. Because she couldn't. Instead, she rubbed at her face and rolled her neck slowly as I politely lifted my hand from her body. 'I feel a bit weird, Odette, what's wrong with me, I don't feel right.'

'You've had too much to drink. Come on, let's go.'

And O stood up, no problem at all. Fucking typical. I went over and punched her in the face. She promptly sat down again. Fell down. Collapsed. Died. No, not that. She breathed. I know because I saw her chest move up and down, from where I sat with Just again, having to travel to and fro between my women.

Just moaned softly. 'What have you done to me, Barney? I feel... fuck, I feel, feel...'

'You feel nothing, you stupid bitch. Go to sleep, there's a good girl. And, O, what to do with you.' Being a gentleman, I hurried, ambled, walked very slowly over to her body. Gently slapped her cheeks. Eventually, she opened her eyes and, after looking more than a little lost, she rubbed them and shook her head. Closed her eyes again, opened them, closed them.

Opened them with intent. 'What have you done, you bastard? You've given us something. You've drugged me.' She peered around my body to peer at the now-unconscious woman sleeping the sleep of the Just. 'Jodie, wake up. What have you given us, you fuckwit?'

'Not enough, clearly. Don't worry, it's only a mild sedative – no long-lasting dire side effects will rain down on you. Grace actually loves the stuff, so give it a chance. It should chill you out, and believe me, that would be most welcome in your case. Why not lie back and enjoy? Relax. Give yourself up to it.'

'Fuck off.'

'Then I'll have to tie you up. Not something I do lightly, but as you refuse to succumb to the Valium, you leave me no other recourse. And don't fight me, because I'll win, although physical restraint would not be my natural go-to. It's most unlike me, in fact.'

Taking the unmessy cable ties from my inside jacket pocket, I easily overpowered Odette the Objectionable and, securing both her hands and feet, I checked on Jodie. Fast asleep. I tied her up as well to make my life easier. I checked on O again. Eyes shut.

But I didn't believe her.

Running, sprinting, walking, crawling, moving back to her, I dragged her over to the heavy table and fastened her to one of the legs. There. Snug as a bug and stuck. I ignored the fact my body and mind seemed discombobulated – each doing their own thing. *Weren't they?*

Scanning the room, I could only hope that the women were unable to escape. I could hope. I did hope. I prayed. I laughed a bit and scarpered out of the small door off the sitting room, off to the utility room, off to Grace. Off, off, off.

34

———

ME

'Here I am, Grace. Me to the rescue.'

'Hello, Barney. You're late.' She paused and seemed to think about it. 'Aren't you? I can't really tell.'

'Does it matter that much to you?'

Smiling broadly, she shook her head and opened her mouth. I didn't even have to ask anymore. She was positively gagging for her 10ml top-up. Couldn't wait for the soporific effects to take her to a softer world. I imagined it a nice feeling. In less strained and busy times, I promised myself a syringe full – just because I could.

A softer world would always be welcome.

'I come bearing news, Grace. How would you like to see your besties?'

'What?'

'Jodie and Odette are in my sitting room and they can't wait to see you. I'm presuming you feel the same and are teetering on the edge of your seat with anticipation?'

Her response was slow and her slowness in general was beginning to seriously irk me. 'Jodie and Odette are here?'

'Yes, they are indeed.' I de-radiator-ed her and allowed her time to regain the feeling in her wrists, arm and legs. For the last couple of days, I'd left her, not bothering to come to this room to bully her. My conversation with Bully Bertie had been fruitful and enlightening – there was no sport in victimising a person who was quite patently weaker than oneself. Far too easy a project and little to no value would be gleaned from that game. I'd ignored her instead, only seeing her for doping and feeding times. During which, she'd never stopped chatting, pre-Valium. It was all most unpleasant and unnecessary.

My body appeared to be vibrating with excitement as I waited impatiently for her, my limbs all a tingle. Her very presence so repellent, I couldn't fucking *wait* to bring her up to the others. I worked on the premise that her revoltingness would be diluted when mixed with Just and Objectionable.

'Listen to me, Guilty. You've told me, during your delightful stay with me, how you've always wanted to be fully accepted into Jodie's group. It brings me great pleasure to announce you *are* the star attraction. In fact, you could say, you're the founding member. You were the first woman I captured, so you have that to be proud of. J and O came *after* you. You won. I know from your ramblings that will be important to you.'

Holding her hand, I led her; she on shaky legs, me on a shaky mental footing but enjoying myself. 'Under the circumstances, Guilty, don't feel you have to bring anything to the party. I'm only expecting you and your very charming chatter. Although that will be dimmed due to your medicine, but any-hoo, let's crack on. Don't worry about not turning up with chocolates or wine, but thanks for the thought. You shouldn't have.'

A sound like a giggle escaped her and, hurrying, I pulled her along behind me and through into the sitting room. 'Ta-da. I bring you Grace, which this party has been sadly lacking. It's been an utterly grace-less affair, on every level imaginable.'

Just made no movement at all, stretched out cold, nestled in her beanbag like a present waiting to be unwrapped. Objectionable stared at me, struggling to maintain the stare without closing her eyes. It was a shame. Guilty Grace was an idiot, Just was out of the picture, so I was left with an audience of one. But O would have been my first choice anyway – to be my sounding board. Not for long, but long enough that I could get it all off my chest. Fair's fair and all that. My story would be short and sweet though. None of the breast-beating that had proceeded it, and needless to say, none of the *fucking lying*.

Pushing Guilty into my recently vacated beanbag, tying her hands and feet again, I addressed O. I wanted to scream and shout, but understood that any sabre rattling was pretty redundant, as my enemies were all in different levels of consciousness – Jodie completely under, Grace so desiring of that state, that she lay, as Vulnerable as Vera, waiting for it to take her. And the redoubtable Objectionable fought it, her eyes open but slow-blinking, her brain clearly having problems keeping up, taking its sweet time to understand the spoken word as if on a time delay.

'Are you listening carefully, O? Then I'll begin.' I bowed and stood over her, my hands on my hips. 'I'm afraid you'll have to accept my ire, which is three-fold thanks to the trio of women before me, but as you are the only one paying attention, you'll get the full tirade – a solo performance. I hope you appreciate the good fortune that has been granted you.'

'Fuck off, Barney.'

'Disappointing, Miss Tight-Arse-Bun woman. I expected more from you. Something a bit more illuminating and understanding. You have a brain – use it.'

With a prod of my foot, she managed a snort and spoke before the noise became a snore. 'I'm giving you nothing.'

'Okay, fair enough. Lie back and listen, then. And enjoy.

You can throw roses at my feet when I've finished.' Dipping at the waist again, I took a minute to take in the tableau around me, which was missing the bleeding obvious. Hesitating, I couldn't decide on the order of play and, O, with eyes still open, picked up on my dithering immediately.

'Forgot what to do next, Barney? Not thought this through?'

'It's all thought through, don't fret.' *I am fretting.* I couldn't wait for the next chapter, but knew it would have a bigger and better impact if I showed restraint and waited for it. *Fuck it.*

Putting my hands on my knees, I put my face closer to O's. 'Do you know Grace's lie? Because I do. We all know she did nothing to save her sister. But that's not the full story. There's a much nastier element to it. The point is, she *could* have saved her drowning sister, but *chose* not to. It was something she said when she confessed to me under the influence of Valium. A bit tame in the grand scheme of things, don't you think? When you juxtapose it with the horrors committed by you and Just.'

O's eyes had briefly shut but I found I cared little. She could hear – that was good enough. But I prodded her left hip with my foot because I did care. She *needed* to hear it.

'All three of you, Jodie, Grace and you, Odette. Just, Guilty and Objectionable – you are all evil bitches. Each of you has no idea of the wrongness of your actions. *It wasn't murder, it was justice.* And you, O, your *mother's* release *from life.* What a crock. And poor pathetic needy Guilty, *I wanted to beat my sister at* some*thing.* I've never heard anything so selfish and misinformed and wrong. All euphemisms for killing a person, a husband, a mother and a sister. Euphemisms you all wrap yourselves in, like a warm blanket, to keep out the cold hard truth. It's more than contemptible, it's despicable and totally beyond my comprehension.'

Prod.

To give the woman credit, when she opened her eyes,

comprehension suddenly shone in them as she made sense of what was going on, and she looked victorious. Another quick prod with my foot kept her on the ball, engaged her mind and elicited an instantly snotty answer.

'Boo-fucking-hoo, Barney. You missed the point. Because it's beyond you.'

'I missed it because it was pointless, you fool. And do you know the true horror of it? None of you see your murders as anything other than *good*. You all cover yourselves in glory and boast about doing no harm, when you have all committed the most heinous act that man can perpetrate on one another. You lie and lie and lie and think that keeps you safe. After killing people you all loved, in some form or other, you hide behind your respectable middle-class façades, your shiny veneers, believing yourselves higher and mightier than the rest of us.'

Bending down as if to kiss O, I instead spat in her face. *That* made her open her eyes again – better than prodding. 'You make me want to vomit, you self-righteous bitch. How dare you kill your mother? How fucking dare you? Just who is the psychopath around here? Is it me, or is it all of you?'

O's expression was so relaxed it almost disappeared and slid from her face, not having the strength to stay in place. Smiling briefly, she said, 'You're the fucking psychopath, Barney. Don't worry, you've won that title hands down.'

Fury had taken hold and I found him shaking me from the inside, as if I needed to get a grip on the situation. As if I should hurt all three women.

I explained to him, in my head, *I am not like them. I am not. I will not show them real anger. It would be wasted on them. My way is infinitely better and will be appreciated by each of them. Given time.*

I was going to teach them a lesson they would never forget,

and one I learnt from my mother. The only person whc ever really understood me.

My ladies will all lead my life now, *my* life, with *my* rules, and they shall all obey.

These bitches will have no choice but to follow my lead.

For I was not asking their permission. I was taking what was mine. The women were mine, and I'd improve them.

Do not waste any tears on them. I shall show them the real world and they will prosper under my care.

'Now it's time, Objectionable. I can't delay anymore. The time to set myself free and return to the fold. For you three, well, you'll have to wait and see. I think you'll be amazed and impressed and ultimately, you will accept, for you will understand that what I'm offering you is, indeed, something to be truly grateful for. I give it with love, although none of you deserve it.'

For a second, O's eyes opened and looked into mine but she kept her silence.

'I give it to you, with all the love from me and my dolls.'

And now, finally, it was time to prepare my women.

35

ADELE

Adele had been standing outside the interior door to Barney's flat for some time. Had been camped there for the last couple of hours, sitting cross-legged, waiting to hear... She wasn't sure what she was waiting to hear, but whatever it might be, she wanted to be there. For her son. For the women. For herself.

As if in a daze, over the last weeks, Adele had foolishly stepped into Barney's frightening and accelerating mental breakdown with her eyes wide open, but at a loss as to how to save him. She had compounded that mistake when she'd agreed to ring him tonight on his mobile. And he'd talked to her as if she was someone else. So, now she was inextricably involved. Caught up in the strange fantasy world in which her son was living.

Adele knew she was losing him, *had* lost him, and yet, here she was, still standing by him, stupidly holding his hand in support. Condoning and encouraging him. Timothy would be furious with her. *She* was furious with her.

She worried what Timothy would think of the choices she'd made, but didn't allow herself to explore that concern too deeply. Adele had failed. She knew that and Timothy would tell her so, but he wasn't here because he was dead and she was all on her own.

With her psychopathic son.

Not knowing what would alert her to the end of the evening, Adele had decided to knock on the door at around eleven o'clock. She would insist on coming in. Would not take no for an answer. She wanted to check that everyone was well and happy and the evening had gone well.

Wanted to check that everyone was still breathing.

She looked at her watch for the thousandth time in less than five minutes. The big hand finally pointed straight up, and the little hand to the eleven. It was time.

Adele rapped her knuckles on the door, a quick rat-a-tat-tat – businesslike but with a jolly cadence as if she were bringing happy news. If Barney refused her entry, she wasn't sure what she'd do.

The door swung open and the beaming pink-cheeked face of her son greeted her. He held his arms out wide and she walked into them. His embrace was tight as he hugged her to him. 'Marvellous Mummy, come in, I've been waiting for you. Come in, come in, right now, this minute.'

Her heart felt as if it were tripping over itself, and her mouth was so dry it scratched the back of her throat. Before she could ask him why he'd named her like one of his dolls, Marvellous Mummy had her answer. And the sight of his sitting room chilled her. As she shrivelled inside, goose pimples fluttered across her flesh, covering her from head to foot.

'What have you done, Barney? Jesus fucking Christ, what have you *done*?'

He didn't seem to hear her, but danced around the room, his face shining with happiness. 'Look, Mummy, look and see.

Aren't my dollies the most perfect things you have ever seen in your whole life?' He stopped and wiped his face and his expression changed to a look of confusion. Adele watched as realisation hit him. 'And I'm crying, Marvellous Mummy. I'm *crying*. I've never cried before. But they're tears of joy.' His voice was full of awe and delight and Adele, not being able to bear his madness, tuned him out.

Adele tiptoed through the china dolls laid out on the carpet. Like an army, their shiny glass eyes seemed to follow her, their mouths seemed to laugh at her, and their arms seemed to grab at her. Hundreds and hundreds of them, some of them so small she had to be careful not to stand on them. They sat, leant and stood – all of them positioned so they appeared to be looking at her.

The three women were tied and unconscious, lying and arranged face-up in beanbags, their faces painted – bright red lipstick, rosy rouged cheeks, reshaped freshly arched black eyebrows – all of their eyes shut, displaying extra-long false eyelashes that lay softly on their cheeks. Like cherished dolls, they were displayed carefully.

And then one of the women opened her eyes and looked straight at Adele. Her eyes were stretched wide as she watched Adele's timid approach. Adele, guilt and fear making her a coward, quickly dropped her own eyes. Shame made her feel faint.

Making herself ignore the woman's gaze, Adele saw how carefully the women had been positioned, their ankles neatly trussed together, their lower limbs held awkwardly. They seemed smaller than they really were, swallowed up by the beanbags. With their wrists bound tidily together and resting in their laps, as if waiting politely for a treat, Adele took them in quickly, desperate to unsee them. But she could still hear. The woman with her hair in a bun, the one who'd opened her eyes, said, 'Please help, whoever you are, please help us.'

Adele's throat locked and she made no reply, her eyes filling with tears of despair. She dared a look and saw the woman's face harden.

'If you don't help us, who'll help you?'

Barney's voice was singsong and out of context. 'You'll find no help here, Objectionable, and don't ask again – it's very naughty of you.'

When she felt her son's arm at her elbow, Adele had to stop herself from jumping from his grasp. She heard him speak softly to the woman again. 'Really, Objectionable, shh, or I'll fast-forward your lipping procedure.' He gripped Adele's forearm, and steered her as if she were on some sort of a tour. 'The two sleeping women are Just Jodie and that, over there, is Guilty Grace. But, Mummy, this one, who opened her eyes and pleaded for help, is Objectionable Odette. Odette, this is my mother, Adele. Now, say hello to each other nicely and maybe later you can play together.' He laughed. 'If you're both *very* good.'

The woman's eyes weren't bright and alert and Adele guessed she'd been given Valium. But there was no denying Odette knew precisely what was happening. Adele watched as Odette's face expressed a blurred version of hatred aimed most decidedly at Adele, and then there was confusion, followed oddly by amusement.

'Your name is Adele? Christ, I thought Barney said, "This is my mother, A-Doll." That would have been a scream, right? And a *huge* coincidence. Considering the company we're currently keeping.'

Barney had stopped moving and stood very very still. He whispered out the two words, as if awe-struck. 'Adele. A-Doll.' He stared at Adele and she didn't know what to say, or how to stop the inevitable train of this thought from escalating. The seed had been planted.

After a long silence as Barney scrutinised her, he unexpectedly bent double and laughed and laughed and laughed.

He wiped his eyes and studied his wet fingers. 'And these are tears of understanding. Total comprehension – at last. I've *finally* understood. Is this destiny, Mummy? All this time, and you never even told me, not ever, all this time, my whole life, you've been masquerading as my mother and the *entire* time, you've been a doll in Mummy's-clothing. You're a doll, just like me. It's *per*fect.' His hands covered his mouth as if to stop himself from screaming with the wonder of it all. 'We're *both* dolls, and I never even guessed. We're both perfect on the outside, but the difference is, now we're also perfect on the *in*side. Because we have realised who we truly are. Together. Mother Doll and Son Doll.'

Her voice, when it came, shook and trembled. 'Barney-Boo, I am *not* a doll. I'm your real mother. I'm Mum, the same as I've always been. Stop being silly, darling. Please.'

'But don't you understand? Now we are king and queen of the doll world, *our* world, and united we will rule the only real life worth having. A real world with no nasty lying – it will be filled with the truth of perfection. Look what we've created.' His arm gesticulated wildly and loosely, indicating the hundreds of dolls filling the room.

'We have to let the women go, Barney. They don't belong here. It'll be so much better just the two of us. Trust me, darling, I know I'm right.'

'Don't be ridiculous. The women are the whole point. Have you seen Jodie and Grace's lips? They have dolly mouths now. They have become my forever-dolls.'

Slowly, Adele moved over to the woman nearest her, who was wearing a red dress. She bent down to inspect the woman's face with her cupids-bow red shiny lips. Adele's nose was nearly touching the poor woman's forehead, before she saw it, and Adele reared back, her hand clamping her mouth shut.

'What have you done, Barney?'

'I superglued their lips together. I haven't done Objectionable Odette yet, as she's still awake and communicating – but I will. Anyway, see here? I've left a tiny hole in the middle of their glued lips, the size of a straw, so they can drink and take nutrients and live forever and ever.'

'You have to let them go. Keep me instead. They'll die – they can't exist forever on liquids only. They'll need food. What will you do then?'

Her son laughed. 'You are a silly-billy, Mummy. Why, I'll get another one of course, just like that.' He clicked his fingers. 'Easy-peasy. The real world is *full* of women who will happily become my dollies. I have an unending supply. Aren't you proud of me now, Mummy? *Really* proud, I mean? Now, I'm your Bestest Boy Barney, and we'll live happily ever after.'

Adele stood and wept, a feeling of exhausted inevitability crushing her. Her own defeat made it hard to breathe. *Forgive me, Timothy. I cannot leave my son on his own. I have no choice but to stay with him. God help me.*

God help these women.

I am no longer a wife, but I can still be a mother. That's all I can be.

'You won't leave me, will you, Mummy? I've created a perfect world and we can live in it together.'

How could she desert him now? Adele had given birth to him. It was her duty to love him. It's what mothers did. She couldn't abandon her little boy. He sidled up to her, slid his hand into hers, and squeezed it. 'I'm all better with you here, Mummy. Now I'm completely normal.'

Adele spoke through her tears.

'I'll always be with you, Barney, and I will never leave you. I made you, and we'll stay here together, in your beautiful world. And it *is* beautiful. It's more than that. It's absolutely perfect.'

'Thank you, Mummy. For everything. I knew you'd understand. That's why I do so love you.'

'And I love you too, Barney. Always and forever.'

THE END

ACKNOWLEDGEMENTS

First of all, and as is always the case, huge thanks to the whole of the Bloodhound team – they've all been fantastic and I couldn't be more grateful.

This was my first time working with Abbie Rutherford, as my editor, and she did an absolutely bang-up job, and made it a far better read, for which I thank her wholeheartedly. She was a pleasure to work with.

Big thanks to Donna Wilbor, my always-beta reader, who has never failed to support and encourage and tell me if and when I get things wrong. Thank you.

An especially very huge thank you, to Dr Charlotte Stevenson, for also beta reading this novel for me. Her input, copious notes, comments and suggestions, were invaluable and showed a great generosity of spirit and kindness. As well as a big brain on all things psychological. I also feel very privileged that she took the time to read this in its infancy, as I respect her enormously as an author, and her book, The Serial Killer's Son, remains one of my all-time favourites.

And mostly, as always, all my thanks to Francesca.

For everything.

A NOTE FROM THE PUBLISHER

Thank you for reading this book. If you enjoyed it please do consider leaving a review on Amazon to help others find it too.

We hate typos. All of our books have been rigorously edited and proofread, but sometimes mistakes do slip through. If you have spotted a typo, please do let us know and we can get it amended within hours.

info@bloodhoundbooks.com

9 781917 705585